A Shape

Julia Ibbotson

First published by Endeavour Press Ltd in 2017.

Table of Contents

Prologue

1500 years before

Lady Nymue, her mother, is rising from the mere like a spirit: tall, slow like a dream, over-gown falling in slim folds from her waist. Vivianne sees her in a haze of mist, like magic, an illusion. She feels it, that enchantment, and it is enfolding her, but making her shiver, too. Her life-giver, robes dry despite the water, is coming towards her as she stands anxiously on the bank, waiting impatiently, calling out urgently, hopping from one foot to the other, tangling her feet in her earth-sweeping kirtle, longing to rejoin her playmates who are chasing around the village pretending to be Roman soldiers. Her mother, reaching out a hand to her, is shaking her head, but laughing. Be more patient, my little Lady Vivianne, she says, I have not completed my rituals, but let me wrap you in my cloak, for I must return to the mere. But she is only a little girl and something is making her feel cold, frightened. No, she calls, sticking out her lower lip, I want to play! I want to be Honorius this time! They promised! Eleanor will play my wife - or maybe my lady servant.

Her mother is ruffling her soft curls. Well, then, she smiles, I will return later to finish. She is lifted onto her mother's horse, in front, held close. Dry, warm, comforting. Riding back to the village. Her care-giver is taking her back to play with her friends again. Her mother turns to the special hall which her father, Sir Tristram, called "sacred" and where she is only allowed to go sometimes.

And then, fire, flames, the acrid smell of smoke. Looking across to the great hall, terror strangling her heart, stealing her breath. Running towards the wooden building, through the ash and cinders and the roaring, screaming now, choking. Someone holding her back, pulling her.

Darkness.

Waking up in her little bed. A big red-faced man in the shadows, haloed with a fair unruly beard and thick wild hair, telling her that her parents were dead, burned in the fire. Her mother and her father, both of them. An accident with tallows. She knows those tallows; they are always on the altar in the sacred hall. They are only spoken of in whispers. But this man is speaking in a strange way, loud, too loud, and it seems to her, sneering, as she peers at him through the darkness.

Chapter 1

Viv blinked through the darkness of the apartments' communal hall, struggling to escape the strange thoughts that invaded her mind.

"*My little Lady Vivianne*" – where had that come from? Had her mother called her that? But it was so long ago … her parents were gone, way back. And the man, speaking loudly in that odd determined way, as Pete sometimes did, but yet certainly not Pete … this one, a disturbing voice, vaguely heard on the air … Darkness and unwanted thoughts, so vivid they seemed like memories.

But a flick of the brain and they were gone. She was shattered after four nights with little sleep, and her mind out of kilter.

Her eyes adjusted to the dimness after the glaring sunshine of the courtyard. As her vision cleared so did her brain. She unlocked her own apartment door. Pete would be back soon from his four day IT conference in Belgium. She could hardly wait.

Viv planned to make his favourite meal and then … mmm …

She dropped her work bag on her desk in the little study. Tired already, she'd had a busy day at the university but the thought of Pete spurred her on. Quickly she changed from her business-like work suit into the slim jeans that fitted her long legs and rounded bottom snugly, and the floaty chiffon top that showed off her firm breasts, knowing these clothes were Pete's favourites.

Pulling out of her bag the manuscript she was working on for her undergrad students, the new translation of the long Anglo-Saxon heroic poem *Beowulf,* she took it through to the kitchen and opened it on the table to glance at as she began one of her favourite activities, cooking a special dinner for the two of them.

Soon wafts of Il Divo singing *Nella Fantasia* drifted out from her sound system, and she hummed along with it as she lifted the casserole dish out of the oven to stir it, breathing in the rich earthy smell of the venison in red wine. Not only was Pete coming home, it was also the fifth anniversary of moving in together to this wonderful flat.

As she prepped the meal, she kept peering through her reading glasses at the manuscript, trying to work out one particularly difficult passage. She had the candles ready for the table and she grinned to herself as she thought of the silky basque she had bought for tonight. He would smile at her across the table and take her hand in his; they'd leave the dishes there and he would lead her into their bedroom … She squirmed deliciously and forced her attention back to her tasks.

She was slipping the casserole dish back into the oven when she heard the front door slam and Pete drop his briefcase on the hall floor.

"Hi, darling," she called out to him, snatching off her glasses.

He didn't respond. She looked up and saw him standing in the kitchen doorway, leaning his well-built rugby-player's physique against the doorjamb, staring into space.

She smiled at his unusually serious face, his piercing blue eyes, and the way he raked his hand through his thick fair hair which looked almost golden in the early evening sunlight. He was growing a beard and had a distinct dark shadow across his jawline. He looked tired. But she felt the usual shiver of desire run down her spine as she moved over to him and wrapped her arms round his neck.

He bent to her, eyes closed tightly, and nuzzled her neck. "Mmmm …" he murmured something into her thick wavy hair but she couldn't hear him as she felt his strong arms surround her slim body and pull her into him. She felt the familiar tingling in her abdomen and the warm ache. His mouth sought hers and he kissed her deeply. Oh goodness, he'd clearly missed her so much. She felt herself melting into him as his fingers burrowed urgently into her hair. Maybe the dinner could wait half an hour … His teeth almost bit through her lip and she caught her breath with the pain. This was not Pete's normal gentle exploring first, that usually sent shivers of anticipation through her body, but an immediately desperate demand. He tugged at her hair. An almost brutal force.

She snapped open her eyes. He was looking through her as if he was seeing someone else in his arms.

He pulled away.

She shuddered and frowned, searching his eyes. "What …? Is everything all right?"

"No, actually. I - er - I need to tell you something." He frowned. Viv straightened up and felt her heart thrum in her chest with foreboding.

Was he ill? Or maybe something had gone wrong at work. Had something happened to their finances? He looked disturbed.

"What's the matter, hun?"

He turned away from her and rubbed the back of his neck. "Look, Viv, I really didn't want to spoil the day. But I can't …"

Viv's breath seemed to be burning in her throat. "Oh Lord, you *are* ill!" She reached her hand out to his arm and stroked him. He twisted round to her and touched her hair, her cheek. But she saw that his mouth was distorted.

"No, it's nothing like that." He bit his lip. "Look, I – I do … love you, you know that. It's just …"

"Yes, I know." She tried to smile but could feel that her lips were trembling.

He grimaced. "But … oh god …I'm sorry, I *am* really sorry, although you may not believe it, but …It's just that I can't go on living a lie." He took a deep breath.

"A lie? What do you mean?" Her whole body was shivering, this time not with desire but with fear.

"Oh, Viv. I'll always love you, as a friend, whatever happens." Pete reached down and took her hand in his. "There's no easy way to say this." He looked down into her eyes and she saw a flicker of something odd there. "I'm leaving you."

"What?" The kitchen seemed to be shifting dizzyingly around her. The walls wouldn't keep still. The floor felt as if it were shuddering as her legs trembled.

"Viv, dear Viv. I'm sorry to have to say this, but … I've … I've found someone else."

What? He was having an *affair*? Good god. She'd had no notion, no suspicion of anything like that. She'd been sure he was so faithful, so loyal, so principled. After all, she'd known him since they were at school together. She knew him so thoroughly; she knew his thoughts, his desires, his worries. Didn't she? Surely she would have suspected something. She would have known.

No, it couldn't possibly be true. But he *said* he'd found someone else. What alternative meaning could that have?

She was swaying, buffeted by pushing, urgent waves. Water crashing over her, swamping her in fear. She was drowning.

She had to clutch on to the back of the high kitchen bar chair with her free hand to keep her balance. She knew that her mouth was gaping open. Her brain seemed out of gear. Someone else …

"What? Who?"

He made a dismissive gesture with his hand, as if it didn't matter, but she kept staring at him, and she saw him crumble.

"It's Gwyn."

"Gwyn?" she echoed blankly. "*My* Gwyn?" What the hell was he doing? Gwyn, from university, along with Ellie, three of them pals, helping each other through broken relationships, awful boyfriends, disasters, a hundred triumphs. "My friend Gwyn? No. Good god!"

She knew her face was expressive and that her expression right now was of horror and disbelief. Even disgust. Pete dropped her hand and she snatched it to her breast, to herself, to her possession again, and shrank back. This was a stranger standing in front of her, in her kitchen, for god's sake. A lightning strike of memory of his love-making, his kisses, his touch, all now for someone else, for *Gwyn*, jolted a shock of electricity down her spine.

She felt sick.

Pete sighed and she could hear the impatience, the softness gone. "Yes, of course 'your' Gwyn. How many others are there?"

His face looked somehow unfamiliar. Blank. Hard. He moved away from the doorjamb.

Everything seemed to Viv to drift out of focus.

"Pete …!"

He swung around towards her and looked at her as though he was surprised she was still there.

"What?"

"I just don't know what to say … Why …?" She clutched the chair back.

"Viv, please don't start anything." He sighed. "I'm sorry and all that, I've tried to be nice, but you just have to deal with it. Listen. I'll be back in a few days when you're a bit calmer. I'll have to get my stuff and make arrangements."

"Arrangements?"

"Well, obviously we'll have to sort out the sale of the flat."

"Sale of the flat?" Her voice echoed his words around her head.

"Viv, I need the money." He turned to go, stooping to pick up his briefcase in the hall. "For the business. We're expanding. You know that." He spoke deliberately slowly as if she were a child, then twisted round to her. "And, listen, please don't try to ring me. I'll be at Gwyn's place and I don't want you pestering her." For a moment he stared at her, mouth twisted, and she watched as his lips curled up, baring his teeth. She thought she was watching an animal snarling his attack. This wasn't her Pete. Not the Pete she knew. She shivered violently.

Viv heard the front door slam shut behind him and sank on to a bar chair. She felt as bleak and cold as she had twenty years ago, when she was nine years old and her grandmother had told her that her parents were dead.

*

For two hours she sat there, frozen, blank. When she heard the hall clock strike eight, she realised that she hadn't moved since Pete walked out. The smell of burning roused her senses and for a moment she had no idea what it was.

Oh god! The venison casserole. As she opened the oven door, a cloud of black smoke blinded her. Viv grabbed the oven gloves and manoeuvred the pot onto the counter top. Inside, the meat was dried up, blackened. She scraped it out with a spatula and dumped it into the bin. Destroyed, dead, cremated, like her relationship. God, she'd loved him so much. Hadn't she? But maybe she hadn't loved him enough. Maybe it was all her own fault. He'd sounded as though it was. Sick with shock, she pulled open the fridge door and grabbed the gateau that would have been their pudding. Viv tipped it, plate and all, into the bin on top of the charred remains of the venison.

He wanted the flat sold. Even with a half share, she wouldn't be able to buy anywhere else. Not now she'd sunk most of the money her parents had left her into Pete's venture, only too happy to help him get on his feet properly at last, working for himself. And she didn't want to buy anywhere else anyway. This was her home and she loved it.

But now what the hell was she going to do? Viv wandered from room to room as though committing each one to memory, as though she would never see them again after tonight. Certainly it was no longer properly hers, her home, her safety, her security. It was the place she loved to come back to after a long day at the university. It was a place of peace

11

after sorting out her students' troubles, a place of beauty that she had designed and decorated herself in calm, soothing colours, a place of relaxation after a day with her third year finals students.

She picked up from her desk the prospectus for the Anglo-Saxon studies programme she established and led. She was proud of what she'd achieved. Her parents would have been, too. Viv loved her job, she worked so hard, nothing was ever easy, but she found a haven in her home, where she felt she could be truly herself. A home that was so much a reflection of herself – and Pete.

No longer.

She stared in the full-length mirror in the bedroom. What was wrong with her? Was she *that* unattractive? Viv drew in her breath and looked critically at herself. So, maybe her boobs were too big for Pete, or, thinking of plump comfortable Gwyn, too small. She peered at her wide grey-green eyes and saw the mist in them, the creased pale skin of her forehead. Her thick curly auburn hair was loose, tumbling free and wild over her shoulders as Pete liked it. Or had said he did. Had he - or was it *all* a lie?

How long had he been with Gwyn?

Her birthday party! She'd teased Gwyn about flirting with Pete. Never for one moment thinking anything was going on … but it was all true, wasn't it? Oh god. Their flushed faces when they emerged from the kitchen together. And she'd thought it was the champagne. Stupid. Stupid. Why hadn't she realised …

Back in the kitchen she grabbed a bottle of Merlot and unsteadily sloshed out a large glass and gulped it down. Her stomach felt queasy and it occurred to her that she hadn't eaten since breakfast. Her lunchtime had been taken up with student and colleague emails at her desk and she'd forgotten to take a sandwich. She ought to eat something. But she couldn't face it. Her throat felt constricted. She knew she couldn't swallow anything solid. She poured herself another glass of Merlot.

Viv stared into space, empty.

Later, much later, hand shaking, she fetched another bottle of red from the wine rack in the kitchen and put it on the coffee table in front of her, but when she collapsed back on the sofa, she fell into a disturbed nightmarish stupor, full of harsh voices and waves of fear, her mother calling to her, terrified, looming mountains and the darkness of water.

How she managed to crawl to bed in the middle of the night or to work the next day she never knew. She had called a taxi to take her in to the university campus. With her head pounding she couldn't be certain that the effects of the previous night's alcohol had gone from her system. And she knew that Fridays were always quieter, nobody wanted classes or tutorials or meetings on a Friday. So instead she slumped in front of her computer and caught up with emails, reading them through twice before clicking "send", just in case, and keeping well away from everyone …

Viv shuddered at the mental images of herself last night. If only she could delete it all as easily as she could obliterate words on her computer.

*

She glanced at her watch as she opened the outer door to the apartments. It was seven thirty. Another late working day. Viv unlocked her own front door and bent to pick up the pile of mail that clogged her hallway. Why did she always get so much on a Friday? The flat was empty, silent. She shivered.

She flicked behind her ear a wayward strand of hair that had escaped from the ponytail which she had roughly twisted up for work, and sifted through the post. A formal letter from the university calling her to interview on Monday afternoon for the senior role she'd applied for. Could she even do it now after what had happened? The corner of her left eye twitched and she rubbed it. On top of everything else those disturbing dreams last night and those wild thoughts that kept plaguing her mind made her feel drugged and she was struggling to concentrate. What was it? Something about a lake … her mother? Water … repelling her … or drawing her? She shuddered and shook her head; she needed to keep those persistent images out of her mind.

Viv forced her attention back to the post. Mostly unsolicited junk mail. She tossed several onto the hall table.

But one envelope caught her breath. It was from Donaldson and Eger, the solicitors that she and Pete had used to buy the apartment. Frowning, Viv tore it open and stared at its curt single page.

"Dear Dr DuLac,

Re Our client Mr Peter Adamson

As you are aware, we have been consulted by your co-habiting partner, named above, regarding the sale of your joint property 1, The Coach House, with the purpose of discharging the collateral used for the development of the business Adamson and Knightly at 261b Uttoxeter Road, Derby. We are instructed by him to execute matters as soon as possible …"

What? It didn't make any sense.

She peered short-sightedly at the date at the top of the page: nearly a week ago. So, delayed in the post. And written before Pete had told her the awful news about Gwyn. Before he had told *her* he wanted them to sell their apartment.

She pulled her reading glasses out of her bag and read it again. Discharging the collateral for his business … used to pay off his business loan …but she knew nothing about it. How could he do that legally …surely he'd need her signature? Pete couldn't use their apartment as collateral for his business without her knowing. Could he? The flat for which she shared the mortgage payments, in fact 75% of them. She had agreed to stand the bulk of the mortgage to support him while he was setting up the business, despite his parents' generous help with the capital. And hers. Where on earth had all that money gone?

And since when had the business been Adamson and Knightly? That was Gwyn's name: Gwynneth Knightly.

The letter contained a paragraph and a list of bullet points in legalese that she didn't immediately understand and then …

"We would suggest that you now seek independent legal advice, taking this letter to your new solicitor, in order that we may then proceed to give effect to the above provisions.

Yours sincerely …"

No, surely not: he was selling their apartment from under her and she would have nothing. Is that what it meant?

Viv's hand shook as she clicked on his mobile number. The voicemail message informed her that Peter Adamson was unable to get to the phone at the present time, so could she leave a message after the tone? Yes, she certainly could.

She yelled down the phone, "What the hell's going on? I've had a letter from Donaldson and Eger about the flat. Collateral for your business? What's happening?" A few more choice words, and Viv clicked on the red button.

She sank on to the sofa, dropping her mobile into the cushions beside her. Clutching the letter in one hand, she reached for last night's unopened bottle of red wine and a glass on the coffee table in front of her. Her worst nightmares had come true. Now she was losing all the security she had built up. And after the bombshell last night. She sobbed.

Viv stared at the letter in her hand and at her mobile nestled where she had thrown it amongst the plump burgundy cushions. She willed it to ring and for it to be Pete and yet she dreaded hearing his voice again. She poured another glass of wine and drank it quickly to dull the pain.

But the phone didn't ring and the bottle emptied.

In the end, she had to escape the claustrophobia of the empty silent flat and to walk to try to clear her head and allow herself to think it all through. Viv wobbled as she kicked off her heels and unzipped her suit skirt, pulled on her jeans and slipped on her ballet flats. An automatic glance in the hall mirror as she passed it showed a pale ghostly face and huge darkened eyes, and her high sculpted cheek bones looked skeletal.

Her watch told her it was eleven thirty. She quietly let herself out of the flat, tiptoed across the hallway so as not to disturb Tilly, her upstairs neighbour, and opened the front door of the apartments. The door clicked shut behind her.

With careful concentration Viv placed her feet on the old cobbles that seemed intent on moving around, and cursed herself for drinking all that wine. In the moonlight she could make out the dark walls of the old abbey rising up to her right. Converted now into flats, there was only one light that she could see still on, one family or couple still up. She'd bet that everyone else was curled up in bed, relaxed and content. Oh, how she loved this place. How the centuries of history called to her. Dear god, she'd lost Pete - she couldn't lose her home as well. It was all she had left. She had to fight for it. Somehow.

But her thoughts wouldn't organise themselves. She couldn't make sense of any of it.

Gwyn. She saw the image in her mind of how they'd met at the Nottingham university freshers' party over the coffee machine, introducing themselves, Viv reading Medieval Studies, Ellie business studies, and Gwyn maths. They'd stuck together and supported each other through the three years and beyond.

Viv had tried to ring Ellie twice since the evening before, but each time she tapped the green button for her number in her iPhone's memory, she had immediately tapped red. What would she say to her? What if Ellie knew already? She shuddered to think how she could handle that conversation.

She walked without conscious direction or purpose, yet somehow irresistibly drawn, over the fields, still muddy after the rain last weekend, and followed the narrow path through the woods at the edge of the village, until she found herself on the banks of Cooney's Mere. How many times had she felt enticed to the lake, this mystical place, where old legends drifted like mists between the dark shores, fascinated by something intangible and haunting. She stared at the ancient stretch of water, black in the moonlight, thinking of the centuries it had been there. Her mind flickered over the memory of how, a long time ago, she'd found it marked on a medieval map and read that it dated back to well before the dark ages, even before Roman times. Possibly Celtic times, or Iron Age, if the artefacts found nearby were anything to go by. Hmm, she always meant to research it properly. Her academic parents, with their archaeological interests, would have been pleased. But somehow in her busy life she'd never found the time. And now … well, now was a different world …

A sharp breeze arose and she watched the ripples on the mere grow into turbulence. The reeds and rushes around her rustled and swayed in the wind. She felt her shoes sink further into the mud and she shuffled to release herself. It felt like quicksand beneath her feet. Her shoes would be wrecked, but she hardly cared now.

The shiny black water stretched towards the little village in the heart of the English countryside that she had happily made her home. She was out of sight of the road in that remote spot, but nobody would have seen her anyway, as the darkness of night had long since enveloped the land.

How could her life have collapsed about her so totally and so quickly? And with no warning?

She stared at the inky- black before her. The ghosts in her mind were screaming: fear of losing everything she'd fought for, fear of a lonely future that loomed, fear of the water, yet the pull of it … too much red wine …a muddled, hazy brain.

Was it really only twenty four hours ago that it had all started, this nightmare? Her mind drifted back again to the previous evening, coming home from work at the university, happy and relieved that the busy week had nearly ended - Thursday, so nearly Friday and then a whole weekend ahead with Pete… now she recalled the snatches of melodious music that drifted across her brain to become a distorted screech in a cacophony of violins; comforting smells of rich cooking that became the sourness of bile in her mouth; feelings of excitement at Pete's return that evening from his conference - feelings that became a judder of cold terror … And now, tonight's letter …

She heard the chime of the church clock in the village. Midnight. The hour of witches and ghosts. The hour of magic.

Viv stared across the meadows towards the church that she had loved the moment she saw it. Memories of house-hunting in the area with Pete flickered across her brain, searching for a home in a village just outside the town yet within commuter reach of Nottingham and Derby. She remembered how they had explored that church, hand in hand, delighted at its history: Norman but built on the site of Romano- British and Anglo-Saxon remains. Her historical interests, her home, her job, her love-life; it all fitted together so well. A perfect jigsaw. She'd fallen in love with the flat too: the converted mews in the grounds of the ancient abbey near the church. It had all been ideal. She'd worked so hard to make it homely for them both. She couldn't imagine living anywhere else. And alone. She just couldn't do it. Her breath retched into a sob that wracked her body.

A sense of movement behind her made her swing round, but there was nobody there. She felt chilled yet somehow she couldn't move away. Rationally, Viv knew that she needed to get home, tucked up safely in bed. She needed sleep; on Monday there was work, a lecture to give, a tutorial, and the interview for the new role at the university. Oh god, she couldn't be tired for those, it was imperative to be on the ball. She'd given so much to get to this point. Yet how would she be able to sleep? Viv felt the tears begin to course down her cheeks. God, why did it all have to happen now, when she needed to be on top form. Oh, why did it have to happen at all. Everything in her life was crumbling away. Pete, what have you done to us …

Again, a movement behind her, a parting of the rushes. The sense of a dark figure at her back. She swung round. Nothing. Then she turned back to the mere. A shadow on the water. She stared at the ripples but the image diffused and disappeared. Hardly daring to look she glanced round again. Nobody. She was alone.

Viv shuddered, her eyes fixed on the water in front of her. She must get out of here, get safely home, but somehow she couldn't move. She was transfixed and held against her will, as if her body was bound with invisible ropes. The mere and the world around her juddered, swept away and then returned, misty and echoing in her head.

She felt herself cry out. But it was a cry, not for help, but of despair.

Then a hand planted firmly on her back, pushing her. She staggered but felt the inexorable push towards the dark murky water. As she fell, she had the odd sensation of someone breathing on her neck, falling with her. Her hand reached out to save herself, to grasp anything that might halt her tumble. She scrabbled wildly at the undergrowth but felt the branches break as she tried to clutch hold of them.

The cold water rose to meet her and there was no longer firm ground beneath her. She flailed about but it was hopeless; the cold stole her breath and her strength. Something was pulling her downwards, sucking her into the murky depths of the mere.

My little Lady Vivianne.

She was sinking, as if there was someone below her who was grasping her ankles and pulling her down. The water covered her head and, even at the last, when she managed to struggle her head above the surface she saw that she was much further away from the bank than she had imagined. She could no longer fight, and with that realisation, the water covered her head for the last time.

Chapter 2

A deep male voice came faintly from far away and slowly entered her consciousness.

"Lady Vivianne!"

Viv felt a strong arm grip her waist and then she was floating, being drawn gently through the water. She gasped for breath as she rose, and her mouth filled with balmy air, sweet and fragrant. Oddly, it was light, and the sun was just starting to sink into dusk.

"What …? In heaven's name …?" Viv spluttered, as the man lifted her up and over his broad shoulder and, splashing through the shallows, carried her to the bank. The world swirled around her and she found it hard to focus. She tried to draw in her breath but her chest felt too tight. She was trapped against him. Her body felt strange, her dripping sleeves seemed wider than they should be, her jeans somehow flapping against her legs. She was soaked through but yet the mere seemed to be calling her back again. She tried to twist round to it but the man only held her tighter. She grabbed hard at his shoulder and a piece of wet cloth tore away in her hand. It felt strange, not a fabric she was familiar with, thick and closely woven, but not rough.

He lowered her to her feet and grinned down at her. His eyes were dark like smoke, skin olive and exotic, and he ruffled his long dark curly hair to flick away the water that soaked it. She stared at his large wide mouth and the dark shadow that swept his chin and upper lip. His smile was intimate, as if they shared a secret. For a moment, Viv felt her brain somersault. Her mind was drifting in and out of consciousness.

She was aware of movement around her and she tore her eyes away from him. There were people, men, their figures moving out of focus behind him, their voices echoing as if from far away. There were trees that she didn't remember being around the mere. It seemed wilder than it should have been. Yet everything within a few feet of her was exceptionally bright and clear, the light picking out all detail: the veins on the leaves, the knobbles and crevices of the tree bark starkly sharpened in high relief. Beyond that, all she saw was misty and swirling.

As she clenched her hands into fists she realised that she still held the torn fragment of cloth, and made to thrust it into the pocket of her jeans. The pocket was no longer there. She looked down and saw that she wore a long skirt, the dark wet fabric clinging to her legs. Good god, what was happening?

Viv looked back at the tall figure before her. He was dressed in some kind of loose cream tunic, dripping with lake water, with a brown leather belt that was finely tooled in gold, and as she stared he pulled on his boots that he had left at the water's edge.

She looked wildly around her. The other men were dressed likewise in tunics, though not so fine. There were horses higher up on the bank-top; she could hear their loud snorting and feel the juddering of the earth as they stamped their hooves. What was this? What was going on? Her brain didn't seem to be working properly; she felt confused, dull-witted. The sun was sinking behind the trees, leaving a trail of bloody streaks, red and orange, in the sky. Yet she had stumbled into the lake in the dark. She remembered staggering, a hand on her back, clutching for the branches to halt her fall into the water, floundering, or being pushed? Her clothes … her peculiar-feeling body … these people.

Her hand found a pouch hanging from her waist within the folds of her soaking skirt and she thrust the fabric into it, hiding it, though she had no idea why she needed to.

"Sir Roland," murmured one of the men, holding out to the dark-eyed man a large, heavily embroidered crimson cloak which her rescuer swept around his shoulders and pinned with a huge gold brooch, covering the torn seam. As he did so, he glanced at Viv and smiled intimately again, his glance insolently drifting down to the clinging folds of her skirt and the pouch where the fragment of cloth nestled. His eyes found hers. Embarrassed, she turned away.

"My thanks, Arfon," he said to his helper. "And now we must bring Lady Vivianne back to the mead hall with all haste." He grinned at her. "She may need to change her gown first, though; it is not fit for public view."

Viv felt a shudder rise up through her spine. She had the odd feeling that she should be in the lake and that he should not have rescued her and brought her out of the water, that she had been where she belonged, where she felt the magic, not here out on the banks, on dry land. The feeling was a wisp of thought that rose and fell inside her, catching her breath.

"Come, Lady Vivianne." The man called Roland stretched out his hand to her. "We must make haste. Sir Pelleas has thus far not noticed your absence. The thegns are too busy celebrating our return from battle in the borderlands. When I left to follow you, he was well into his cups, and hardly noticed anything."

She felt impelled to take his hand and he guided her up the slope of the bank onto a path where the horses stood, bedecked with embroidered and jewelled purple saddle cloth and head dress. The largest steed, a huge grey that looked to her as big as a carthorse but more lithe, turned on her approach, bent his head and pawed the ground, as if readying himself for her. As if she was expected.

Viv shook her head, bewildered. She made to move away but with a swift movement, Roland lifted her up onto the embossed leather seat, so that she sat side-saddle, and then swung himself up astride behind her. She could feel his big warm hands around her waist, steadying her against him, the side of her body pressing against his chest, his breath gentle on the top of her head. He wrapped his dry cloak around her wet garments and enfolded them both within it. It was embarrassingly intimate, and her heart quivered with a confusion of fear, excitement and anger.

"How dare you!" She tried to swivel sideways round to him but yet he held her captive. "This is madness! Are you some kind of enactment?"

"Enactment?" echoed her captor.

"You have no right! You ...you are abducting me!"

"Abducting you? Is that what I am doing?" and she heard the laughter in his voice. "My Lady of the Lake! Ha! Men, ride on!" He held her with only his left hand now as he gripped the reins with his right, but his hold was firm and sure.

A painful jolting wracked her body as the horse moved off and took away her breath, preventing any further speech. Her back hurt, her thighs hammered against the horse's sides as he gathered speed. If this man let go of her, she would be thrown off and crushed under the hooves. She feared she might slip and leaned her left shoulder in closer to him for safety. She breathed in the scent of bergamot clinging to him, and she heard his quick sigh as he gripped her even more firmly.

Any fear she might have felt gave way to a fury that she was forced to be dependent and cling to this stranger. Yet she knew she had no choice if she were to survive. And survival seemed, at this moment in time, the most important thing for her to focus on.

At the side Viv could only see the exposed gnarled roots of ancient trees as they sped by and the hooves thundered on the hard earth. She twisted her head to the front and saw that they rode through an old holloway, the track carved into a smooth dip by years of footsteps, horses' hooves, cart wheels, and weather. The trees reached low, bending over their heads in an archway. She stared at the dusty track and the thick trees and undergrowth as they flashed past, her head throbbing, until it all became dazzling and out of kilter. A confused hazy memory drifted through her mind, of a little girl on a pony, of doting parents, before … before … darkness.

Her mind seemed to be slipping out of gear. Even behind her closed eyes she could see images, misty, floating, dark rolling towards her. Dizziness overwhelmed her. She was falling … falling … into nothingness …

*

The sound of the horse's hooves clattering on stones shattered her reverie and Lady Vivianne opened her eyes to the huge spreading mead hall before her. She stared at the wooden building with its thatched roof as if seeing it for the first time. Somehow it looked different: less clear, more misty and blurred. Yet this was the place of feasting, drinking mead, discussing community affairs, business and dispensing justice that she knew so well. It was the hall that her father had built, and that Sir Pelleas had taken on Father's death: Pelleas, whom her father had rescued, a lost tattered boy, a cast-out Saxon, and, recognising his nascent military prowess, brought up as his own lieutenant; Pelleas, who had become her 'protector', and her suitor.

She glanced towards her own timber sleeping hall, her chamber, which stood beside the great hall, alongside all the others that surrounded the mead hall at the centre of the settlement, approached by the ancient Roman stone-paved streets built long before her birth and long before their Roman protectors had abandoned them to their fate.

Serfs ran out to greet them and lifted her from the mount. Roland slipped from the saddle and moved to catch her arm, but she shrugged away from him, frowning, and looking around for her lady-of-the-chamber. She heard the shrill voice before she saw her.

"Move away! Let me through!" A sturdy woman in a long green peplos pushed through the throng and curtseyed, gesturing that she should follow her quickly. "Lady Vivianne, I am glad that you are back in time," she grumbled. "I do not know how long we might keep Sir Pelleas distracting."

"Distracted," Vivianne corrected with a toss of her head.

Her woman shook her head and sighed. "Why do you do this, my lady?"

Vivianne took a deep breath in, filling her chest, and clearing her mind. She straightened her back and tossed her head. "Guin, you know full well what happens on these days when I am drawn to the lake."

"So like your mother…" muttered Guin, but Lady Vivianne chose to ignore the comment and pursed her lips instead. She followed after her lady-of-the-chamber, into her sleeping hall, conscious that she deliberately slowed her feet a little, in annoyance. She would not be hurried, not for Pelleas, not for anyone.

But pushing past Guin and sweeping into her hall in front of her maid, Vivianne's palm curled over her pouch and she felt the piece of fabric in a wet clump inside it. She felt a heat suffuse her body and she fumbled furtively in her pouch, slipping the cream cloth out. Lest it might be regarded as a lord's favour, she quickly tightened her grip around it, knuckles white.

"Be pleased to dry my pouch, Guin," she said as she held up her arms for her lady-of-the-chamber to release the leather bag and lay it carefully before the fire that blazed in its hearth at the side of the chamber.

As Guin bustled around her, tugging her wet dirty gown from her and stripping her of the thin linen shift, Vivianne clutched the cloth and hummed a little tune she remembered from her childhood. It was one that her mother used to sing to her, before her life changed so devastatingly. And she made a show of drying herself on the linen cloth that Guin held out, keeping her hand out of sight behind it.

Vivianne was aware of Guin tugging and mumbling as she dressed her, pulling a clean and dry light blue kirtle over her body. It felt soft and

23

Vivianne glanced down to see the way it skimmed her body and fell in gentle folds to the floor. She held out her arms, with tight fists, for Guin to fix the gold clasps at the sleeves, and then helped her to slip the rich burgundy overgown on top and arrange its drapes and folds. It was one of Vivianne's favourites for the evening, trimmed with light blue to match the kirtle and edged with ermine. She chose a large gold brooch from the wooden board that Guin held out to her. It was decorated with the curled white dragon of her family and it reminded Vivianne of her lost parents. She bit her lip as the maid fixed it on the over-mantle. Guin signalled to Vivianne to hold up her arms as the brown leather girdle-belt was slipped around her slim waist and looped through the buckle and back around its length to fall at the front.

Guin paused, admiring her handiwork.

"My pouch?" Vivianne prompted. Guin reached for the tooled leather pocket and hung it from the girdle.

"I did not forget, my lady. I know I am simple, but not *that* simple," Guin snapped. "I know that you are minded to keep it by you at all times." Tutting her annoyance, Guin moved behind her and dragged the harsh bone-comb without mercy through Vivianne's long hair that reached to her hips. Vivianne glanced sideways, seeing her reflection in the piece of precious glass propped on the table, and saw that her curly flowing locks shone bronze-red in the flare of the flames lit in the wall sconces. Vivianne quickly and quietly slipped the cream cloth back into her pouch to nestle against the tiny silver crucifix she kept hidden there.

"My lady, your hair!"

"It will be fine. I shall imagine it beautiful. We see what we want to see."

"Hmph, none of your imagining magicking it right, my lady. It is still damp and it smells of mere water." Guin sniffed. "I shall have to braid it." She sighed. "We really do not have time to do this! I am a martie –"

"Martyr."

" – a martyr to you, and have always been, ever since you were a girl and your sweet mother was alive." Vivianne heard the break in Guin's voice.

Vivianne moued her lips, then relented and smiled, despite herself, if a little guiltily. "I know you will do your best for me."

Skilfully with busy fingers, Guin worked her hair, and Vivianne felt the tugging as her maid draped two long thick braids down her full breasts. Then she was aware of Guin standing back and knew that, as always, she frowned critically at her handiwork.

"Hmph," Guin muttered as she pulled a few strands of purple flowering thyme from the pot in the fireplace, and wound them into the braids.

"Thank you, Guin. That smells lovely. And I am sorry that I caused you such worry."

"Hmph. You are too high-thinking for your own good," muttered Guin, frowning.

*

Vivianne entered the great mead hall. Roland, also changed into dry warm clothing, met her, graciously bowing, in the ante-room and gestured for her to walk through the great door before him. Inside, there was a noise of boisterous revelry and a thick cloying smell of hops, barley and honey pervaded the place. The stink of sweat, distinctively male body odour, and the chamber's pots overflowing with urine and vomit, met her as she stepped a few paces in. As the serfs noticed her, they hastily ran out to do their rounds of emptying the pots again.

Her eyes swept the hall with distaste. As she became used to the gloom, she could make out the wooden benches and tables set on folding trestles down either side of the hall, that were littered with the debris of an extravagant feast: hunted venison, domestic mutton and beef from the burg, goose and swan from the riverside, and fruits, nuts and berries from the hedgerows, lay ravaged and discarded, bones and branches of thyme flung to the side. Ale and mead jars overturned and golden liquid dripped unheeded onto the wattle mats on the floor, even as the only women present, the cup-bearers, hurried round yet again with the communal ale-bowl. The flares were already flaming in their sconces on the walls, the hanging cressets shedding an oily light, the fire pit in the middle of the hall flaming up, licking towards the roof, black choking smoke clouding the air as it rose to the thatch.

She watched a couple of drunken guests staggering and rolling together, no longer capable of caring whether they were supposed to be fighting or embracing, grabbing for balance at the rich tapestries hanging on the walls. One swept his arm wildly at the carved icons glowing in the light of the flames with their gold figures and enamelled cloisonné garnet eyes staring unnervingly at their assailants. Vivianne winced and clenched her fists. She remembered when this hall belonged to her royal parents and the company was polite, respectful, and the court recognised the old values of courtesy, chivalry and honour; when the entertainment was learned and cultured, with poets and musicians, acrobats from the east and dancers from the south. A time when Roman Christianity was overt; splendid gold crosses, paintings and icons revered, not hidden or knocked aside like common pottery.

But now, on the dais set in the centre of the gloomy right-hand benches, she could see the large stocky red-faced man with a fair unruly beard and thick, wild, dirty hair, the colour of the moonlight, sitting on a huge carved wooden seat. He was in his usually adopted place of honour at the centre of the top table, mopping his scarlet forehead with a cloth. He swung a gold goblet as he sang along, showering out spittle in all directions, with his raucous friends:

"And she tumbled from the stallion
Nymue's earth muddied and mucked her
Robes awry I glimpsed her breast
For Venus's sake I fell upon her and ..."

Suddenly he stopped, goblet still raised in his hand as his eyes caught hers at the far end of the hall. He had clearly not missed her at all. The bawdy song petered out and a hush fell through the room. Sir Pelleas with his piercing blue eyes and greasy golden hair stared at her for a moment. Then he seemed to recover himself and raked his fingers through his hair. Vivianne had the oddest feeling of seeing him somewhere else too, somewhere strange, in a small chamber, leaning against a door lintel, a sense of cooking pots with unfamiliar smells and unusual haunting music. She shivered.

"Vivianne, my betrothed," shouted Pelleas merrily, and the court began to murmur again with relief. He rose quickly and strode across the hall, arms outstretched, the dark heavy cloak stretched like the wings of a vulture hanging from his arms.

He grasped her shoulders with a strong grip but gazed at her face with a lopsided smirk. "Come, my lady, my love. Let us to my chamber. Oh, now that I am battle-victorious and home again, how I long for our hand-fasting ceremony at the next moon, and then I can lie beside you every night." Then his expression mutated into a leer, and he glanced meaningfully around at his drinking companions, "Or, indeed, on top of you ...,"

Vivianne shuddered, smelling his beery breath in her face, and drew back a little, out of his clutch. He had hardly missed her presence, she thought, clearly revelling in the rowdy company of his thegns.

He reached out for her again, gripping her arms even tighter, his florid sweaty face thrust into hers, and pulled her to him, crushing her into his broad, hard chest. His hands groped her back and as she pulled away he swiftly flicked one hand between them and grasped her breast. She staggered back, pushing against him.

"How dare you, *Sir* Pelleas. You know that I do not want you. You take my father's place as chieftain, yet you are nothing – *nothing* - compared with him." She raised her hand to slap his face but he caught her wrist. She yelped in pain as he twisted it. But her eyes met Pelleas's in a stare that she knew was defiant and disdainful. She wrenched her hand from his grip. "You are ..."

She felt a firm strong hand on her arm, catching her and moving her away. But she caught the flash of anger in Pelleas's eyes and twisted round to see Roland move to her side, his hand still on her arm. For a moment the hostility between the two men was palpable. Then Pelleas's body was racked in a loud belch, his stare faltered and she heard Roland speak in his calm, even tone.

"My lord Sir Pelleas, I believe that the scōp has arrived."

"What? Well. Good," Pelleas caught his breath and nodded. "And the glǣman also? I feel the need for a bawdy story-teller and jolly musician tonight." But as he turned away to follow Roland back to his place on the dais, he swung back to Vivianne and, leaning in towards her, he hissed, "As you will, my *dear*. But mark me, I may find myself a bed-mate elsewhere." Someone nearby giggled. Pelleas's face contorted into a sneer. "Do not cross me, *lady*, or refuse me. We marry as soon as the moon allows. I allowed you that delay because of your ..." He flapped his hand towards her lower abdomen. "And then we shall see ..."

Vivianne shivered under the threat. He had taken it to the Witan council and her settlement had approved that she, high-born and father-less, be given to her protector. She knew he wanted to breed on her as soon as they were hand-fasted, even before the formal marriage. And there was no more guile for delay she could use.

In a moment, Guin was at her side, and as she ushered her back to her sleeping hall, she glanced at Vivianne's face and murmured, "My lady, you have no choice. With your father and mother dead, and you alone. Except for me, and our lord Sir Pelleas ..."

"Guin, this is not a judicious man, he is not a noble warrior, he is not worthy to lead this settlement. He is neither a royal Brythen, like my family, nor from Roman descent, like Sir Roland's. He is disgusting and boorish. He is a foul brute and he is a *Saxon*!"

Vivianne felt the bile rise in her throat and her heart thrum loudly in her ears. The room juddered and swept with mist before her eyes as she fell.

*

Viv gasped for breath and grabbed the half-submerged branch that clawed at her elbow. Her eyes cleared as she struggled out of the water and pulled herself to the safety of the dark muddy bank. Her shoes were gone. She sank onto the ground, wrapping her arms round her knees and tried to fill her lungs with air. Her breath rasped and her chest hurt. Her jeans and top were ruined, torn and soaked.

Good god! But at least she was alive. Slowly her hearing returned and the sounds of night drifted around her. Beyond the mere, she could hear the occasional lorry on the dual carriageway that by-passed the village and followed the line of the ancient Icknield Street south to Birmingham. Not much traffic at this time of night.

She shivered. Shock, she assumed, at falling into the water and nearly drowning. She hugged herself tightly and felt an uncomfortable lump against her leg. She fumbled in the pocket of her jeans and pulled out something she thought at first was her wet handkerchief. It felt wrong. And as she stared down at the fine cream cloth lying in her palm, she heard the church clock and counted the twelve chimes.

Chapter 3

"Hi, it's Ellie. Please get back to me, Viv. I ... er ... just *please* get in touch!"

Viv leaned against the kitchen island bar, trembling hands wrapped around her "I'm a medieval geek" mug that slopped coffee as she listened to the voicemail. Ellie sounded anxious, concerned, just as she did when Viv had been ill that awful time at university. OK, she could always ring her and then end the call if it was difficult – if Ellie knew all about what had been happening with Pete and Gwyn. It was her worst fear, that she was the last to know. She would feel so idiotic, even more betrayed.

She remembered staggering back home at midnight last night, across the fields, head full of strange nightmarish dreams, woozy from the wine and the images of mead halls and red-faced chieftains swirling around her brain. Had she somehow been drugged? But she hadn't even taken a paracetamol; she rarely did, let alone anything stronger.

Yet she had fallen into bed and slept deeply without dreaming, waking that morning feeling somehow refreshed. Then when her hand had groped for Pete in the bed beside her for their slow lazy Saturday morning love-making and found his place empty, she had remembered Pete's announcement, the letter, and the devastation had returned in force.

Her torn and muddied jeans were still on the floor in the bedroom awaiting their fate. A small fragment of damp cream fabric sat on her dressing table. Where had she picked that up from? Maybe as she grabbed for the undergrowth when she fell at the side of the mere. Maybe it was tangled up in the branches and roots there.

Her coffee was getting cold as she stared at the phone, unusually indecisive. Then she reached out. Go for it.

Ellie picked up straight away, after only two rings.

"Oh, god, Viv! It's awful. I had no idea. Well, I suspected that something was going on with Gwyn, she was being a bit ... secretive, suspicious ... but not ... oh god, not with your Pete."

29

"So how did you hear?" Viv sank onto the bar chair with relief.

"She left me a rather curt message on my voicemail last evening. She sounded … distant. Well, she would be, wouldn't she, announcing that Pete was moving in with her. It was like … *don't argue with me, this is it …fact*. It was so unlike her, comfy, homely Gwyn. I tried to get you last night but there seemed to be something wrong with the signal – odd, I don't usually have a problem here."

"Oh, Ellie. I think I'm still in shock. Something else has happened too. I need to talk."

"Listen – I'll come straight over. Stuart's in and he said he'll look after the kids while I come right over to be with you. Amazingly there's no golf today, and a Saturday too."

*

As Viv opened the door to Ellie, they fell into each other's arms.

"Oh god, hun, oh god. Babe, what can I say?" wailed Ellie as Viv released her shock and grief and sobbed into her best friend's neck, her voice muffled by Ellie's thick, luxuriantly glossy and flowing locks.

Viv pulled away first. "Goodness, I'm suffocating in there." She swiped her tears away from her cheeks with her palms, trying for a brave smile, and drew in her rasping breath. "So …. Coffee? Wine? Although I for one have had far too much over the last couple of days. But come on in before Tilly upstairs hears us and comes down for a nosy." Viv sniffed loudly. "Hearing like a bat, that one, and the curiosity of a Miss Marple."

"Yes, wine o' clock – it must be. And I can get a taxi back if needs be, and collect my car tomorrow."

Viv's will crumbled. "Oh, go on then."

They settled on the sofas in the sitting area of the huge living room. Viv sipped her wine slowly, conscious of her over-indulgence these last nights, and leaned her head against the sofa back, telling Ellie about Thursday evening and then the letter last night.

"I just can't get my head round it all," said Viv. "I had no inkling, none at all. I mean, were they in business together? Why not tell me? I haven't seen Gwyn since, goodness, must be my birthday party in the spring. I'd begun to wonder if she was avoiding me, but when I texted her she just said she was very busy at the school …And I've been up to my eyes too …"

"Yes, I know! And has he replied to your voicemail yet?"

"No. There were no signs, no indications at all that anything was amiss. The relationship, the flat ... I don't understand what happened."

"No, I know. Me neither. And – I mean ... I'm not being funny ... but Gwyn, well, I know we've all been BFF for years, but ... she's just .... Hardly a femme fatale."

Viv made a wry face. "No. I don't know. Maybe that's what he wanted. Someone homely and unambitious, a simple soul. Not like me, studying, going for promotion, doing research, presenting at conferences all over the world. Maybe it was just too much for him."

Ellie spluttered. "Oh for god's sake, Viv. He knew what you did before you moved in together. You haven't changed. And why the secrecy?"

"Oh god, I don't know what to do. I wish ... I wish Mum and Dad were still here."

Ellie put down her wine glass and reached to squeeze Viv's hand. "Oh, hun. I know it's not the same as real family, but Stuart and I are here for you. You're not entirely alone, you know."

"I know. And thank you. You've always been there for me. I do appreciate it." She paused as she gulped more wine. "Ellie, I may have lost Pete but I'll do anything not to lose the flat as well."

"God, the rat!" Ellie shook her head. "He doesn't need the money, surely? Aren't his family wealthy? That's just vindictive."

"But I don't even know why he would want to be vindictive. That assumes getting back at someone for something they've done. And I don't know what I've done."

"Yes, but some men can't cope with taking guilt and blame, so they feel happier hurting the one who they prefer to imagine is to blame. It makes them feel as though they're justified for doing what they're doing." Ellie picked up the wine bottle again, then realising that it was empty returned it to the table. "And, anyway, didn't you use most of your parents' inheritance to buy it? He shouldn't get that."

"Oh, it's not as straightforward as that, Ellie. Yes, I used my inheritance to help set up his business, but Pete also contributed, or rather his parents did."

"But his parents will buy him another place and you've used your inheritance already. That doesn't seem right!"

"I never thought ahead. I suppose I should have done."

Images swirled around Viv's mind: decorating the flat together when they first moved in, laughing together at the silliest things, reading to each other from books they loved, taking romantic holidays, running hand-in-hand along the beach at sunset on a snatched holiday in Nice, making love in the afternoon sunshine that time in Perugia ... pulling Pete's shoes and stained clothes off when he came back drunk from a night out with the boys, covering up for his temper tantrums when he'd offended someone, fobbing off his parents when they called and Pete was in bed fending off a hangover.

"So – o – o, what is your thinking about the flat then?" Ellie brought another bottle in and topped up their glasses.

"It's my home. I love it. I love the village. I feel more at home here than I have felt anywhere else for years, since my childhood home with Mum and Dad in that old converted rectory outside York. Even more than my home with my grandparents. Well, I guess that wasn't really my home, not in the same way. And here I love the feeling of a connection with the past; there's so much history here. The Iron Age barrow, the pre-Roman and Anglo-Saxon finds at Cooney's Mere ... it all fits with my medieval research ..."

"I can see that you wouldn't want to move. Cooney's Mere – yes, it's lovely." She paused in thought. "Funny name, though. Why is it called Cooney's Mere? It always makes me think of George Clooney ..."

Viv smiled. "Yeah, everything makes you think of George Clooney! No, it's a corruption of Cūning's Mere, or Lake. Cūning means King in Old English. "

"Oh, right. So, King's Lake, but why?"

"Well, there's a legend about an early pre-Anglo-Saxon king or chieftain hereabouts, and his lady who turned out to be the lady of the lake."

"God, Viv, are you OK, you've gone very pale?"

"Yes, yes, I'm OK. Just shock still, I think."

But she looked down, aware that her hands gripped her baggy old jeans, and her knuckles were white.

*

Later, she waved Ellie off in the taxi, and closed the front door quickly in case Tilly upstairs heard. She liked her crazy neighbour, but knew she couldn't cope with her just now. Viv pulled the heavy curtains over the large arched glazed doors onto the courtyard and sank onto her comfortable squashy sofa, curling up like a foetus. She felt so exhausted. Her stomach was queasy from the spaghetti Bolognese Ellie insisted on making for her. She reached for the remains of her lunchtime wine propped up against the sofa, but her hand seemed to have lost all its strength. Well, at least I'll sleep, thought Viv.

And sleep she did. She was vaguely aware of a knocking at the door and, as she'd heard heavy footsteps on the stairs, she guessed it was Tilly and didn't rouse herself to answer it.

Her dreams were garish and confused. Dark smoky noisy rooms, a sweaty red face thrust into hers, Pete hissing "don't you cross *me*", and turning away from her, a tall dark figure brushing her arm, staring down at a piece of cream fabric in her hand, Gwyn tugging brutally at her hair, pushing at her back, knocking her off her feet, staggering … water …

Viv woke abruptly feeling very nauseous, and ran to the bathroom. Sinking onto the tiled floor in front of the toilet bowl, holding her hair back with her left hand, she heaved and vomited. God, why had she drunk all that red wine? Two nights running and then lunchtime today with Ellie. So unlike her. Such a bad idea.

A loud, urgent banging assailed her consciousness, and she realised that someone was trying to attract her attention at the courtyard doors. She pulled herself up to her feet, flushed the toilet, rinsed with minty mouth wash, splashed cold water on her face, and straightened her clothes as she returned to the sitting room. She pulled the curtains back and jumped as she saw Tilly's round red face framed with her wild frizzy blonde hair pressed against the glass. She was gesticulating wildly for the courtyard doors to be opened. Peering at the glazing again, Tilly rubbed her sleeve over the sweat marks from her forehead that smeared the glass.

"Oh, my!" sniffed Tilly as she slipped in through the double doors that Viv held open for her. "*Someone's* been going at it a bit with the old vino."

Viv opened both doors wide to let the early evening air in.

Tilly stepped across the threshold and peered at Viv. "Hey, you're not …?"

"No."

"I've been trying to get your attention for *hours*, sweetie-pie." Tilly plonked herself down on the sofa and folded her arms under an ample bosom threatening to burst out of her tight low-cut top. In one hand flapped a piece of paper. "What *have* you been doing? And where is that Mr Gorgeous Sexy Hunk of yours?"

"Umm. The gorgeous sexy hunk has left. And I've consumed far too much wine."

"Hell's teeth. That's why this place stinks like a gin palace. Why's he left? Another woman? Not enough sex? Too much sex? Not enough of the right sex?"

"Hey, hey! *Please*. It was just the other night. I'm feeling fragile, Tilly. I can't deal with an interrogation."

"Sweetie-pie. I may be a few years younger than you, but I do know about sex. It's pretty much my research project! It's *always* either not enough sex or not the right sex. Take it from me. Chris did a bunk because I stopped the bondage stuff. Well, my wrists and ankles were raw, *raw* ... they got infected, and, well, you should have *seen* ..."

"Aaagh. Would you like a coffee?" Viv turned quickly to the kitchen area.

"Love one. So what's up with the hunk? Honestly, *men*! Did I tell you about James at work? I've given them up, men."

Viv turned in surprise. She'd certainly heard male voices recently on the stairs.

"Well, not literally. I mean – can't live with them, can't live without them. Just want them when I need them. Did you read in Cosmo, the big O a couple of times a week or more keeps you healthy? Good for the heart. Keeps your skin smooth. Exercise, you see. Pumps the blood. Who needs a relationship to clog things up?"

"Clog things up?" Viv shook her head and handed Tilly a mug of white coffee. She'd made her own black and strong. She wished she hadn't asked that question. What on earth was Tilly going to spout now? She could hardly keep up with her at the best of times.

Tilly reached forward to place her mug on the coffee table in front of her, and tugged her tight bubblegum-pink skirt over her substantial thighs a centimetre nearer to her knees.

"Life. No, keep it simple. Live your own life. Keep a man in the background for what he does best. And I don't mean changing light bulbs or taking out the rubbish." She winked and picked up the paper that she had rested on her lap, and flapped it towards Viv. "But, sweetie-pie, this is what I came for. To ask your opinion." She carefully unfolded it and held it out to Viv. "It's a new design. For a replica tapestry. The brief was difficult. Exactly who and what had to be included. Very specific. But has to look like very early Saxon." She wafted her fingers over the paper. "I normally do much later fabrics, Georgian, Victorian and stuff. I have done some earlier artefacts but not tapestries. You're a medieval thingy. What do you reckon?"

Viv knew that Tilly was a designer for a firm that specialised in making replica jewellery and artefacts for theatre productions and re-enactments. She often asked for her opinion and ideas, but usually about a completed piece for a much later period. Tilly's field was art not history.

"I looked it up on the internet, but it was a bit confusing so I'm not sure it's right."

"Well, I would say so. The style of the figures and hunting dogs do look authentic to me, and the stylised buildings, oh and the boar – nice touch! It's a little out of my field, the art stuff, but, yes I guess it gives the right impression. What's it for?"

"Oh," Tilly flapped her hand in the air. "It's a TV thingy … drama … a new series, fantasy and stuff. Thing is, now they all have high res HD and the pause button, we have to be so careful. I've looked at so many pics, I'm going blind!"

*

When she finally got rid of Tilly, Viv turned on the wide screen smart TV and sank again on to the sofa. She flicked through the channels and selected a movie she'd seen before. She didn't want to sit in solitary silence in the flat but music made her cry and somehow she couldn't focus on reading a novel.

But her mind wasn't on the movie. She couldn't push the images of her drunken dream out of her mind: the clothes styles, the mead hall, the décor, the language, it was all so familiar from her research work. She forced herself to picture Lady Vivianne looking down at her dress, staring at Sir Pelleas and the mead hall, eyeing Sir Roland. She saw again her 'maid', Guin. What she saw would place it in the so-called 'Dark Ages', between the end of the Roman Empire and the main Anglo-

Saxon invasion. Early middle ages: what, maybe 450 to 500AD. The time people dismissed as uninteresting, unrefined, uncultured, even barbaric. The time that people forgot. The time Viv had begun to investigate again, revisiting her post-doctoral research into early Old English language and literature, fifth century origins of Beowulf, and King Arthur.

Yet there were oddnesses too; things which were not what she would have expected from her research. The fabrics were soft and flowing, in deep and bright colours: blue-green, burgundy, crimson, not the thick rough fabrics of her research, hemp and sacking-like, in drab colours. Plain, not richly embroidered. There should be simple wooden saddles, not bejewelled purple saddle cloth. She thought of all the tooled leather in her "dream", the gold brooches, and the rich and varied food. That was not how it was supposed to be. That did not seem rough and unskilled and barbaric.

Viv bit her lip to stop the sadness that threatened to engulf her, and manoeuvred her box file from under her laptop and took it to the sofa. It was the only thing she felt she *could* focus on just now. Her work. Neutral, unemotional. She sat, cross-legged, unclipping the lever arch and pulling papers out. A paper on the Romano-Britons, the departure of the Roman legions, the warring tribes from small 'kingdoms' or 'chiefdoms' dealing with each other and with invaders from Scotland, Northumberland and the continent. There was little to go on, so little had survived, but there had been recent archaeological finds, like Lyminge, that possibly suggested a more cultured, wealthy and organised society than previously imagined.

She shuffled through the papers and found her own draft piece entitled '*Pagan or Christian? A clash of cultures or an intermingling? The mix of cultures that sheds light on the "Dark Ages" of post-Romano-Brython England*'. She had never finished the paper for publication. She'd got side-tracked onto the new Beowulf commentary that her publishers had commissioned. Well, perhaps now she might take it up again.

But right now, as always, she became absorbed with scanning paper after paper, making two piles beside her on the sofa: 'evidence' and 'questionable'.

In the background the movie droned on.

Eventually Viv felt the strain in her neck and, wincing, rubbed it. She circled her head from shoulder to shoulder, as she did in her yoga classes, then stretched her body out, resting her head against the sofa back and closed her eyes. A dozen thoughts swirled through her brain. She remembered an argument she had become involved in with a colleague the other day. It lodged in her brain like watching a television debate:

Colleague: *"But it was a dangerous, barbaric period. Most of the evidence, the little that's survived, indicates a lack of skill in the dark ages, a rejection of the Roman influences ..."*

Viv: *"Yet those Roman influences and skills are seen again in the finds from the Anglo-Saxon times – Sutton Hoo, for example."*

Colleague: *"Sutton Hoo demonstrated new influences on English culture."*

Viv: *"Yes, in some ways, but surely the richness of coins, tapestries, brooches and buckles from the Roman period would not have disappeared completely on their withdrawal from England, then suddenly been crafted again after the main Anglo-Saxon invasion and settlement? The culture and ideas, the religion and practices, surely couldn't have just suddenly vanished."*

Colleague: *"Remember that the economy all but collapsed after the Romans withdrew from England."*

Viv: *"OK, so the economic scene changed but surely it would have been a gradual process, beginning in the Roman occupation and continued after their withdrawal?"*

Colleague: *"So you're saying that the "Dark Ages" can't logically have been so very dark?"*

Viv: *"Yes. OK, it's easy to focus only on that so-called "dark" period between the Roman withdrawal and the coming of the Saxons, as though it was bleak and fallow, as though all the Roman inheritance was left to rot, but was it really like that? Surely some things would have continued through. Yes, some Roman buildings and civic structures may have been abandoned and fallen into disrepair, finally crumbling. But not all. I can't see it myself."*

Colleague: *"But there's no evidence ..."*

Viv: *"There's little evidence either way. We just make assumptions. Surely some folks would have continued traditions, cultures and ways onwards after the Romans. Was there really a sudden fall into barbarism after the Romans left? Why should people suddenly change their lives so completely? I don't think so.*"

She rubbed her neck again and felt herself frowning.

So what if the things she 'saw' were more true to that time than the source books indicate.

And if what she saw was the truth, then was she dreaming … or experiencing a reality?

She was so tired. Viv must have dozed off because the sound of her antique grandfather clock in the hall woke her. Midnight. …

Her mind threw itself into top gear, despite her physical exhaustion. Viv picked up her paper on '*Pagan or Christian*' again. She wondered if different communities really started falling out and fighting each other? Surely there must have been some cooperation between groups, relationships, intermarriage. Religion and beliefs meant a lot to early societies. Just suppose there was an interweaving of paganism, magic and Christianity that bound different communities together. Or did it cause suspicion, fear, feuding? So many questions burned through her brain.

In her drunken dreaming the night before, she created in her mind a Germanic-looking pagan Saxon Sir Pelleas, a red-haired Romano-Brit-Celtic Lady Vivianne, likely Christian with her silver crucifix, a Mediterranean olive-skinned Roman Sir Roland. If that was a true historic story, it would be fascinating.

But how could it be true …she was dreaming, surely? The alternative was truly terrifying.

That she was going mad.

Chapter 4

Someone was moving around in her room. Gingerly, she opened her eyes, just enough to see the fringe of her eyelashes. A shadow crossed to and fro at the end of the bed. Oh, strange, she couldn't remember getting to bed at all. She could not, at first, make out who the person was. But it seemed by their movements that it was somebody who should be there, not an intruder.

"Oh, Lady Vivianne, you are wakening." Guin's voice, low and soft, lulled her senses. "I was worried for you last night, when you fainted. I was obliged to accept help from Sir Roland to carry you here to your sleeping hall."

Vivianne reached her hand below the bedcovers and felt her linen night shift that was tangled round her feet. She frowned. For some reason she expected something else.

"Come, my lady. It is time for you to break your fast."

Vivianne opened her eyes fully. Guin was standing beside the bed, holding open a heavy robe trimmed with fur. Early morning light filtered through the thatch and the fire blazed up in the new-fashioned hearth which stood at the end of the room, not in the middle like the traditional halls. Its warmth revived her body after a night of disturbing dreams and she breathed in the comforting aroma of wood smoke tinged with the sweetness of purple thyme which Guin always added to the pine logs. As she swung herself out of bed, she felt her head ache with the images of Sir Pelleas, the crowded, noisy, threatening mead hall, and a nameless fear of losing her home, her life, all that she held dear. A drift of memory like a wisp of smoke: cream fabric, a friend hugging her tightly…

Guin wrapped the robe around Vivianne's tense body, and turned to lift the wooden boards away from the window openings, letting the light flood in.

"See, I have laid out for you some fresh spelt bread, still warm from the brick, and honey from the hives, cold meats left over from the feast last night, and hedgerow berries."

Vivianne sat at the small trestle table by the fire. Guin turned to the table, poured from an earthenware pitcher and handed her a bowl of mead. As Vivianne sipped, the warm rich honey-laced liquid soothed her throat and began to clear her foggy head. She felt her huddled body relax its grip and her muscles ease. She sighed.

Guin bustled around the room, tidying the bed covers and laying out clothes for the day, as Vivianne ate, breaking her fast hungrily. She was so very glad that Pelleas had not demanded her presence in the hall for 'first meal' that day.

"I assume Sir Pelleas broke his fast at some ungodly early hour," she murmured to Guin, "and is now with his thegns, hunting in the woodlands?"

Guin turned away from her so that she could not see her face. "I would expect so, my lady."

"Then I am happy. It seems I have the day to myself, before he demands my presence at feasting tonight." Vivianne returned her attention to her meal.

"My lady," began Guin. Vivianne looked up from her food and nodded as her maid stood in front of her, twisting a shawl in her plump fingers.

"Yes, what is it?"

"My lady, I was wondering whether your fainting last night was perhaps a symptom of a … er …womanly condition?"

Vivianne stared for a moment, frowning, then realisation dawned upon her. "Goodness, no!"

"I simply wondered whether you were with child, and whether we needed to make …adjustments."

"How on earth could I be?" Vivianne could hardly bear the thought that some day Sir Pelleas, her *betrothed*, might even touch her in any intimate way. It made her feel quite nauseated. Her whole body reviled the thought of what, she supposed, was her future inevitability. Yet women often did have to marry a man they disliked, even hated, especially high-born yet abandoned women like herself. How could she do it? Yet what other future was there for such as she?

But she noted that Guin's smile bore a relief that seemed to be not only for her lady. An odd, secret smile that she quickly turned away from Vivianne. And the hesitancy and modesty which was not Guin's normal robust manner. That modesty reminded her more of her own mother, wrenched from her so long ago.

"Guin?" Vivianne pushed her platter of fruits away from her across the little table with her left hand and drained her mead bowl with her right. She replaced it on the table and wiped her mouth with her hand. "Guin, you were with my mother before she passed over to the higher world ..."

"Yes, indeed, my lady. I was only a young girl, not so much older than you are now."

Vivianne raised her eyebrows. She had always thought of Guin as perpetually old, like Pelleas.

"But she was so kind to me. It was my first service and she showed me what to do and how to do it well. I was with her when Sir Pelleas came and when she and your father died. You were a mere child of ten harvests, five long harvests ago," she sighed. "So I felt I had to stay to serve you and see that you grew well into your inheritance."

"I have no inheritance," snapped Vivianne. "Pelleas saw to that."

Guin looked at her sharply. "You will have what you share with Sir Pelleas, when you marry. He has restored the fortifications against the marauders, the village houses and streets, the old Roman roads to the settlement, and the halls, and kept your parents' properties well ... my lady."

"This is not how it looks to my eyes," retorted Vivianne, rising and sorting through the clothes on the bed, picking them up then flinging them down again. "He has taken them over as lord, chieftain and king, and he has them as his own now. It is irrelevant that I should marry him to *share* my property that is rightfully mine alone. It only reinforces his own position to his thegns, all the freemen ceorls and the peasant geburs ... and makes him secure on the dais in the mead hall."

Guin stared at her and there was anger in her narrowed eyes. "He looks to care for you and protect you."

"Hmm. I wonder if he would do so if I was ugly and sickly?"

Guin smiled briefly. "You are certainly not that, my lady. Young, beautiful and strong." She thrust Vivianne's kirtle at her. "And I am sure that you will bear Sir Pelleas a brood of healthy, strong and clever children to inherit and continue the line." She turned away abruptly.

Vivianne grimaced. "Guin, you tended my mother and yet you seem to defend Sir Pelleas most readily."

Guin glanced back at her but turned away quickly. Yet Vivianne still managed to take note of the angry blushes that suffused her maid's cheeks.

As Vivianne dressed, aided somewhat brusquely by Guin, there was a hearty knocking at the door.

"One moment!" called Guin, adjusting Vivianne's pouch onto the wide leather girdle, before making her way to the door and opening it cautiously. "Oh, Sir Roland! You are not with Sir Pelleas out hunting?"

"Let him in, for goodness sake, Guin! Do not hold a conversation in my doorway." Vivianne sat down by the fire again.

Sir Roland strode in to the sleeping hall, grinning at Guin's startled look, and with him came a drift of bergamot.

"But, Sir Roland, if I may, sir … this is not right, to enter my lady's chamber."

"Guin," said Vivianne firmly. "Sir Roland is hardly going to ravish me." She glanced at him and only just caught the twinkle in his dark eyes. He motioned his head to indicate that he wished Guin to retire. Vivianne frowned at him, but acknowledged his unspoken request. "Leave us for a moment, please, Guin. Take the food bowls but leave us the mead pitcher and two drinking bowls."

"Well!" spluttered Guin as she gathered the remains of the breaking-fast, and swept out, banging the door behind her. Vivianne waited until she heard her maid's footsteps retreat outside.

"May I?" asked Roland, gesturing at the stool but drawing it up to the fire opposite Vivianne before she had time to answer, sitting down, long muscular legs wide apart. He rested his strong tanned forearms on his knees and gazed across at Vivianne. His large presence dominated the chamber and she could not help but notice the depth of his dark eyes, the glow of his olive skin, and the broadness of his generous mouth – and his strong thighs – that made her heart flutter, her body flush and her abdomen contract with a warm ache. Quickly, Vivianne looked away and reached out for the mead pitcher, filling the two drinking bowls with a hand that was not as steady as it should have been.

"Would you like anything to eat, Sir Roland?"

"No, thank you, I have already broken my fast with Sir Pelleas before he went out hunting. I simply wished to speak with you. That is why I declined to go with them. I said that I had business with the treasury."

"Well, that would not be denied, then," snorted Vivianne. Roland smiled and raised his eyebrows.

"No indeed. But my business *is* with treasure and, indeed, warnings."

"I see," Vivianne said slowly, "I am intrigued."

"Lady Vivianne." Roland lowered his voice, but still looked directly and openly into her eyes. "I overheard a conversation, an intimate conversation, that involved your lady-of-the-chamber, Guin, and your betrothed, Sir Pelleas."

"*What?*"

"I am sorry that my words are abrupt but I wish to tell you before there is any interruption." He glanced towards the door. "I chose to come to you whilst the thegns and Sir Pelleas are out hunting, and the geburs are busy with the day's beginning."

Vivianne inclined her head in acknowledgement. "So what is so secret and mysterious?" She laughed nervously but a moment later her laughter fell silent.

"I was passing Sir Pelleas's sleeping hall late last night, after I had ensured that you were safely in yours, and that all the flares were extinguished in the mead hall ... and I saw your lady Guin enter. She looked around suspiciously and moved silently, clearly not wanting to draw attention to herself. I was puzzled and slipped inside the ante-chamber in the shadows. I heard her giggles as she ... I am sorry, my lady ...as she embraced your lord."

"Oh, my god in heaven!" Vivianne slumped on her stool and shook her head. She did not care about Sir Pelleas, but she cared that Guin was disloyal to her.

"I distress you too much, my lady."

"No, no, I need to know what business my maid has with Pelleas and what has been betrayed."

Roland reached over and touched Vivianne's hand. Because she did not snatch it away, he enfolded it in his own. Vivianne felt her cheeks redden but kept her hand in his. It felt so comforting, so reassuring.

"He pulled her into his sleeping chamber, but as he did so, I overheard him asking if she had done as he asked and found the Vortigern chest, and whether it was possible to open it without arousing suspicion."

Vivianne's hands flew up to her mouth, stifling her cries. "No, oh no!"

"I knew that the chest is the one that Lord Vortigern from the south had sent up to your father."

"Indeed, I remember my father telling me that there was a precious chest, hidden safely. I do not know where. It was filled with the gold and silver to support his rebuilding after the legions left."

"And *I* also know that it is your secret inheritance that he kept for you that no Germanic Saxon husband would know about."

"And how do *you* know about it?"

"Because your father revealed to me that he hoped for a Christian Romano-Brython husband for you … but he feared that it was not to be when the pagan Saxons began to arrive here."

"Father …" Vivianne faltered, then gathered herself again. "Father certainly did not trust the pagan Saxons. That's why I don't understand about Pelleas."

"Your father was a good man. He could not stand by and allow a poor abandoned child, alone, as Pelleas was then, to be refused. And so he took him in to his mead hall. But he did not intend for Pelleas to marry you."

"And … and … you? What did he intend for you?" Vivianne saw the hesitation on Roland's face, the frown across his eyes.

"Your father asked me to watch over you. I have tried to keep his faith." Roland pulled out of his pouch a small shiny object which he held up to show Vivianne. It was a gold crucifix.

As Vivianne stared at the Christian symbol which now they both kept secret from the pagan Saxons and therefore from her betrothed, she felt as though the pieces of a broken pot had reformed themselves into a whole again.

"I see. And the Vortigern chest?"

She reached out to touch the gold crucifix, but the sound of footsteps approaching halted her hand. "It is Guin returning. Make haste, Sir Roland. Meet me tonight after the meal, outside the mead hall, and we can talk further."

Vivianne ushered him to the entrance. As he opened the door, she touched Roland's arm. "I must apologise." Vivianne raised her head and looked him straight in the eye. His deep dark handsome eyes. "I behaved abruptly to you the day before. I know that you were only considering my best interests. And I also understand that you carried me here to my sleeping-hall when I … er …fainted."

Roland shook his head and gestured a dismissal of his action.

"No, I wanted to thank you, Sir Roland. It was good of you. I was agitated at being summoned out of the mere."

Roland looked at her and his eyes were gentle. "I know," he murmured. "You do not need to explain."

"You called me 'my Lady of the Lake'." Vivianne lowered her voice to a whisper. "Why?" He fumbled with his pouch and thrust something into her hand and she felt the cold of metal in the shape of a key. His eyes flickered a warning.

But there was no time for his reply, as Guin rounded the hall. Vivianne thrust the key into her pouch along with the silver crucifix, and her head spun around with a new fear. And with images of a glinting chest, gold and silver crucifixes, a large bronze altar cross, gleaming bejewelled helmets and brooches, sword hilts, a gold key held in her father's hand, and … fire, flames soaring and consuming in the darkness, smoke choking her, struggling to catch a final terrified breath, her mother screaming, her father shouting … her mind slipped into the shadows.

Chapter 5

Viv's heart pounded and she breathed in deeply, trying to still her trembling. She snapped her eyes open. The shadows of her bedroom moved, shifted and resettled into the dark shapes she recognised. She hesitantly crept her hand to her throat and felt lower to her breast. Yes, she was wearing her familiar PJs, the smooth cotton t-shirt top and, as her hand explored lower, her leggings. Relief. And yet she had felt so totally at one with Lady Vivianne, in her body and her mind. She seemed to feel her emotions, too intensely for a mere dream, think her thoughts, fear her unease.

A strangled sound startled her and she held her breath.

The grandfather clock, inherited from her parents' house, clicked into action and began to strike, and she counted the twelve sonorous chimes. It had happened again. Time had stood still; at least in her own world, if not in Lady Vivianne's. No, that world had moved time on, as if she was occupying a story. She shivered.

But … wait … when she last heard the midnight chimes, she was surely in the living room, on the sofa. That was the last thing she remembered. How had she got into bed? She had absolutely no recollection of moving.

And what about the water, the lake: that seemed significant before, but this time it was nothing to do with the dream. Why? She'd just been sleeping, on the sofa, in bed. Her academic training made her seek the logical explanations, but none of this was remotely logical. She shook her head. Everything was knocked out of kilter.

She was wide awake now, and knew that the only thing for it was to make a mug of Suchard hot chocolate in the Tassimo to try to settle herself off again. As she pushed herself up in the bed to turn on the lamp, her hand touched something cold lying beside her. She groped for it in the darkness. It was a small gold key.

This was ridiculous. She'd dreamed about a key. But how had this one got here? Viv ran her fingers over the hard metal, feeling the coldness of the smooth surface, yet, as she stroked it, sensing also an underlying warmth of another hand. A trembling of memory shimmered up her spine to her fourth vertebra and around to her ribs, her heart. A drift of gentle dark eyes flickering a warning, strayed across her vision. She saw a hand, strong and masculine, a tanned forearm, and her heart fluttered. "*My Lady of the Lake*" a soft, deep voice whispered in her ear and she pulled the duvet up over her head to muffle the sound that wouldn't leave her mind.

For the rest of the night, Viv's sleep was disturbed, lying wide awake then drifting off for half an hour, then waking again. But even when she slept her mind was crowded with strange images, like flickering black and grey movies, not like the narrative she had now experienced twice. That dream had felt real, so very real. So much so, that in the darkness she could hardly distinguish the two.

She was beginning to get seriously worried about her mental state and her lack of sleep. She had to be OK for Monday at work. She couldn't be tired and unfocused for the teaching or the interview. And the latter was make-or-break time. A chance to break into the higher echelons. A senior colleague had retired and his post was available. There was not a great deal of staff turnover so there may not be another chance for a long time. God, if only that awful day hadn't happened. Why wasn't Pete still here, with her? He knew about her nervousness over the interview. Didn't he care? Clearly, he didn't. But could she make him care again? She wanted him. She needed him. Then the image of his lip curling back in an animal snarl rose behind her eyes and she knew. The man she'd been intimate with for so long, didn't even think about her warmly any more. It was over.

*

Viv dozed restlessly on and off, then hearing the church bells ringing out across the village for Sunday service, she realised it was approaching nine o' clock and she should be getting up. Ellie would be here in an hour or two, to pick up her car that she'd left last night. She would stay in for Ellie and have a coffee with her. She suddenly felt a yearning to go to early communion, but it was too late. Viv rarely attended the service, but she liked the atmosphere in the ancient village church; it was calming. Anyway, much as she would have loved it, especially at this confusing and frightening time, Viv didn't really feel up to it today. She was reluctant to be with people from the village who would ask after her – and Pete. What could she say?

Viv hadn't been to church that much here in the village, especially as Pete didn't go, even derided it, but she must try to do something that would make her feel human and alive again. She couldn't cook for one today. She didn't even know if she'd have any appetite. Perhaps she could wander down to the canal marina and have a drink at the bistro on the waterside. Nothing too demanding. Although she knew that she must go through her interview notes again tonight and try to get focused. She had never felt less like thinking. She felt torn and twisted and battered: Pete, her flat, her job, the peculiar, disturbing things that were happening to her.

Viv threw all her clothes into the washing basket and found a clean pair of Levi's 501s and a pretty Aqua muted-pink silky top that always made her feel better. She rifled through her chest of drawers, pulled out a lacy ivory balconette bra and bikini pants set from la Perla that she had bought herself as a treat for her birthday (or really for Pete...) and took them into the bathroom. In the doorway, she stopped and clutched the lintel. What was the point? She turned back and thrust the underwear back into her drawer. Instead she rummaged for a plain t-shirt bra and white sloggi knickers, pushing the drawer against the mess she'd made, for once not caring to fold and pile neatly.

The warm water in the shower felt soothing on her skin. Viv closed her eyes and turned her face up to the spray. She loved the feeling of water on her body. As the sound of the splashing filled her senses and brought her comfort, she sighed and, in that moment, heard, low but clear, as if the voice was in the room with her, a deep gentle masculine whisper, "*My Lady of the Lake*". Her eyes shot open and she grabbed the towel that was hanging on the top of the screen door, switching off the shower and shielding her body with the towel in one startled movement. The screen door was steamed up so she pulled it open a little, just enough to be able to survey the small bathroom. Nobody was there. There was nowhere anyone could hide.

"My god, am I really going mad?" Viv said aloud, taking deep breaths to slow her heart rate. When it stilled, she stepped back into the shower cubicle and turned the water back on, massaging the shampoo into her long auburn hair, but keeping her face to the room. Just in case.

This was crazy. Viv pulled on her clothes clumsily and her fingers shook as she buttoned her top.

She didn't remember opening the bedroom window, yet she watched as the light voile curtains fluttered in the early summer breeze. She leaned out and breathed in the sweet air of the courtyard. The Gertrude Jekyll roses that tangled and scrabbled over the archway along the ancient Lady's Walk across the cobbles, were already starting to bloom and their musky old rose fragrance mingled with the gentle scent of the French lavender they had planted to keep the greenfly away from the blossom. Someone on the far side of the abbey was up and out already, mowing his lawns, and Viv smelled the fresh cut grass and listened to the deep lowing of the motor.

The rumble of a car on the lane reminded Viv that Ellie was coming over for her car, and she moved away from the window and rubbed her hair in its towelling turban, before drying it thoroughly with the hair-drier and brushing it up into a top-knot. A flash of eyeliner and lipstick, and a whisk of blusher on her cheeks made her feel less pale and drawn, and a little more human.

The living area still smelt of wine so Viv flung open the high arched courtyard doors and let the perfumed air drift inside. She filled the Cona coffee machine and cooked herself a little porridge in the microwave, then made herself sit at the kitchen bar instead of wandering around the apartment eating. She surprised herself by feeling quite hungry after her shower. Remembering that she hadn't eaten much for a day or two, and throwing caution to the wind, she splashed double cream on the top and a dribble of honey. She needed the sweetness of comfort food. At least she felt a little better physically, not quite so drained.

Viv picked up the papers from the sofa, the articles and materials that she had been studying the day before, and that she had left in piles on the chesterfield and the coffee table. She couldn't help a slight grimace of satisfaction when she thought of how annoyed such a mess would have made Pete. But he wasn't here to see it, and she could make all the mess she liked. A small comfort, and just as swiftly, she felt the heavy lowering sadness again.

She was just struggling to focus on the paper on Lyminge when she heard the sound of a motor in the parking area and realised that it was probably Ellie's taxi arriving.

"Hiya!" called the familiar voice as Ellie's heels clicked over the cobbles and she appeared at the courtyard doors. "Oh, hun, you look a bit better this morning! " They hugged and Ellie said, "My lovely Stuart is looking after the kids again so we can have lunch and I don't need to be back home until teatime. Look, what d'you say we go to that wonderful bistro at the marina? You need to get out and it might cheer you up a bit."

Viv couldn't help but laugh. "Huh, great minds, etc! I was thinking of that myself, but it'll be so much nicer not to be on my own."

"I've got my trainers so we can saunter down there." Ellie waved her hand in the air, clutching her pair of Converse.

"Why didn't you put them on to come over here?"

"Oh, you know me. I couldn't come out without my heels. Not in front of the taxi driver!"

Viv shook her head and snorted affectionately. "What *shall* we do with you, Mrs Glam?"

"Well, I'm just glad I make you smile today, hun. I was very worried yesterday."

"Shock. It comes back in waves. I guess it's a good thing we didn't have kids to complicate matters."

Ellie glanced at Viv, then turned away. "Umm …" Then, as if making a decision, she looked back at Viv and lifted her arms to hold her friend's shoulders. "Viv. Sweetie." Her eyes were full of sympathy.

"What? Oh god. *What?*" Viv felt her breathing tremble.

"I'll have to tell you 'cos you'll find out sooner or later and then you'll feel awful if I've known all along. I had a text from Gwyn last night, very brief, just saying … oh god … that she was pregnant. And that I was to tell you."

Viv felt bile in her mouth. "When? I mean, obviously before Pete left, while he was still with me …Oh my god. Pregnant with *my* partner's kid. Couldn't she wait? Couldn't *he* wait?"

"Well, it's horrible betrayal, but … well, at least you didn't want kids at the moment yourself, did you? I mean, you weren't *trying* for one, were you?"

"No, not till I was further on with my career. But that's not the point. I didn't expect Pete to make them with someone else."

Ellie flung her arms around Viv and held her tight against her. "I know, and I'm so, so, sorry about all this."

"Well, it's hardly your fault!" Viv knew her voice was muffled against Ellie's t-shirted bosom and she pulled away enough to be able to speak, but not far enough to break the comforting hug. "We'd always planned … oh, at least another couple of years. Oh god, Ellie …"

Ellie's hand stroked her back gently, just as she did with her boys when they were distressed. She didn't speak, and Viv knew there wasn't much she could say.

Eventually, Viv pulled away and brushed her tears from her cheeks. Her heart was indescribably bleak and empty. That was that, then. Not some brief fling, not a temporary decision about the flat. She was cold and numb. "Well, there we are. It's a kind of finality, isn't it?"

Ellie grimaced. "A cruel finality."

Heart-sore, Viv stood up. She had to move as if action would obliterate the pain. She moved heavily to the Cona. Viv poured two coffees, one white for herself and one black for Ellie. She remembered that Gwyn too liked her coffee black. Black, thick and strong. She remembered that, away from her sheltered life with her elderly grandparents, when she and Ellie first met Gwyn at the freshers' convention it seemed odd but quite exotic and not in keeping with the jolly and kind but ordinary-looking girl in front of her in the queue for the coffee machine.

Why had that thought crept into her mind?

She and Ellie carried their coffees outside into the courtyard and sat at Viv's little bistro table within the shelter of her big courtyard doors. As Viv rested her mug on the mosaic table top, she recalled Pete and herself searching for a table set like this in Derby, just like those they had seen in Perugia, had held hands over at the little bar up in the Umbrian mountains.

They talked about restful, gossipy stuff, nothing to do with Pete, and gradually Viv's heart slowed and quietened.

Until there was a shriek from a few yards away, in the direction of Tilly's front door, next to her own. "Oh, hell's teeth!"

Ellie's eyes raised to the heavens as Viv swivelled round and called, "What's up, Tilly?"

Her neighbour skipped across, thighs in worryingly short shorts and forearms in a sleeveless gym top wobbling manically. "Oh my! Just been to the gym. Didn't go to the loo before I left. Desperate!" She hopped from foot to foot, dropping her open hobo bag onto the cobbles, and blowing a puff of air up to her brow where a lock of straw-fair curls straggled from her untidily pinned banana-clip. "Can't find my key. Think I left it in the locker! Wooee!"

Viv jumped up. "Come on in and use my bathroom. We can look for your key afterwards." She ushered Tilly through and gestured at the bathroom, although of course Tilly knew it well already. As she returned to Ellie in the courtyard, she heard Tilly's shriek, "Aaah! Oooh!" and the rush of copious pee into the toilet bowl. Viv scooted back to the bistro table.

They stifled their giggles as they heard the flush and the sound of the bathroom door opening.

"Oh, sweetie-pie, thanks a million. Now if I can only find my key ..." She scrabbled about in her bag, then a whoop of relief and she pulled out a brass front door key and held it aloft. "There's the little bugger!"

The sunshine glinted on the key and as Viv watched Tilly wave and skip off to her own door, she had a sharp stab of memory. A shiny key. Slipping it into her pouch. Finding it in her bed. Slipping it onto her bedside night stand.

"Viv, are you OK? You've gone a bit green. I know it's all a shock. How can I help you?"

"No, it's fine ... at least ..."

Ellie peered at her old friend's face and Viv knew that she wouldn't be able to keep all this dream stuff from her. Ellie could always see through her. "It's not just Pete and Gwyn, is it? What else has happened?"

"Ellie," she began hesitantly. "Oh, I don't know where to start. It's ridiculous. I want to tell you something. I need to share ... but it's crazy..."

"Look, just try me. Don't keep it bottled up."

"It's ... mad. Strange things have been happening to me. I thought it was a dream. Or stress from what's happened. But maybe I need help," and she poured out all that had occurred over the last couple of days. "So," she ended, "do you think I'm going completely insane?"

Ellie reached out and stroked Viv's hand as it clutched the handle of her cold mug. She said slowly, "Of course you're not going mad. But you *have* been under a lot of strain. Peculiar nightmares I'm sure are to be expected. In the circumstances. Maybe it was some kind of trauma reaction…?"

Viv turned to her and grimaced. "But it seemed so real – it *was* real, I'm sure of it. And the fabric and the key – they're real. I didn't imagine them. You can see them if you want!"

Ellie flushed. "Well, I don't know. I mean, perhaps you picked them up and just put them down somewhere different? You were in quite a state. Understandably. When your mind and emotions are confused … Um, maybe you're suffering PTSD, it wouldn't be surprising after all, hun, and when you're stressed you forget things you've done, even a moment ago. But they can't have just appeared in your flat – oh, hun, things like that just don't happen, do they?"

"They did to me. Oh Ellie …" Viv's heart heaved into a sob and Ellie wrapped her arms around her as she burrowed in to her friend's hair and cried until she could cry no more. All the horrors of the last couple of days wracked her body until she was empty of all and only the dregs of sorrow were left deep in her soul.

"Viv, it's OK to let it all out. It's best. Let it go. Oh, my dear girl." Ellie hugged her and stroked her back till Viv quietened and moved. "Here." She rummaged in her bag and passed a large tissue to Viv.

"It's everything," Viv hiccupped, dabbing her eyes and blowing her nose. "But this Lady Vivianne business has me torn. I know I'm vulnerable with Pete and the flat. But I think I'm going crazy, too. I mean, I feel her feelings, I think her thoughts, Ellie, I *am* her. It really was like I slipped in to her time, her life. Oh, Ellie, I think I …I kind of time-slipped. No, I'm certain of it. And I brought back real items with me. I know it's madness. And I'm too logical a thinker for all this … Yet …Oh, I know it can't happen. But, Ellie, it *did*. Where does that leave me? Insane?"

Ellie bit her lip and absently patted Viv's hand. "Look, hun, it's just as probable that there is a perfectly scientific explanation for all this."

"So you *do* think I may be going potty?"

"No, hun. But," Ellie frowned. Then abruptly she smiled a little too brightly and took Viv's hand. She drew in a deep breath, stood up and pulled Viv to her feet too. "Come on then, show me this gold key and let's do some rational thinking."

Together they tried the key in every lock in Viv's apartment, all the cupboards, her parents' old bureau, the antique desk, everything. But it didn't fit anywhere.

"OK, so we know it isn't likely to be one of yours. I suppose you could have picked it up from somewhere else and ..." Ellie's voice petered out uncertainly as Viv grimaced at her. "Well, why don't you boot up your computer; let's have a look for key designs in – what? – the fifth century, did you think? I'm sure we can find out if it's genuine or a replica maybe." Ellie's eyebrows shot up. "Hey, isn't it possible that *Tilly* dropped it in your flat and it's one of her bits for a film?"

Viv peered at Ellie and sighed. "Are you trying to humour me?"

"Would I do that?"

Viv wasn't sure, but she shook her head anyway.

Viv propped her laptop on her knees and did a google search. "The design's strange, isn't it? Unusual. Hmm, let's see ..."

Ellie peered at the screen and turned the key over in her hand. "It kind of looks genuine except it's shiny, but – what do I know?"

"Right." Viv scrolled down the screen images. "Fifth century, late fifth century." The date 499 whipped across her mind. Where had that come from? "Here we are. So, mine looks like a solid gold rotary key with hasp decorated with knotted circles, a bit like the Staffordshire knot design. It's certainly very well done, detailed."

"Aaagh, glory. Look here! It looks like this one," gasped Ellie, jabbing her finger at the picture.

"Oh my god," whispered Viv, bending forward towards the screen. "Yes, the size is the same. Oh lord, if that's right, it's a post-Roman ... Romano-Briton ... pre-Saxon ...oh wow, it's quite rare ... no, *extremely* rare."

"Goodness, it does look like it!" Ellie peered over Viv's shoulder at the pictures and blurb on the website. "But yours is so bright, in fairly good condition considering. If it *was* that age it'd surely be grotty-looking, wouldn't it? Doesn't that mean it's a fake, a replica?"

Viv stared at her. "But, Ellie, it wasn't very old when I was given it in 499."

She realised what she had said. And what that implied. She also realised that it was what she truly believed, madness or not. She was aware that Ellie's eyes were fixed on her own.

"O – kay," said Ellie slowly. "So, where do we go from here? Let's suppose that, however you came by it, it is real and that presumably means it's worth a fortune." She rubbed her brow. "So, why don't you get a valuation. I mean, putting aside where it actually came from, if it really is valuable, you could sell it and buy Pete out of the apartment. You really need the money now, hun."

Viv's head hurt. The laptop screen juddered, the words scrambling into nonsense. Her eyes lost their focus and a drift of screen-saver floated across in front of her, the words "*my Lady of the Lake*." She saw a hand, two hands on a golden key, one thought: the Vortigern chest. And then her screen filled with a jumble of letters that appeared to form themselves into one: *help*. Then just as abruptly it was gone, her sight cleared and she saw again the page of information. But a feeling lingered in her heart: the certainty that someone somewhere was reaching out to her, imploring her.

She rubbed her eyes and twisted round to her friend. "No, I couldn't. Firstly, nothing could be that valuable and secondly it'd be treasure trove, I suppose – I think that means it doesn't belong to me to sell. And anyway, how would I explain how I found it?"

"Well, we don't know how you 'found' it, do we? Make something up. Say you found it in the fields."

But Viv shook her head. "Well, that *would* be treasure trove! But much as I'd love to buy out Pete and restore my inheritance, I couldn't sell it. I think ..." she glanced at Ellie, and bit her lip, tasting blood, "I know it sounds crazy but the more I think about it, the more I feel that it appeared with the... the dream experience, and I think it was given to me to bring back to the present day for a purpose. I don't know what yet. But it's something important. Oh dear, yes, I know that does sound crazy!"

To her surprise, Ellie's expression changed from scepticism to reflection and she nodded slowly. "Well, I don't know what to say. I need to think. But okay, hun." She patted Viv's arm and grimaced. "I hear what you're saying. I just don't know at the moment how to respond. Just – I'm always with you." She shrugged helplessly and picked up her Converse.

*

The bistro on the marina boardwalk was packed with people enjoying Sunday lunch with their families, but Viv and Ellie found a little table for two in the corner looking over the canal. Viv fiddled with her bag, reassuring herself that she still had her purse safely there where she had hidden the precious key; it felt safer to keep it with her than leave it in the apartment. She was aware that Ellie was trying her best to make normal conversation with her, but her mind was swirling around wildly.

"I'm not terribly hungry," began Viv, flicking over the pages of the menu without really seeing the words. "I did have a bit of porridge for breakfast."

"You must eat," said Ellie sternly. "This is doing you no good at all. What about the rack of lamb and cous cous? I fancy that."

"Oh goodness, no, too much for me. I'll just toy with a small starter-sized Caesar salad."

"Well!" murmured Ellie under her breath and peering over Viv's shoulder at someone behind. "I fancy *that*, too!"

"What?" frowned Viv, swivelling round. All she could see was the broad shoulders of a tall man with thick dark curly hair, leaning towards a pretty waitress in her blue and white uniform.

"Wait till he turns round," whispered Ellie, "He is *gorgeous*!"

"And you a married woman and mother of two!" teased Viv. Just at that moment he turned towards their table and Viv gasped. He had olive skin, deep dark smoky eyes, neat designer stubble across his strong jaw and upper lip. Viv stared at the large full mouth with a warm, intimate smile that he trained upon them. She felt a jolt of recognition and held her breath. "Sir Roland!" she breathed again.

"What did you say?" Ellie reached over and shook Viv's hand. "You've gone awfully pale. What's the matter?"

The tall dark man approached their table and Viv turned back to Ellie. "It's just that he looks like …"

"Hello, ladies. What can I get for you? A drink first, perhaps?"

Viv looked up at him and for a moment their eyes locked. He frowned.

"Don't I know you from somewhere?" he asked quietly.

"I … er …I don't know," Viv stuttered. She was aware that Ellie was staring at her strangely. Viv felt herself flush very hot and she brushed the back of her hand over her forehead, blowing her fringe to cool herself. She smelled the woody masculine bergamot fragrance of his cologne. OMG! Her lower abdomen felt hot and a quivering ache suffused her. She felt dizzy; the room was trembling around her, and her body did not feel like her own. Oh god, no. It was happening again.

"Can I get you some water? You look a little pale." He signalled behind him and almost immediately a waitress appeared with a jug of iced water floating with fresh cut lemon slices and poured her a tumbler.

Viv sipped slowly and tried to compose herself. As if from far off, she heard the man persist, "Maybe it's from the university? Do you work there?"

"Er … maybe … I'm a senior lecturer … in medieval language and literature …" Viv felt nauseated and a sharp pain flashed at the right side of her brow. Oh, no, a migraine. She hadn't had an attack for years. In fact, she'd forgotten she'd ever had them. Stress, probably.

"Aah! I guess that's where I've seen you. I'm doing my PhD in early medieval religious iconography. I'm taking a little time out from my real job to finish writing up the thesis and helping my mother running this joint at the same time. Sucker for punishment. Even God took a day off, after all."

"So what *is* your real job, then?" Viv heard the flirty flutter in Ellie's voice.

"Don't run away too quickly, but I'm more usually to be seen in a clerical collar, I'm afraid! I'm the new chap at St Michael's. Known as Rev Rory, for my sins … Rory Netherbridge … pleased to meet you …" He held out his hand. Viv stared at it and her body shook. Those fingers had held a mead bowl, and had cupped a golden crucifix, had handed her a gold key …

"Sorry," she squeaked as she pushed herself up from the bistro table, grabbed her bag and, pulling it over her shoulder, ran outside, onto the boardwalk along the canal. She was aware that people were staring at her. She staggered. Why was it so slippery under her feet? Why was it so misty? Why was it so crowded? People were pushing at her, shouting …Was that Pete and Gwyn walking towards her, hand in hand? What were they doing here … how dare they, knowing she often came to the marina? Her head was throbbing and a stab of pain seared her forehead. The world shuddered around her, as she heard, in the distance, Ellie's voice calling and a man's deep gentle murmur, "my Lady of the Lake", and she slipped and fell sideways, losing her balance and feeling the water rising up to meet her.

Chapter 6

"Lady Vivianne!" Someone was shaking her shoulder. "Lady Vivianne! Wake up!" Someone was splashing water on her face. "Lady Eleanor has returned from the eastern plains and wishes to see you."

Vivianne opened her eyes to another splash of cold water. "Stop it! You will drown me with your agitation." She pushed Guin's bowl and cloths away and as she did so, she knocked the goblet on the table before her, sending a spray of red wine over the floor. Guin hastened to mop up the spillage with her cloths.

"Oh, leave it!" grumbled Vivianne and wriggled upright on the bench before the fire. Guin indignantly dropped the cloths on the floor and Vivianne stared at them. The wine stains looked like blood.

"You were in a deep sleep, my lady."

"Yes, and now I am wide awake, thank you." Vivianne stood and straightened her crimson overgown and matching robe trimmed with smoky cream fur. The fabric skimmed her figure softly and flowed smoothly in gentle drapes to the floor. She adjusted her gold-tooled leather belt and slid the pouch across to the front. Her long hair, newly washed in soft rainwater, was scooped up on her head and Guin had, that very morning, after Sir Roland had left, pinned it with pretty jewelled brooches.

Vivianne bit her lips and tapped her cheeks to raise some colour to her face. "I am ready for Lady Eleanor now."

Guin nodded and, picking up the bowl, hurried out of the chamber.

Vivianne smiled at the prospect of seeing her friend Eleanor again. The past six months had been long without her sweet laughing presence, while she travelled on quest with her new husband. The door opened and Guin ushered in Vivianne's tall, beautiful childhood friend. Vivianne noticed that she walked a little awkwardly.

"Eleanor! My dear precious friend! How are you? How did you survive? What adventures have you had?" Vivianne ran to embrace her, holding her firmly to her bosom. Her dear friend was clearly not as slender as she had been before her travels.

"Vivianne! So many questions. Let us sit and I shall tell you all that has befallen us." Eleanor hugged Vivianne and arm in arm they sat close together by the fire. In the dimness of the chamber, Vivianne held her friend away from her a little and drank in her so-familiar face, her so-familiar scent of lavender. How wonderful to see her again. And yet … a strange feeling shivered through Vivianne's body, a confusion; she seemed to recall seeing her not so long ago, talking, eating some unusual food, in some crowded hall, and a waterway close by – but that was impossible. Eleanor had been travelling east since her hand-fasting with Aidan, along with their train of geburs and lower thegns, in order to supervise the trade exchange with the coastal folk of the marshes and with the warriors from across the wide seas.

Eleanor frowned at Vivianne's scrutiny. "What ails you, my beautiful friend?"

"Oh, nothing, nothing at all." Vivianne patted Eleanor's hand and pulled herself away from her visions. "But *you* look well. And do I detect a thickening of the stomach?"

Eleanor smiled shyly. "Yes, indeed, I am five months with child!"

"Oh, Eleanor, that's wonderful. What glorious tidings you have brought back with you. I am so very pleased for you. And Aidan of course."

"Indeed, he had much to do with my present condition!" laughed Eleanor, stroking her belly.

"So, tell me all about your travels. Did you bring many goods back with you?"

"Goodness, yes. You would not believe until you see with your own eyes, the fifty packs! The horses were laden. We have exchanged our tapestries, goblets, our mead jars, honey, our potatoes, herbs and salted meat, for the most wonderful glass goblets with long stems to hold them, amphorae of wines and precious olive oil, spices, gold and silver. And tools for eating and crafting. And, oh, the softest cloth that ripples like water!"

"I long to see it all!"

"Indeed. The geburs are unloading now. Oh – and Vivianne! The traders from the seas brought brooches intricately decorated in the new fashion, glass beads and jewels. And …" Eleanor fumbled in the pouch at her belt and lowered her voice, "these!" She held out both hands cupped over something which she carefully revealed to Vivianne as she lifted one hand away.

Vivianne gasped. Two small gold crucifixes on delicate chains nestled in her palm. The figure on the cross was finely wrought, even the tiny face showed agony in the eyes and mouth. "But they are so much like the one my mother gave me, worked in silver. She must have been given it by the traders from over the seas. I always thought it was from the Romans, inherited from my father's family. The faces are the same. Look!" She pulled her own silver crucifix from her pouch.

A noise outside made both of them quickly thrust their neck adornments back into the secrecy of their pouches and turn in alarm.

"Lady Vivianne! Are you hiding from me?" the loud rough voice was Sir Pelleas's. Eleanor and Vivianne sprang to their feet as the door was flung open, crashing back against the wall, and Eleanor's hand flew up to her mouth. Pelleas stormed in through the doorway. He glared at both ladies, then gestured rudely to Eleanor, "Get back to your husband, lady!"

"You are back early from your hunting, my lord?" stammered Vivianne in confusion.

"Not at all. It is late. The morning sun is high. And we have great trophies. Now I am ready for my betrothed!" He wobbled on his thick legs, already this early intoxicated with mead or beer.

Eleanor glanced at Vivianne with a trembling smile, nodded and ran out. Vivianne moved to halt her but she felt Pelleas's hand grab her arm and pull her back. She staggered under the force. "Sir Pelleas!" she protested. "Unhand me and show some courtesy!"

"Courtesy?" roared Pelleas, swaying, and retrieving his balance with a hand to the wall. "When you avoid me – me, your betrothed - for two days? How dare you not come to the mead hall last night and again fail to join me for breaking-fast this sunrise!"

Vivianne pulled herself up to her full height, straightening her back, and looked him in the eye. She was trembling with anger. "And how dare you come like this to my sleeping chamber, sir!"

For a brief moment he glared at her. Then before she could move, he grabbed her round the waist and threw her onto her bed. He tore off her belt and pouch, and, pushing her fighting hands away, flung the leather onto the ground. She heard the hide split open and the chink of silver on the hard floor. She tried to push him off her, but he pinned her arms with his. Vivianne bucked and twisted her body away from his but even as she did, he laughed derisively at her efforts and, taking one hand away from her arm, he reached down lower to her thighs. His eyes locked on to hers and he stared scornfully, lip curled.

She gasped with ragged breath and as he pulled at her garments she struggled against him, kicking and biting like a wild boar, but he hit her across the cheek with his ringed hand and as she cried out with the sharp pain, he pushed up her skirts and trapped her with his legs. "You are my betrothed," he growled, breathing mead fumes into her face, "And I am weary of your delays. I demand that you now behave like it." He grunted as he fumbled with his tunic and shifted his position over her, pushing her legs apart, and thrusting his groin between them so that she felt his hardness at her pelvic bone. "See if you like *this*!" He moved to better place himself to enter her.

She screamed. As loud and forcefully as she could manage.

There was a scuffling at the doorway and Vivianne could sense a presence in the chamber. She could see nothing beyond Pelleas's broad back heaving as he struggled with his clothes.

"Help me!" she screamed to whoever was there.

She felt the pressure from Pelleas's weight lift from her and a deep voice saying calmly, "Sir, you are required urgently at the counsel."

Vivianne sensed a slight hesitation, a slackening against her, then the movement of the bed as Pelleas stood. She twisted her head and saw him adjusting his clothes. She gasped for breath in relief, her chest heaving, her heart pounding. She tugged her skirts to cover her nakedness and straightened her gown, then wriggled herself to standing. Sir Roland, eyes turned away from her, had his arm round Pelleas guiding him towards the doorway.

"She avoids me, yet she is my betrothed!" Pelleas whined. "How dare she cast me low! How dare she …," he belched loudly, "…not want me to have her!"

"Sir. I think she cannot."

"Cannot?" Pelleas stopped, staggered a little. "What?"

"See," Roland gestured to the red wine soaked cloths on the floor. "The lady is indisposed, sir."

Pelleas looked blankly, then back at Vivianne, and, wrinkling up his nose, turned away and nodded, "Ah, her time of the moon, her curse. At last. That explains her reluctance. Not about me at all." He hiccupped, and leaned against Roland's shoulder. "That is *almost* acceptable, then. You are most observant, Sir Roland. An admirable quality in a second in command." But he looked back at Vivianne one more time, and then to Roland and his expression was one of drunken confusion. "And so the hand-fasting will be soon. I can wait no longer, lady." He gestured towards Vivianne's bed. "As you have reason to know."

Roland glanced over his shoulder at Vivianne and raised his eyebrows. He mouthed "Eleanor." But although Vivianne was grateful for her friend fetching help, she was not happy that Sir Roland had referred to her intimate womanly things. She glared at him. He grinned knowingly and turned to half-carry Pelleas out of the chamber.

She tidied up the cloths, thrusting them into the woven basket for washing. Certainly, at times that man could be helpful, as when he warned her about Guin and Pelleas, referring to the Vortigern treasure chest. But he could also be quite insufferable. What gave him the right to be so familiar with her? Even the way he looked at her smacked of an intimacy that she told herself she had never encouraged. Never.

"Vivianne, are you unharmed?" Eleanor rushed in to the chamber.

"Yes, I am quite well. He did not get very far with his intentions."

"Thank heavens. And Roland came to your rescue?"

"Indeed."

"He is very courteous and kind," smiled Eleanor slyly.

"He ... he can be ... on occasion," granted Vivianne. "But he can also be very annoying."

Eleanor smiled. "I must go to rest now before the meal." She stroked her stomach.

"I thought I might go for a ride to the mere, then, while you rest, and we can talk again later."

"I do not think that you should ride alone today, my lady." Roland strode in. Vivianne looked up in surprise. "The door was open," he explained, grinning and gesturing behind him. "I will accompany you."

"That would be very courteous," smiled Eleanor, turning to Vivianne.

"I do not need ..." she began.

"I am sure that you do not, Vivianne, but you must not take risks."

"Exactly so," nodded Roland. "I came to tell you that there have been sightings of marauding brigands again further north, and to be careful."

Vivianne huffed. "Marauders are unlikely to breach our settlement. We are well protected and fortified on this wooded hill."

"Indeed, but there is danger in the forest, river, mere and meadow, surrounding the village. You know that, my lady."

"Well. I shall be careful," insisted Vivianne.

"No. You will allow me to accompany you. In case there is occasion for you to be protected from … anyone." Roland looked Vivianne straight in the eye. She felt her heart flutter and her body flush again, despite herself.

Eleanor glanced from one to the other. "That is wise," she nodded. "And now I shall go to rest."

"Hmmm. I know when I am defeated." Vivianne kissed her friend and turned to Roland. "Come, then," she said briskly, averting her eyes and busying her trembling hands in straightening her dress again. When she glanced up at Roland with a frown, he was grinning.

*

The horses chomped at the grass as Vivianne and Roland sat at the mere side. She felt an almost unbearable desire to walk into the water. Something was tugging at her. She looked at the smooth mere before her. That was where she needed to be. The water somehow gave her such comfort.

She drew in her breath sharply. She desperately needed to ask him for information and clarity. "Sir Roland, I know that we said we would meet to talk after the feast tonight. But I am impatient and I did not think that we would cross our paths before nightfall. So, let us talk now. Tell me about the Vortigern chest, the Lady of the Lake and the golden key you pressed into my hand. Why? What is it all about?"

Roland turned to her and raised his eyebrows. "You do not know?"

"I am not sure."

"Vivianne, the chest was very important to your parents and that is why they kept it in the sacred hall. That is the key to the chest."

"What use is it to me? The chest was lost."

"It was never lost. It was in my safe-keeping. Hidden until your marriage, as I promised your father. The problem is that Guin has managed to discover where it is. And she will guide Pelleas to it. But the key I gave you is the only one that opens the lock."

"And have you unlocked it before and looked inside?"

"No, my lady. It requires the hand of the pure heir."

"The pure heir. So..." Vivianne paused in reflection on his careful words, "So is this ... *magic?*"

Roland drew in his breath deeply before he spoke again. "The magic of the Lady of the Lake."

"And for some odd reason you called me that. Nobody else calls me that name. Why?"

"Vivianne, there is said to be a lady, a spirit, of the mere who guards it and protects the waters for the village's use. But there is also a dark side. A certain chieftain of a neighbouring settlement, who took a liking to her, over-reached his powers and tried to take her. She lured him to the mere and he drowned."

Vivianne shivered. "Oh."

"There is more. The legend is from many, many years ago. Hundreds of years ago. Yet they say that the lady of those times was your mother."

Vivianne gasped. "My mother? Hundreds of years ago? How could that be?"

"There was a magic around her. The old magic."

"But she followed the Christian ways. When she was betrothed to my father, she took the Christian religion to her heart, and left the Brythen magic of her forebears."

"There are things that are not too dissimilar."

Vivianne looked across the water of the mere and a strange vision came into her mind. *Her mother, rising from the lake like a spirit.*

And now Roland was speaking to her. "They say that the magic of the Lady of the Lake is passed down from the mother on her death to ...."

"But if she had magic, the old magic," interrupted Vivianne eagerly, "how was it that she perished in the fire? Surely she could have used her magic to survive...and to save my father."

"They say that she could not complete her rituals in the mere, that they were interrupted that day, so she did not have enough protection from the fire. The water magic was not there with her to save them."

Vivianne covered her face with her hands. "It is my fault."

"No. How could it be? You were a child."

"I disturbed her rituals. I insisted she came from the mere to take me back to the village. Then it was all blank and dark. I smelled fire and burning on the air."

"You were distraught. Sir Pelleas had to calm you. I did what I could, too. You were a child and distressed. That was why Sir Pelleas was elected by the counsel to be your guardian and protector, and to rule for you until you came of age. You were too young and vulnerable to inherit. But I fear …"

"He is not right to lead after my parents. He cannot follow their ways. He is not one of the old religion, he is a pagan. He hates our religion. I keep my symbols hidden from him." Vivianne's hand flew to her pouch - if only her pouch had been where it was supposed to be. "Oh no! My pouch! My crucifix! The key! I left it on the floor in my sleeping chamber!"

In haste they galloped back to the village, and ran to Vivianne's hall. She rushed inside and to the side of the bed. Her pouch lay half hidden under the bed. She tore it open, shaking it upside down. But there was nothing inside. Frantically, she scrabbled around the bed, under the covers, throwing them on to the ground. Roland took the bed apart, pulled up the floor coverings, moved the table, the stools, scouring everywhere. A noise outside. Vivianne looked up. A flash of a deep blue robe. A grim smile peering in through the doorway. Pelleas?

She sank to the floor. The gold key and silver crucifix were gone. She buried her head in her hands and mumbled up to Roland. "You said that the magic of the Lady of the Lake is passed down from mother to … who?"

"To her daughter," whispered Roland as he knelt beside her. "You must continue your mother's work for the sake of the village. And that is why I called you the Lady of the Lake, and that is why you need to awaken the magic again and bring it back to the village. You are the only one who can open the Vortigern chest and use the riches for good."

"But I do not know how! And now I have lost the key. Still more, I have lost the crucifix and if Pelleas has found it he will destroy me, you and all the others like us." She raised her eyes to the roof. "Pelleas, you barbaric heathen!"

Her desperate sobbing filled her mind.

Chapter 7

She felt strong hands lift her and lower her gently to the ground. Fingers feeling her throat, her pulse. A warm face against hers. Masculine woody bergamot fragrance.

Viv snapped open her eyes. "What are you doing?" she demanded.

"Saving you," came the brief, and rather amused, reply.

"Well … well, don't!" she snapped.

"Don't?"

"Just help me up, please. I'm fine." He took her arm and helped her to her feet. He picked up her bag from the boardwalk where it had fallen from her shoulder, and pressed it back into her hand and she clutched it tightly to her. She became aware of the crowd around her. A slight disturbance alerted her senses: was that Pete and Gwyn pushing through the parted crowd and out of sight?

She shivered. Her clothes were wet. Not again! Her Aqua blouse was soaked. She looked down. God, it was almost transparent. Quickly she folded her arms round her chest.

"Right." His voice was almost cracking with suppressed laughter. He looked slowly down her body, his eyes amused. Viv couldn't help but notice the crinkly laughter lines …

She forced herself to frown and spluttered, "Aren't you supposed to be a reverend?"

"Sorry, I didn't mean to embarrass you. Yes, but even reverends are human, you know. Think of Sydney Chambers in Grantchester. Into jazz, whisky, crime, women. But I'm not really into crime."

She sensed a movement in the crowd again and this time Ellie pushed through.

"God, Viv! The ambulance is on its way. You'd better lie down. Or sit down. Or something. Rory, she shouldn't be standing up. She'll be in shock."

"Well, I didn't have much choice in the matter. Your friend is very … um … strong-willed. Ah! What's that?" He bent down and picked something up from the boardwalk. "I think you dropped this." He held out his hand. As he uncurled his fist, she saw that it was a silver crucifix.

They sat in the bistro nursing glasses of wine. Reverend Netherbridge ("call me Rory, for goodness sake") had asked the waitress and the sub-manager coming back on shift to take charge. The ambulance staff had examined a protesting Viv, declared her fine and driven off. She felt a little calmer now, as she held the little cross between her fingers. Rory was only looking out for her, after all. She felt warmer towards him with all his kind solicitations. She realised that she was staring at his strong, tanned forearms as he raised his wine glass and her breath caught at the sight of the dark hairs and the large hands, long fingers ... Oh, that feeling low down there ...She looked up quickly, guiltily ...But he was looking intently at her face, over the rim of his glass, with a worried expression.

"So, is there something you need to tell me?" he asked Viv quietly. "There's clearly something wrong. And I may be able to help. I'm trained to listen."

"Thank you, but I really can't." Viv shook her head but saw the pleading in Ellie's eyes. "To be honest I can't even begin to put it into words." She didn't want to go through it again, and she had no idea whether he would laugh at her for being fanciful.

"Just tell Rory what you told me," said Ellie earnestly. She turned to him. "It concerns another life. Viv thinks she may be in touch with another world. I think she ... we both need help with it."

"Oh, come on, Ellie, it's not quite ..."

But Rory nodded. "Okaa - ay." He stared questioningly at her.

"It's just stuff that's been happening to me ... magic and ancient Romano-Christian beliefs," added Viv, thinking that would put him off.

Rory perked up. "Really? Now this is a bit more interesting than the usual stuff I have in my pastoral duties. Hmmm, my kind of thing too. Tell me about it."

"No, honestly. It's stupid."

"Viv, nothing is stupid." Rory looked in to her eyes and she felt a strange sense of peace and reassurance. What did she have to lose, since she was likely to lose everything that really mattered to her anyway?

"Well, umm, well ... it started at the end of the week, when I was very upset because," she paused, not knowing how much to reveal, how much she wanted to reveal, without sounding completely insane. Yet a vision of Sir Roland slipped into her mind and somehow she felt as though she could talk to this man without fear.

"Her bugger of a partner, Pete, walked out and went off with our old uni friend, Gwyn. God, I ..." Ellie stopped and threw her hand up to her mouth. "ooops, sorry, vicar ...er, Rory ... I said bugger, and God."

Rory smiled. "It's OK. I hear far worse than that from some of my parishioners. Go on, Viv."

She sighed and hesitantly recounted the story again, but did not describe Sir Roland or mention her shock at the similarity between him and Rory. Maybe there was some weird Freudian issue there.

"The strange thing is that it happened just now and twice before definitely at midnight. I heard the clock strike both times and yet it still struck twelve when I 'woke up'. Today, it clearly wasn't! That's odd. And then twice it's been somehow connected to water, but last night it wasn't at all! I just don't know what to think of it all. It's all so real. So strange." Viv looked up into his deep eyes, then lowered hers and whispered, "I don't know what's happening to me." Ellie reached over and touched her arm.

Rory sat silent for a moment, stroking his chin, then he said calmly. "I have reason to hear what you're saying, Viv, without prejudice. The time thing – well, um, all I can say is that the effect in time was the same. You slipped at the canal side but I was following you out and I pulled you from the water straight away. You hardly even had time to go under. Yet your time in the ... let's say ... 'dream' or 'other world' was, what, hours? So it appears to be an instantaneous slip but a varying passage of time at each end of the ...hmmm ... That's rather a fascinating concept. And water is something to do with it, but not the only trigger."

He lifted his wine glass again and frowned contemplatively. Viv forced herself not to look at his forearms and hands.

"So, what do you make of it?" urged Ellie, leaning over the table. "I don't know what to make of it myself. I don't know whether it's scary or unbelievable. It's like a glimpse of another time and space, but that's impossible...hmm. Is it stress, PTSD, what? Does she need counselling?

I know Viv's normally very sensible, very logical, she has to be for her job, but this ..."

Viv snorted. "Oh, you make it sound like Star Trek or something. Or that I'm going bonkers. What on earth is happening? And why me? I can't get my head round it all."

"Maybe," said Rory carefully, "your state of mind after what happened with your partner perhaps ..."

"I thought that too," interrupted Ellie, a little too eagerly.

"State of mind? You mean temporary insanity?" gasped Viv, hands pushing back her hair from her burning cheeks. "It was so real, you know."

"Well, these things can be," whispered Ellie, catching Viv's hand and holding it between hers. "At least, I don't know, but I would imagine so."

"Or," said Rory, looking straight at Viv and holding her gaze, as she had the strangest feeling that he looked right into her soul. She saw too an odd expression of familiarity in his dark eyes and she shivered. "Or you just happened to be in the right place where something called to you across the time continuum." Viv felt Ellie loosen her grip on her hand and draw in a sharp breath. "And you were especially vulnerable to that call because you were distressed and in a – forgive me – a highly emotional state. At those times we seem to be more in touch with the shapes on the air."

"Shapes on the air?" Ellie echoed.

"That's what I call them. The imprints, if you like, that I believe are all around us from those who have gone before, from events that have been significant, but that we aren't normally receptive to."

"Ghosts?" gasped Ellie.

"Well, not as we normally envisage them. Spirits may be a better term. But I use 'imprints' or 'shapes' because it suggests something that doesn't have an independent matter."

"Before this happened to me, I would have thought you were barmy, saying that!" said Viv. "Oh, sorry, Reverend Rory, that sounded so rude."

Rory's smile reached his eyes again and Viv saw the crinkling at their edges. He nodded. "Well, maybe I am "barmy". Maybe all vicars, priests, are, in that we believe in what many folks think are fairy tales, magic, superstition, other worldly … the resurrection, the communion, the sacraments … To some people that would be regarded as magic and fantasy."

"And magic in early Christianity, is that …?"

"There are things that are not too dissimilar."

Viv froze. She had heard those exact same words somewhere before. The same voice. Pretty much. The same tone. A vision drifted across her mind. Another attractive, tall, muscular man, olive-skinned and dark eyed, someone else with a soft gentle voice, reassuring her, explaining to her. A lake, a mere. *The* mere, *Cooney's Mere.* Then a panic, a loss.

She gripped the crucifix in her hand and ran her thumb over its contours, the tiny figure nailed to the cross, the contorted face. Then she remembered. Lady Eleanor and herself, or Lady Vivianne rather, comparing their crosses, her friend's beautiful shining hair, her gentle manner and smile, her assurance. "But Ellie, you were kind of there, too. In my … Lady Eleanor, Vivianne's good friend, she reminded me of you. In this other world, I mean."

"Good lord," Ellie shuddered. "Well, I for one certainly didn't dream anything like that, thank goodness! Stuart would think I was …"

Rory looked across at her thoughtfully, "I guess you haven't had any traumatic experience, though?"

"No, I haven't. So you think that was what triggered Viv's strange dream-experience? Trauma? Like an incidence of PTSD, as I thought?"

"I do believe that people who have recently suffered something traumatic are often more … er … susceptible to what is usually hidden from most of us, and I myself …"

"Vicar!" A very attractive girl in a figure-hugging ivory contour dress hurried over to their table and placed her hand on Rory's broad shoulder. Head tilted to one side, she smiled and fluttered, "Oh vicar, I'm *so* glad I saw you. *Rory.*" She appeared to be stroking his back. "Excuse us," she added, looking Viv and Ellie up and down under her long dark lashes. "We have some things to discuss."

Rory twisted round to look up at her. "Do we, Fi?"

"Yes, it's about the curate."

"Fi, I am, as you know, on sabbatical for six months. However, if there is an urgent matter, of course I am available to all my parishioners. Perhaps you could make an appointment tomorrow at the church office?"

"Oh." Fi's face fell.

"I can spare half an hour for a coffee." Rory smiled. A very engaging, even sexy smile, it seemed to Viv. He held his left hand up in a gesture of confirmation and she glanced at his third finger and saw a gold ring nestling there. It was not like any wedding ring she had ever seen before, though. It was a band with what looked like a buckle on a belt. But it was wide and bright, such an explicit, unquestionable symbol that she was surprised she hadn't noticed it before. Her heart jerked. She felt Rory's gaze turn to her and quickly, guiltily, looked up.

She saw Fi flush and then smile back at Rory, nodding. He turned back to the table and to Viv. But she was watching Fi's pert bottom in its close-fitting skirt wiggle back out of the door. As Fi sashayed along the boardwalk, Viv noticed that she turned back to look through the window and raised her arm to wave at Rory. But he wasn't looking at her so she dropped her hand, glared at Viv, and walked on out of sight.

"So," said Rory firmly. "Where were we?"

Viv fumbled in her purse and drew out the gold key, holding it out with the crucifix in her palm. "These are the items I seemed to bring back with me from my dreams."

She watched Rory's face and she saw him pale. For a moment he sat very still. Then his hand covered hers. His touch made Viv flush hotly and she was sure that she blushed all too publically. He seemed to be struggling to speak.

"I … er …I think that it would be best to keep these private. Do you have a safe at home?"

"A safe? No."

"Most folks don't. Mrs N insisted we have one." Ah, he *was* married – of course he was – and there was an all too real Mrs N. She nodded in satisfaction at her deduction. "But, Viv, I would recommend you invest in one. I suspect that these are extremely rare and precious, worth … well, a lot."

"Really? Oh goodness. We looked the key up and did wonder if it was valuable."

"Not only that." Rory grimaced and bit his lip. He looked at Viv. "You see … I've seen them before."

*

71

The Reverend Rory Netherbridge sat on Viv's sofa, this time with his clerical collar in place, and turned the key and the crucifix over in his hand. He looked up at Viv with a slight frown. All Viv could think of was how attractive he was. She had never really thought of vicars being good-looking, sexy. But this one …

"Thank you for agreeing to my visit tonight," he said and Viv noted the formality in his tone and pushed her thoughts away. "I'm sorry that your friend Ellie couldn't make it, as she's quite involved with the story, although sceptical, but…,"

"I guess anyone would be," interrupted Viv, "except me and maybe you. But that's OK. I understand that, actually, you really wanted to speak with me in private."

"Yes, I do. There are things that I have to admit I didn't want to say in front of Ellie. Um, Viv, could I first ask you about your experience – or rather, what you *saw*? Do you recall much about that mead hall you saw, the people there?"

Viv thought carefully because her response seemed to matter. She described the mead hall she saw and Rory quizzed her on the decorations, the artefacts, the gold, the carvings. As she tried to detail all she remembered, Rory frowned. She wasn't sure if she was saying something that disturbed him.

"And, Viv, can you tell me what the people … what they looked like, what you could make out about them?"

"Yes, it was all strangely vivid." She described the tunics, cloaks and robes, the jewellery. "Oh, let me show you the cloth from a tunic." She went into the bedroom and found the fragment of torn cream coloured cloth. "Here."

Rory held out his hand and felt the fabric between his fingers. He sat very still, staring at the cloth. Then he cleared his throat and murmured, "It's soft as you described it."

"Yes, that was odd because I had always read that in the Dark Ages, the post-Roman pre-Anglo Saxons wore thick, rough shapeless sacking-like clothes when everything went into decline after the Roman legions left. Dull muddy colours. Drab. Yet the ones I saw were fine, flowing, soft. They were well-designed, in bright rich colours. Not at all what I had imagined from research. And there were finely crafted decorative objects, household wares, beads, brooches, religious pieces."

"Hmmm." He frowned. "Have you heard of the finds from the Must Farm dig?"

"Must Farm? Oh, yes, I read something about that recently, but I didn't really pursue it because it's a lot earlier than Anglo-Saxon times."

"Well, I'm interested in archaeology. Goes with the iconography! You know Must Farm was a bronze-age settlement?"

"Yup."

"So, archaeologists made some interesting discoveries there. They found fragments of clothing that indicated that they were made from lime-tree fibres and hems that suggested flowing gowns."

"Ah, so not the rough-hewn home-spun stuff we thought. And by the fifth century it would have been even more sophisticated. There's no real evidence to imply that culture, crafts, arts went backwards in the post-Roman era."

"That's what I was wondering. Interesting." Rory reached down to his brief case, and pulled out a copy of The Times and a glossy journal. "Did you see *The Sunday Times* this morning?"

"No, I haven't had time to even open my computer for the news page."

"Well, it's all in here." Rory handed Viv the newspaper. "I remembered noticing it this morning but I'd only scanned the summary caption briefly. When you said what you did earlier today, I thought I'd pull it out and bring it over tonight to give you. And I found this in the rectory library, too. There is a page marked," he passed the magazine over and Viv read the title 'Journal of Romano-Brythonic Studies', "it's a paper on the finds at the Wilmingham dig."

She felt her heart miss a beat. He leaned over to Viv and opened the page where he had turned down the corner. "It's a report of research into the post-Roman pre-Saxon artefacts they found there."

"Wilmingham dig?" Why did that sound familiar? A dig? Her parents had been archaeologists: her father professionally and her mother, a career researcher, as an academic research interest.

"Yes, just down the road. Beyond Cooney's Mere. And they found evidence that bears out what you experienced."

"Really? I didn't know there had been an official organised dig here. I knew that various items had been found in the area but not about a dig *per se*. And I didn't know any of this." Had she? Had she known it? Why did it echo in her mind?

"Exactly. Yet you experienced and saw these things. Yes, maybe you might have unwittingly read something without being aware that you had taken it in, and then 'dreamed' it in your semi-conscious mind. But equally, maybe it could indicate that you really did experience a time-slip into another universe. That it was real?"

Viv glanced at the copies in her lap. "A time-slip into another universe? So either way, am I going mad then?"

Rory tugged at his clerical collar. "Well, if you are, then so am I." Their eyes locked. "You might need a brandy. Because I was there too."

Chapter 8

Viv wasn't sure whether it made it easier or more weird that the Reverend Rory had also possibly time-slipped as she seemed to have done. According to him. So that's why he was so interested in her story. Goodness, this was terrifying. She hardly dare think of the implications. But how could it be so? They hadn't even known each other then. She shuddered and felt chills at her back as though a draught had swept through the apartment. Her head seemed light and thoughts a jumble.

"But ... so ...," she stuttered. "What does all this mean?"

Rory shook his head. "Philosophically? Psychologically? I can only surmise. You know, in my work, my world as a priest, I have to have faith in things that may seem a nonsense to non-believers. The resurrection, being raised from the dead, the meaning of the communion, transmuting blood into wine ..."

He seemed to have retreated back into himself and was frowning. What did he know? Why was he involved in all this? She picked up the paper and magazine and shook them as if trying to release a truth that they might hold. She struggled to get her head round it all and make some sense of her recent experiences. Everything that had happened over the last few days seemed to swirl in her brain and twist into something else. It made her feel dizzy and sick.

Viv's hand was shaking as she slipped on her reading glasses and turned the pages of the magazine and the *Times*. She scanned the pages, expertly finding what she wanted to read and focusing on those passages. Rory sat quietly beside her, peering over the pages and rubbing his chin as if trying to gauge whether he needed another shave.

"Yes, it says – well, it bears out so much of what I saw, or seemed to see. Oh god, now I feel even weirder." Viv breathed in as much air as she could, then exhaled deeply. Full yogic breath. Calming. Balancing. Struggling to hold on to reality. "Phew. Oh goodness, I need a drink." She also needed to move, to feel her own physical body working. "What would you like, Rory? Coffee? Wine? Or something stronger?"

"A glass of red would be great, if you have it."

Viv rose, passing the papers to Rory. "I'll put some coffee on as well, for after the wine. You've got to drive back."

"Thanks. It's not very far up the lane to the rectory, though, but, no you're right; it wouldn't do for the Rev, albeit on sabbatical, to get breathalysed for erratic driving on country lanes, would it?" He smiled up at her briefly, but then resumed staring intently at the pages in front of him.

In the kitchen, Viv pulled out a bottle of burgundy from Pete's stash in the wine rack. His favourite, actually. But, hey, he hadn't taken it with him, so tough. Served him right. As she poured the wine, she pondered on how quickly she had moved from horror and disbelief to acceptance and a lurking desire for, if not revenge, at least annoyance.

She filled the coffee machine filter with her favourite Taylor's Lazy Sunday, and the jug with water, and flicked the switch. The smell of fresh ground coffee beans was so soothing. So much had happened in the last few days; if she stopped to think about it all, her mind would be in turmoil. Yet, somehow, it was less stressful to think about the enormity and peculiarity of the time-slip business than the reality of Pete's leaving with Gwyn and the demand to sell her home. Lady Vivianne and her world seemed like a part of her working life, her research, her study, and something she could hold on to, something familiar in a sense, however weird it all was. She could grasp that more readily than the real world of Pete, his sudden dismissive attitude, his complete and utter rejection of her and "them", and her future alone.

Carefully, because her hands were still shaking, Viv carried the glasses of wine through to the sitting area and set Rory's down on a gold coloured coaster on the coffee table within his reach.

"Thank you." Rory glanced up from the papers. He smiled; a lovely comforting grin that spread from his wide mouth to his dark eyes. There was something engaging and soothing about him. Probably his training and calling as a vicar, rector, priest, or whatever he was. His face was open and seemed trust-worthy. "This is quite amazing. The detail they have discovered recently fits so neatly with your experience. And with mine." He rested the newspaper on his knees and reached for his glass of wine. He took a sip and raised his eyebrows. "This is very good. Are you the connoisseur?"

"No, I know nothing about wine. Just what I like and don't like. Really I prefer prosecco, light and bubbly. This is, *was*, one of Pete, my partner's, *ex-partner's*, hoard. Oh goodness, I don't even know what to call him anymore. I feel confused, odd, in a whirl."

"Of course. That's not surprising. It's early days. Those first confused, bewildered, days of disbelief, of 'what on earth happens next'. Yes, I know it," he paused in thought. "But I have a patient listening ear if you want to talk. I'm trained in counselling. If ever you want to let it all out, I'm also totally discreet. As a man of the cloth, I don't divulge confessions."

"I'm not sure that I have anything to *confess*. I don't have any idea what I did wrong."

"No, no. It's not always that one of the partners has done anything wrong at all. I didn't mean confession in the sense of guilt, but of getting stuff off your chest."

"OK." Viv nodded. "I'll certainly bear it in mind. Thank you."

Rory looked at her for a moment and she felt once more as though he was looking through her and into her soul. Then he smiled again, that very attractive un-vicar-ish smile that was making her feel very wobbly. "We're getting side-tracked from our medieval quest. So, just go through what happened again, at Cooney's Mere, and what followed."

"OK. Let me go and get the coffee first." Viv drained the last of her wine, and went to the kitchen to pour out two fresh aromatic coffees.

Cupping her coffee mug, Viv recounted her weird experiences again, thinking more carefully about exactly the details she remembered and trying to describe it all to Rory. He sat sipping the last of his wine, then, after a few minutes, lifted his mug to his lips, nodding, and didn't interrupt once. She remembered how Pete would argue with her, correct her, rarely let her finish her sentences … not really listen to her.

It helped to make the effort to recall everything, and to share it. Because she felt no judgement, no appraisal from him. He just looked as if he took in what she was saying and was thinking about it. As she talked, she no longer felt any embarrassment, or fear.

"And so, at the end, before I came round, she was sobbing, 'I have lost the key. Still more, I have lost the crucifix and if Pelleas has found it he will destroy me, you and all the others like us.' That was it."

When she finished, Viv looked at Rory, questioningly. "I don't understand what it means. There was some kind of magic, passed down from her mother, and the magic and the key to the Vortigern chest would unlock riches that would save the village settlement. But Pelleas clearly was a danger to her, her magical powers, and to her Christian faith. Does any of that make any sense to you?"

"Actually, yes, it does. I can't say that my experience of "being there" was the same as yours. But I had strangely vivid dreams last week, in which I saw myself as a thegn, a lord, in an early medieval court. The dreams seemed very real at the time. So real that I seemed to be feeling the thegn's emotions and thinking his thoughts. But unlike you, I didn't bring anything back with me to the present day. Sadly, no artefacts. But my name in the dreams was Sir Roland. It wasn't until I saw you in the bistro that I made any connection. When I looked at you, I saw Lady Vivianne ... by the lake, in the mead hall, in her chamber ..."

"But how can there be, oh, whatever, parallel universes, different worlds existing at the same time, objects existing in both worlds at the same time ... time-slips between worlds ... physically. I mean, if I hadn't got the key and the crucifix, if I didn't feel so totally identified with Lady Vivianne, in her body even, I would have said it was a question of vivid dreams. Maybe because of the trauma of Pete and Gwyn. But it's got to be something more than that. These artefacts are *real*, of this world, yet they're also in the other world too?"

"Viv, there are things in the world that are beyond our comprehension. Just think of the universe. Black holes. Even birth and death. What are they? How come you can suddenly become a thinking person, at birth, and nothing at death. Unless you, or your spirit, continues eternally. Which is, of course, what I believe as a Christian. And if the spirit is eternal, then it follows that there is something else besides the real, touchable world. "

"But I don't really believe in ghosts and spirits and resurrection and eternal life." She glanced at him. "I'm sorry, vicar."

"Stick to Rory. Forgive me for asking, but do you ever go to church? Do you have a faith of any kind? Do you believe in anything outside the physical world?"

Viv considered for a moment. "When I was a child, I went with my parents to church. Every Sunday morning, and evensong too. They were very devout. And I was brought up in a rectory, although not in use as one, of course. The diocese of York had sold it into private use when they built a new rectory the other side of the village. My parents loved the calm vibes there, said it was all those former Christian residents, leaving their goodness behind in the walls. They were ..." she shrugged off the memories. "But they died. In a plane crash. Together. After that, although I was just a child, I guess I lost my faith. I'm not a believer and Christianity ... well, no ...I do go to the village church occasionally, but mainly because I love the atmosphere, the architecture, the history."

"Well," he grinned ruefully, "there's nothing wrong with that, it means more than you think! And that 'atmosphere', that 'history' is maybe you reaching out to something beyond the here and now. Do you think?"

"I don't know. It's more of an unthinking emotional response really. I can't put it down to any definitive beliefs."

"I'm not in any way trying to convince you, or convert you. I wouldn't do that. Certainly not after ... well, let's just say I don't do the proselytising bit. I do believe that everyone has their own way to their 'god', whoever or whatever that may be for them. Each one of us has our own journey to make. There's not just one way, but many. Sorry, I'm sounding a bit preachy and I don't mean to."

Although what Rory was saying seemed eminently reasonable, Viv did not want a sermon or to get it all confused in her mind with religion - she didn't consider herself to be religious, not any more, and she didn't want to argue, not with a vicar, he was entitled to his own beliefs even if she had cast off all that long ago - so she just shook her head. "Oh Rory, I don't know what to make of any of it. Magic? Early Christian religion? How do they connect?"

Rory rose to his feet. "Look, it's getting late. Why don't we meet up for coffee tomorrow at the university bar? Have you got half an hour in between tutorials, lectures and whatnot? I need to go in and do a bit of research on all this." He glanced at his watch. "It's getting late and it's been an interesting day with a lot to think about. But you need your beauty sleep ...oh, sorry not that you need it ... the beauty I mean ... oh good heavens, I seem to be burbling now – tired, I guess. Thank you for the wine ... and your company. Better go!"

*

79

The next morning the sky was clear and bright, unusually so for a Monday. Somehow, much as she loved her job, Viv always thought Mondays were a bit dismal, everyone was shattered after their weekend, hunched over their computers, and today was no different: the staff study corridors were quiet.

"Morning," murmured Jo, her colleague who shared the study with her. Her eyes were glued to her screen and she didn't look up as Viv pushed the door open with her bottom, her arms full of books and papers. "Hope you had a better weekend than me. Running kids around to birthday parties, football, dance class. Geoff decided to redecorate the kitchen so everything's in a mess. Glad to get back to work! How about you?"

"Oh, fine." Viv didn't want to speak about her weekend and had no wish to share her unhappiness about what had happened with Pete. Everyone else except her seemed to have someone. Ellie, Rory, Gwyn now. Even Tilly had her own take on 'togetherness'. So she quickly shed her load onto her desk extension, switched on her computer and took refuge behind her long list of emboldened emails.

Gradually she worked through deleting the spam and all-staff ones that didn't apply to her, before clicking on the latest emails from her students and colleagues. If she started with the most recent, she didn't have to engage in the beginnings of discussions that would almost inevitably have resolved themselves an hour or two later. Such routine tasks soothed her, as she was forced to focus on them and not the events of the weekend. There were all the usual student issues: ones that complained that her electronic feedback could be clearer or even more detailed, if she could perhaps rewrite the methodology section for him instead of just marking up comments in the margin it would help … ones that rambled on with long stories justifying why their assignments were not submitted in time … ones that sweetly thanked her for all her help and support.

An hour later, when she was almost up to date, she grabbed her teaching bag, peering inside to check that she had working whiteboard markers, enough flipchart paper and felt tips for group work, and her flash drive for the PowerPoint. It was a session she'd taught several times before about research methodology, so she knew that it would flow without much stress.

Her teaching session was only a short one this morning, an hour and a half, so she was finished by midmorning coffee time, and after booking in one of the students for a private tutorial in the early afternoon, a chap who was having some problems with the conceptual framework of his research study, she dashed her bag back to her office and left the piling of further emails arriving on her system, to find Rory in the coffee bar.

She scanned the crowded bar before her eyes lit upon the tall, broad figure of the vicar. He was sprawled comfortably on a sofa on the mezzanine, a coffee mug before him on the low table, long legs spread akimbo, and he was swiping his tablet, frowning. He ruffled his dark curly hair with large tanned hands.

"'scuse me, Doctor," came a voice behind her. She swung round and smiled at one of her third year students, aware suddenly that she was blocking the doorway.

"Oh, I'm sorry, Richard. I was dreaming!" She moved out of the way and added, as she headed for the open wooden stairs, "How's the dissertation going?"

Her student pulled a face. "OK, I guess. Just a bit stuck on the data analysis."

"Well, send me an email to make an appointment for a tutorial if you need help."

"Yeah, that'd be ace," said Richard as he flashed a thumbs-up sign at her and turned to the queue for coffee.

"Vicar? Er, Rory?" Viv called as she reached the top stair. "Can I get you another coffee?"

He looked up and smiled, a full welcoming grin. Viv felt too warm. "Thanks, but I asked the girl behind the bar to pop up when you arrived and collect our order. What will you have? Flat white? Cappucino? Something to keep you going till lunch?"

"Hmmm, a skinny latte and a caramel flapjack, please?" She loved flapjacks and often made them at home. She thought she might have baked some recently but couldn't really remember now. In more than one sense, time had stood still. And yet in other ways, it had hurtled on. Pete had loved her flapjacks too. When would she make them again? She couldn't imagine baking just for herself.

"Well, that's a contradiction in terms!" Rory laughed, breaking in to her thoughts. He moved up so that she could sit beside him on the sofa. "Is that a diet or not?"

"No, not really! I just prefer skinny latte to the full fat milk they have here, not sure that it isn't UHT!"

Rory signalled to the bar girl, a student supplementing her allowance, and called out their order before she had to climb the stairs again.

"You're good with your students," said Rory. "I heard you with that ... er Richard, was it?"

"Oh, thank you. Well, it's just part of my job."

"I can assure you that not every lecturer thinks that way." He smiled at her, his eyes crinkling at the edges, she noticed, and Viv felt herself flushing again.

They made small talk until the coffee and snacks arrived.

"So are you doing a doctorate for a specific purpose?" Viv settled back on the sofa and crossed her legs, trying to look as professional and elegant as she could manage.

"Well, I hoped that my doctorate would assist in my goal of returning to a parish in the south where I grew up and maybe eventually doing some lecturing along with my clerical and pastoral duties. Only ..." he smiled that lazy intimate smile, "only now I rather like it here, so I'm not sure that I want to move back down south."

"It is lovely around here. I wouldn't want ... don't want ... to move."

"Yes. I can tell. I understand the current stress. And of course, for me, that's all a way off. My six month sabbatical is to ... er ...," Did Viv see him biting his lip? "well, to complete writing up my thesis and then I'm back to the grindstone at St Michael's. And what about you, Viv; what are your plans?"

For a moment Viv felt caught off-guard. She automatically glanced at her watch.

"Actually I've got an interview at 4.30 for the head of subject role here in my faculty."

"What? This afternoon? You should have told me! You don't want to be fiddling around with all this nonsense when you should be preparing."

"No, no, honestly it's fine. I'd have said if it wasn't." Viv thought how Pete would have reacted so differently, with casual dismissal of her attempts at promotion. "It takes my mind off it a bit – and the other things that have happened ... you know, with Pete and the apartment and all that."

Rory grimaced sympathetically and nodded. "Yes, indeed."

"So, what have you found out this morning about magic and early Christianity and parallel worlds and such like?"

"I'll email you some links to the research I've found. But you just won't believe what I've discovered about a find at Wilmingham …"

*

Rory's mind-boggling news filled her thoughts that afternoon and stopped her feeling as much stress and anxiety as she might have done normally in an interview for promotion. She had tried before for a similar role at that level of seniority, but was pipped by a colleague from a different team, with more of a Chaucerian angle than Anglo-Saxon, which the panel believed was more business-growth-favourable.

This time there was a man on the interviewing panel who seemed particularly interested in early medieval studies and understood that she was also perfectly capable of leading on other areas of work. He talked to her about the influence of the Must Farm and Lyminge digs on perceptions of early Saxon literature and thinking. She was so pleased that she had read up on these after Rory's emphasising their importance. She breathed a silent thanks to him. She even mentioned the Wilmingham site, with just a hint at the news that the vicar had brought. Without discussing the context of her special knowledge she was able to theorise on the insight her time-slip experience had brought her.

The interviewing panel had nodded sagely and seemed pleased with her enthusiasm for her field, but she had no idea whether they were as impressed with the leadership skills she had manifested over the last few years and her commitment to the department. She talked about her initiatives, her mentoring schemes for colleagues, her decision-making work on committees, her awards for excellence in teaching and research, her work on the university-wide ethics committee. She remembered to outline her leadership of the cutting edge assessment group and her role as advisor with the government department of education.

But, as always, she could not fathom their reaction. They nodded but their faces were inscrutable. Maybe they already had someone else in mind.

She walked out of the interview room, knowing that she had done her best, whatever the outcome. They had others to interview and had told her not to expect any decisions for a few days. Well, she could do no more. And at least for a couple of hours she hadn't been brooding on her personal situation.

She returned to her study and began to search the emails which Rory had sent her, on time slips and multiple universes, and that's what led her to the site about theories connected to the concept of parallel worlds and falling through one world to another, through a 'portal' …the Einstein-Bridge theory, quantum mechanics …Her heart began to flutter with excitement. So it was mind-boggling, but with some kind of possible 'scientific' theory behind it – maybe not so insane, then.

*

It was only when she returned to the flat that Viv remembered her voicemail message to Pete. The voicemail indicator light was flashing and as she pressed the button, Pete's voice filled the room in an angry outburst.

"I've only just picked this up. Been away with Gwyn. You vile bitch. I'm coming over!"

Her heart stopped and she struggled to catch her breath. The violence of his words slammed into her chest, winding her. Was this really her Pete? She'd bared her soul and body, literally, to this man who called her a 'vile bitch'? Some little voice in her brain told her to record whatever he might say – or do, protect herself from his rage, be sure of what happened … in case …

She heard the roar of a car skidding into the parking area and the slamming of its door. Viv barely had time to slip her small voice recorder into her pocket and unlock the door as Pete pushed it wide and stormed in.

"How dare you send me that fucking message on my voicemail! Gwyn might have heard it!" he shouted, jabbing his finger towards her chest. "I could sue you for slander!" Again she saw his lips curl back and his bared teeth ready to attack, like a wild dog, ready to spring on her, savage her.

"Pete, just listen a moment," she reasoned, trying to keep her squeaking voice calm, as he stood dominating the small hallway and her insides turned to liquid. She saw that his fists were clenched at his side and she felt sweat run down her temples and the nape of her neck. She had never felt a fear of Pete before, but now she did.

She felt in her pocket and clicked the record button. "Pete, listen! Please ...I ... I don't understand what you've done. How can you use our apartment as collateral for your business? I haven't agreed to anything of that sort – and nor would I. It's our – my – home. A chunk of my inheritance was used for the down payment to reduce the mortgage ... and I paid the bulk of the premiums too, in order to help you build your business. I haven't signed anything about this!"

He looked at her, and his eyes were cold and sneering. "There are ways and means. Your signature is not a difficult one." Viv caught her breath and her hand dropped to her pocket to touch the voice recorder there. "And anyway you needed my business to succeed as much as me."

"Not now, I don't."

"Don't be so petty, *Viv!*" He spat her name out with such vehemence that his saliva sprayed her face. "We need the money."

"We? Which 'we' is that? You and me ... or you and Gwyn?"

He shook his head and she could see that his hands were clenched. "That's just bitter, because I don't want to be with you any more."

"You wanted my money, and my parents', and handouts from your own parents too. What did you do with it all?"

He reached out and grabbed her shoulder, shaking it. "A business *costs* to set up and grow. Ah, but you wouldn't understand. An academic. Head in your books all the time. Cut off from the real world, a real job, a business like mine."

She tried to shake his hand off her but he only gripped her harder. She pulled her other hand out of her pocket and held it up to ward him off. "That's ridiculous. You were perfectly happy to take my salary when you wanted it." She felt tears of anger and frustration and confusion filling her eyes. "I can't do this, Pete – fight with you about money and the apartment. If I have to, I'll buy you out. But I'll never understand what you've done."

"Ha! You don't get it, do you? Collateral means the property. Not just my share. The whole property has to go."

"What? To pay off *your* debts? You can't do this."

"Yes, I bloody can!"

"What on earth am I supposed to have done to you, for all this vengeance?"

He did not reply, but glared at her and she saw the hate and viciousness in his eyes. Before she was even aware of his movement, he whipped his fist across her face. God, that was new. She was caught totally unawares. She staggered and her world split into kaleidoscopic fragments before her eyes. Her hand flew to her face as she tasted the saltiness of blood in her mouth. Staring, confused, at her hand she saw the bright red before her vision juddered and she fell.

As her legs folded beneath her, she grabbed at the radiator to soften her fall but she only succeeded in slamming into the unyielding metal. She heard her own scream. The air parted and moved. She felt, rather than saw, Pete storm out in his rage, not stopping to help her, and the aura of fury followed him out. As she slid down the radiator to the floor, winded, she heard footsteps running down the stairs to the communal hall and the stirring of the air as someone knelt down beside her. A whiff of scent.

"Oh, god, are you alright, sweetie-pie? Oh, hells' teeth!"

Someone was wiping her face, holding her hand, stroking her hair away from her forehead, touching her head. Viv felt water dripping down her cheeks. Then, her breath left her body and a darkness fell upon her and in the midst of that darkness she saw her mother and father, their faces right up against hers yet somehow a part of her own body.

She could see their eyes, and the fear in them. She could feel their breath on her cheeks, smell her mother's perfume, always Chanel Number Five, her signature. "Darling Viv," they were murmuring. "It's all right. Come here with us." Something bright, shining. A key. Voices echoing across her mind, fainter and fainter. The lid of an old chest opening slowly with effort. Something gleaming inside. "Look what we found, darling, at the dig … Wilmingham …" Drifting into her mother. Fading into nothingness. People around her, noise, fear. The sound of a plane's engine, juddering, heart swooping downwards in pace with the steep descent, screams, shouted prayers, bumping, shaking, terror. Her stomach lurching. Her head crazed.

Then suddenly totally clear. This was it, The end. The sound of her voice, calling "Be strong, darling. I'm sorry. I'm sorry. Be str …" As the crashing of metal and rock and bone tore through her.

As her breath whipped through her and out and up into the mountain air, she saw the tangled metal and people's lives strewn across the hillside and the sharp crags. As something was soaring up into the sky, as her mind imploded into itself and there was no 'she' any more. But only a wisp of memory and consciousness, falling back to earth, finding a place to embed.

And another wisp, another voice, whispering "Lady Vivianne" over and over, echoing and reverberating in her head. A bright light, blinding, a sharp searing pain swooping through her body.

Blackness.

Chapter 9

"Please, my lady!" A large strong hand gently shaking her. "Please, Lady Vivianne!" The hand wiping her face gently with a cool wet cloth, stroking her head, squeezing her hand. Water dripping down her cheeks.

She knew it was Sir Roland's deep smooth voice, and she opened her eyes to see his olive-skinned face frowning with concern into hers.

Lady Vivianne struggled to sit up. "Oh, Sir Roland, I am quite light-headed, and in pain too. What happened?"

"You fainted away and hit your head. See, it bleeds." He held up his hand that was smeared with her blood. She winced and felt the sting on her forehead. There was a throbbing swelling.

"Yes, yes, I remember I could not find my crucifix and key. Was Sir Pelleas here? My head feels hazy."

"I did not see Sir Pelleas, but I heard you cursing him!"

"Cursing him? What – with evil language?"

Roland smiled, amused. "Oh yes, indeed. I was quite flushed at hearing those words from a lady!"

"You tease me. I do not think that I cursed at all." Vivianne shook her head as Roland courteously inclined his head to defer to her denial.

"You were also calling for your mother and father. As if you were calling through the fire. As if you could see them there."

Vivianne frowned. "Yes, I think I remember. They were saying 'it is all right, all is well. Come with us.' And my mother … she was saying, she had found something. She wanted to show me. How could this be? They were in the fire. I could hear the crashing of the beams as the hall collapsed. I could smell the flames." She shook her head, trying to clear her thoughts. "It does not make any sense to me. Was I there? Surely not. What does this mean?"

"I do not know, my lady. But allow me to help you to your feet, if you feel able to bear your weight and stand. Perhaps your lady of the chamber should get you to bed to rest a little?" Roland wrapped his arms around her and she felt his strength and tenderness as he supported her to her feet. She suffused with heat and knew that she blushed in his arms.

As soon as she was upright and steady, she stepped away from him, and him from her.

"No, I do not need to rest," she mumbled a little too sternly in her embarrassment. "I need to find the key and my crucifix. I need you to show me where the chest is. You said you had it in your care, or knew where it was?"

"Yes, I have it safe, although it seems that Guin somehow has discovered its secret place. It is in a hiding place in the sacred hall, or what remains of it. I will take you, but not until nightfall."

"But how do we open it, if I have lost the key? If Pelleas has it, I will never unlock the chest."

"At least if we can get the chest to safety – at least a more safe place, now that it seems that Guin knows of it, we can …" He shrugged.

"And tell me, my lord, why is it that you failed to inform me of this chest and its whereabouts before now?"

Roland smiled at her frown. "Your mother and father, before their deaths, swore me to secrecy until the time was right. I was to tell you only if you were in imminent mortal danger. Or about to be married to … to another … You are about to be married, and I believe that, although I have sensed danger for you before, on this day you are in true mortal danger."

"I see."

"Do you not trust me, Lady Vivianne?"

"If my parents trusted you, then so do I. But so much has been revealed that I am dizzy with it all." She turned away, fingering her empty pouch. Then she swept round again, back to face him. "I will place myself in your hands, Sir Roland. But only until I suspect otherwise. I reserve my judgement, lest I prove to be unwise."

Lady Vivianne could hardly contain her impatience to go with Sir Roland to recover the hidden chest. They had arranged that the quest would take place after the feasting in the mead hall that night, when Pelleas and his close thegns, apart from Roland, would be well in their cups, and everyone would suppose that they had repaired to their bed chambers.

She paced the village although she still felt a dizziness in her head. She raised up her skirts against the mud and uneven stones, and hoped that her agitation did not show. She needed to think. Where could the key be, and her crucifix? Could she somehow search Pelleas's chamber? She would have to find a way when it was unguarded. She must wait until she could talk again with Roland. There was surely no point in this agitation when at present she could do nothing productive. There was, at least, no danger that Pelleas would see her or accost her now before the feasting, as he was engrossed in the gathering of his thegns, the ealdormen, in their council chamber, discussing security and strategy against the latest threat from the enemy marauders of the north. Those unruly Picts.

Vivianne wished that they did not debar high women from their meetings. She knew that she, although perhaps not so strong in body, was just as strong in reasoning and understanding as most of the thegns. But Pelleas restricted his Witan council to those warriors who could fight off intruders and invaders. So unlike her father. When he was alive, elected women and high born women of the most important families were welcomed into the chamber, and they voted like the men, not by striking shields but by clapping their palms together.

It was so different in the settlement now. Or did she just remember it differently? She was only a child then. But as she surveyed the buildings at each side of the paths, 'the street' as they called it, the weaving house, the wood carver's house, the leather worker's house, all selling at the windows or open doors, she recalled the atmosphere of peace and industry that had marked her father's guardianship. Now – or was she imagining it? - the air was tinged with a frisson of tension and fear.

She called at the weaving house and watched the women at the looms, checking to see how long it would be until her winter cloak would be ready.

"Not long now, my lady," answered the spindle-wife curtly, as if she resented the interruption of her work with her flying spinelhealf burrowing its way through the woollen threads. Vivianne knew that it was desperate for her to earn the high taxes that now had to be paid to Sir Pelleas's coffers.

"And please you remember that I want it dyed with woad, steeping as long as you can. I want a deep blue to go with my crimson overdress." She smiled. "And I thank you."

The spindle-wife nodded but did not look up from her work. In truth, Vivianne cared little for her cloth and colours at this time, but she wanted to keep her thoughts away from the most important matter of her life at this moment, the chest and finding the key.

She wandered restlessly from place to place, stopping at the doorway of the communal baking house that served the villagers, to ask after the baker's sick child, as he kneaded the bread with hefty thumps on the wooden trestle table near the ovens. The smell of the yeast made her nauseous as the small boys ran past her with buckets to take to the mead-brewers in the next house. She knew the baker from her childhood when he would interrupt his work to lift her onto his knee and feed her freshly baked bread torn from a loaf. Now, she sighed sadly at his anxious face. She had bought a small carved wooden doll at the wood-whittlers and she gave it to the baker to pop in his pouch for the fevered child. The baker lifted his head from his work and his tense face softened. He smiled his thanks to her and nodded a respectful bow. Lady Vivianne tried to quieten her thoughts, but she felt agitated, her breathing shallow, her turbulent mind unable to still her hands. She forced herself to keep them from shaking.

"My lady," came a breathless voice behind her. Vivianne swung round to see Mathilda, her young under-maid-of the chamber, the lady Guin's apprentice, hand pressed against her child's precociously large bosom trying to catch her breath, face red and sweaty, wild frizzy fair hair framing her face like the sunshine.

"Mathilda, have you been running after me, child?"

"Yes, indeed, my lady. Guin has …has …," she gasped.

"Mathilda, slow down, catch your breath until you can speak easily. There is no rush." Vivianne reached for the maid's arm and guided her out into the fresh air, away from the heat of the ovens. Mathilda heaved her breath and gasped.

"Oh, my! Phew! I am indeed out of breath."

Vivianne glanced at her maid's youthful but stout body, like a playful piglet, with its heaving wobbling breasts and smiled. "No wonder. You are young but do not need to be so impetuous. Calm yourself, my dear."

"Yes, my lady. But I have to tell you that my lady Guin … your lady-of-the-chamber, has asked me to attend you tonight as she is indisposed."

"Oh, my dear lord. She is sick with the fever?"

"No … nor did she appear to be so just now. But she says that she feels unwell. I suppose it must be her moon-time – she did look drained of blood in her face …"

"Mathilda, I think that we do not discuss lady Guin's indisposition in such terms. It is well for you simply to tell me that she is unwell. I do not need the details from you."

Mathilda hung her head and Vivianne felt sorry for her. "Please my lady, I did not mean to be lacking in …in …"

"Discretion," provided Vivianne. "But no matter. You are very young, child, and not yet grown into the manners and behaviour of a lady's maid." She smiled down at her maid. "We will teach you, and soon you will be a full lady-of-the-chamber."

"Thank you, my lady. I am afeared that my manners are yet rough. But I will learn."

"Now, let us go to the lady Guin's chamber to make sure that she has all she wants tonight in her illness."

They walked together back through the village past the evil-smelling middens to Guin's place, the ceorl's house of her father, and Vivianne looked up at the wattle and daub structure with its blackened thatched roof. There was no smoke and the building looked empty. It was very quiet.

"Guin, are you there?" called Vivianne, but no response came. Tentatively, she pushed the plank door open but she could see even through the darkness within that there was nobody there.

"That is strange, my lady," whispered Mathilda. "She was there clutching her stomach a few moments ago."

"Ah, well, never mind, child. Let us go back to my hall to prepare for the feasting." As she turned away, Vivianne called to a neighbour sitting on a bench outside his house, sorting nuts and berries into bowls at his feet. "Are you cȳββ or cynn of my maid Guin de Ceorlworđig?"

"I am indeed, my Lady Vivianne. But you have missed her. She hurried out a mere moment ago."

Vivianne frowned. "I see. Thank you."

"But I saw her only …"

"Tilda, child, no matter." Vivianne, glancing at the man, interrupted her quickly. "Let us return to my hall and you may organise my dress for tonight."

"Oh. Oh. 'Tilda' My familiar name! Oh, my lady. Such an honour. To dress my lady, who is to be wed to the chieftain." She clapped her hands and jumped for joy. "My lady, I will try my very hardest not to drop anything. Oh, those fine gowns and gold brooches ...! Oh!"

*

Under Vivianne's careful instruction, Tilda did well for her initiation in dressing her on her own and preparing her hair and ornaments for the evening meal in the mead hall. But Vivianne's agitation did not abate. Now she was also fretting about what Guin was doing and why she had lied about being sick, yet revealed a pale countenance.

She asked Tilda to remain at her side during the meal and gave her choice titbits on a platter to take to the young maids' table for her supper for she knew that the geburs worked hard and did not like to see them eating as simply as she ate richly, even though Tilda's plumpness would suggest that her father was able to feed her well. She knew that it was not always the case.

And she needed Tilda on hand for a purpose.

As the darkness fell and the flares in the sconces were lit, and shadows dimmed the hall, Vivianne looked around at the company. Pelleas was slouched at the other end of the table with his thegns as custom dictated that they did not sit together until they were formally married. He was loud and expansive in his tales to his friends, and had clearly drunk much of the pitcher of mead that Sir Roland constantly passed to him. From time to time he thumped the table to emphasise his bawdy jokes and his companions were barely able to sit upright. One even had his face slumped in his bowl of whipped eggs, cream, honey and blackberries. They were all clearly beyond sense. Apart from Roland who looked over to Vivianne and winked.

"Tilda," whispered Vivianne. "Please go to Sir Pelleas and tell him quietly that I have to repair to my bedchamber as I have eaten too much chicken and figs, and drunk too much wine. I will be asleep, in the land of the dreams, very shortly, and not to be disturbed."

Vivianne watched Tilda do as she was told, and saw Pelleas nod drunkenly, clearly too little conscious to try to come after her or even to care. As Tilda returned to her side, Vivianne rose from the table and together they slipped out and made for the bedchamber.

"You do not need to stay to prepare me for bed, Tilda," said Vivianne. "I will just get a little air and then I shall fall into my bed, and be asleep within a breath."

"But, my lady ..."

"Do not concern yourself, Tilda. Guin often lets me retire by myself," she said confidently, crossing her fingers behind her back at the lie.

As soon as Tilda had disappeared and the sound of her footfalls had died away, Vivianne swung her cloak about her shoulders and crept outside. A dark figure was lurking in the shadows by the hall. He came to her side and whispered, "Well done, my lady."

"You left Sir Pelleas in his cups, Sir Roland?"

"Yes, none of them will know a thing until morning breaks. Come."

He led her cautiously through the village, diving into the shadows whenever they heard the moan of someone in their sleep or the cries of a couple's love.

As they crept towards the old withered cinders of the cold and ruined sacred hall, what little remained of it, Vivianne shuddered, and felt Roland's comforting arm slip around her shoulders. She made no attempt to shrug it off: it warmed her heart. He was so kind to her. She could still smell those dreadful smoky flames choking her and the burning timbers crashing around her. She could still hear her parents' cries. Why had they not escaped the fire? Why had they not run out of the hall before it burnt down?

Vivianne felt herself grow hot and her head explode with strange words. Latin? Celtic? Then her own voice: "Mother, help me!" she called silently. "Help me to find the chest, my inheritance. Make everything all right again!" Her words sounded odd to her own ears and she shivered.

The moon was dim in the sky, surrounded by a ghostly aura of light swept by the clouds drifting across it as they walked. Vivianne concentrated on each step she took as her feet in their soft leather shoes padded over the stones and she peered into the darkness to avoid the ruts in the pathway. Roland's hand groped for hers and she felt safe as his fingers entwined with hers. Not only that, but a strange frisson of pleasure shivered up her spine.

And so Roland led her by the hand in the darkness that was lit only by the faint moonshine, round the blackened beams, left for all these years by Pelleas. Ever since he had proclaimed publically in the Witan that they should be left undisturbed, as a mark of respect for her parents and their sacrifice, in such a place of mystery and awe. But Vivianne knew that he feared this place, as she herself did, although for different reasons, and he would surely never come here. Maybe, she had wondered so often before, he was afraid of what might be remaining, not physically but the spirits and shadowy shapes of the dead. The shapes on the air.

The moon moved out from behind a cloud and in the eerie light Vivianne could just make out the shape of the ancient barrow which rose above the village boundary a little way off.

"Here." Roland dropped her hand and knelt down and Vivianne could barely see his figure in the darkness. She had to reach out to feel for him, and at her touch he took her arm and guided her.

The place seemed to be marked only by a small piece of broken pot as far as Vivianne could tell as she knelt down. The pot appeared to be a shard from an amphora. As she reached out to pick it up, her hands felt around a shallow cross-shaped indent in the earth. The pottery lay in the middle of the cross. Nobody could have found this, even in the daylight, or known what it signified. They would probably have thought it was just a piece of discarded pottery of no more use and cast away. The village was littered with such pieces of rubbish.

Vivianne held the cold fragment of pottery in her palm and brought it closer to her eyes. It had symbols carved into its surface and Vivianne traced the shapes with her fingers. A man's body perhaps? Yet the leg seemed to be lying at an odd angle and there were runes at the side of the carved image. The wind drifted through the trees in a hollow sigh like soft footfall, and she looked quickly around her. Her body trembled. Was that a movement in the trees? Was that a dark shadow she could see near the barrow?

Roland drew a knife from his belt and began to dig into the soft earth to the right side of the cross indentation, where the horizontal arm of the cross seemed to point. It seemed like an age before he stopped. All the time Vivianne was glancing behind them nervously. At every sound like the snapping of a twig or the scratch of a rodent, she shivered and clutched herself.

"Look," whispered Roland. Vivianne peered into the hole that he had dug, not actually very deep, and she saw the top of a wooden chest, gold decorations glinting in the weak light from the moon above.

Her heart beat so loudly against her ribs that she thought it would wake the village. "Oh, Roland! This must indeed be Vortigern's chest!"

"Yes, so it is!" came a deep voice behind them and they both struggled to stand, swinging round to see the large figure in the darkness.

"We knew you would come!" laughed Guin. "Thinking that you could make Pelleas drunk and then creep out here together!"

"Never underestimate me!" hissed Pelleas. "You thought, Roland, that I would drink well of the mead, as, I grant you, sometimes I do at the feasting. But we knew what you were doing and unbeknownst to you, I let my gebur drink my mead tonight on the pretext that I suspected it might be poisoned. I am a good performer, do you not think?"

Vivianne felt Roland's hand on her arm as he pulled her closer towards his side.

"And," continued Pelleas, "do you really think we did not know that you were skulking in the ante-chamber when you 'overheard' our planned talk? You are not as clever as you make out."

Vivianne heard Roland's incredulous gasp softly in her ear.

"And now you have shown us where the mysterious chest is hidden, we can safely take you to confinement." Pelleas turned and Vivianne saw figures emerge from the shadows and felt rough hands pull her and Roland apart, pushing her away.

"Leave me, sirs! I am a lady, our late chieftain Sir Tristram's daughter!" shouted Vivianne, trying to shake them off. "Roland! Where are you?" She looked wildly around.

"Here!" gasped Roland as he was dragged back towards the village away from her. "Get help from …" but she heard no more as his voice was lost in the darkness.

"Unhand me, for heaven's sake," cried Vivianne. "Do you not know who I am?"

The men snorted and said, not entirely unkindly, "Yes, Lady Vivianne, we know that you are soon to be Sir Pelleas's wife and therefore under his command. We do as he asks us, as our lord."

*

Vivianne lost sight of Roland as she was taken back to her chamber. Pelleas's geburs hesitated to hurt her or show disrespect but they told her that they were instructed to guard her and that three of them were at all times to be stationed outside her door. There was no escape.

Despite her questioning they refused to tell her where Sir Roland was, or even whether he had come to any harm.

Vivianne watched them leave and heard them murmuring outside her door. She sank onto her bed and dissolved into tears of frustration. They had fallen into a trap. How could they have been so naïve?

Presently, through her tears she heard a familiar voice at her door, and Pelleas strode in. Wearily, she wiped her cheeks and pushed herself up from the bed.

Pelleas stood over her, looking her body insolently up and down, as if assessing whether to ravish her or not. "So, my *betrothed*," he sneered, and his lips curled away from his teeth like a wild boar ready to attack. Vivianne gasped; there it was again. "I have come for the key to the chest."

Vivianne's heart fluttered. If he was demanding the key, then clearly it was not in his own possession. She had been mistaken, then. A frisson of hope rose in her throat. "The key? I do not know where it is."

"Yes, you do," shouted Pelleas. "Guin saw Roland slip it into your hand."

"That may be so," answered Vivianne, standing up to face him, and knowing that there was no point in denying it. "But the key was stolen from me and I tell you again, I do not know where it is. Indeed, I thought that you had it."

Pelleas hesitated a moment as if judging whether she was speaking the truth. "In that case," he said, "I will take my axe to the chest." He turned away from her.

Vivianne's heart leapt. Words seemed to issue from her mouth without her will. "Then I shall curse you!"

Where had that come from? A curse? She had no curses! And why had her voice sounded like her mother's?

Pelleas swung round and she saw the fear torn on his face. He lashed out with his hand and struck her forcefully across her face, so that her head whipped back. Her hand flew to her cheek but as she cried out she felt only the pain of the blow. She fell back against the bed and screamed as she hit the wooden frame and fell to the floor.

"You … you enchantress!" shouted Pelleas, and his voice was filled with hatred.

Flashes of glaring light seared her vision and as the darkness fell, she called weakly after him as he stormed out, "Yes, indeed, I curse you, Sir Pelleas!"

Chapter 10

"Oh, god, are you alright, sweetie-pie? Oh, hells' teeth!"

Tilly. Mathilda. She was there too. Viv moved and winced. She remembered.

"Has he gone?" Viv looked up into the halo of wild frizzy blonde hair and struggled to sit up.

"Yes. I heard the commotion and ran down," said Tilly. "My god, *that's* not a lover's tiff! You're really hurt." Tilly knelt down on the hall floor beside Viv, dabbing rather ineffectually at her face with a dripping wet cloth. Then she scrubbed her own red cheeks with the cloth, swiping at the sweat that had gathered there. "Oh my, oh my!"

"Wooh! Just help me up, Tilly," gasped Viv.

Tilly levered her plump body off the floor with some difficulty, wobbling bosom almost falling out of the low tight t-shirt top, and pulled Viv up with something less than care and decorum. "I'm glad you're alive. When I saw you there, out cold, I thought he'd killed you." She cleared her throat and breathed in deeply. "Right. So, let me get you a … glass of brandy? Cup of tea?"

Viv signalled that she needed a moment and leant against the radiator, taking a deep breath in and out. Her legs felt decidedly shaky and her heart quivery. "Phew. Oh yes, thank you, Tilly, a cup of tea would be great."

With Tilly's help, she made for the sofa in the sitting area and collapsed into its soft enfolding comfort with a groan. Through the courtyard doors she could see the sun dipping lower in the sky towards dusk. She heard Tilly in the kitchen area, making a pot of tea, and although she was only yards away, it sounded distant and strange. Her body felt as though she had been in a tumble drier, bruised and aching, but the worst was her face. Her tentative fingers explored the swelling and the blood. Her lips were ballooning and sore, and her cheek seemed to have swollen up like the time she had an abscess on a tooth. She carefully brushed her tongue over her teeth. She couldn't feel any of them broken. That was something, then. But she felt like hell.

"My god!" exclaimed Tilly as she ledged the laden tray on the coffee table, sweeping the papers and pens onto the floor to make space. "You look like shit." She poured out the tea into large mugs and set one beside Viv. "I found some biscuits. Chocolate digestives. My favourite. Here have one." She proffered a plate to Viv who for a moment wondered where they were from, and then realised they were Pete's little private stash. She'd even laughed to him that he should write 'Keep out!' on the tin. But Viv took one although in fact she felt quite nauseated. Maybe the spasm that whipped across her abdomen would be calmed by having something to eat. She nibbled at it painfully between swollen lips, then abandoned it, while Tilly stuffed most of hers in her mouth at once.

"Yum, yum. So, what the hell happened?" Tilly crunched and mumbled as she reached for another biscuit, spitting crumbs.

"There was a letter," began Viv, as she sipped the strong sugary tea, and slowly she told Tilly what had happened about Pete and the flat.

"Surely he can't do that. And you definitely didn't sign anything about using the apartment as collateral?" Tilly made herself comfortable, cupping her mug of tea, plate of biscuits balanced on the arm of her chair, and wriggling her legs beneath her on the chair, all set for an evening of scandal.

"Of course not! I always read documents carefully and never sign anything without advice."

"So … did he forge your signature then? Wow! In which case you could contest it. Unless it was witnessed."

Viv had not wanted to think of such a foul explanation but Tilly had voiced her own reasoning. And she recalled Pete's voice: *There are ways and means. Your signature is not a difficult one.* She shook her head. "I can't think what else would explain it. I mean, presumably the solicitor saw the original document before writing to me. And he implies that I already know all about the arrangement, and am now party to the use of the flat to pay for the business - Pete's business. Which of course I don't have anything to do with."

"And which is what?"

"An IT consultancy."

"Oooh, I never knew what he did." Tilly put her head on one side. "D'you think he'd consult with me on my new-look website?"

"Tilly!"

100

"Oh yes, sorry. Of course. Not a good time. Forget I said that. Loyalty and all that." She stared at the ceiling for a few moments, munching reflectively. "So … hang on …what has this Gwyn friend – who I never met, incidentally, although I've known you since you and Pete first moved here – odd that, 'cos I've met your other friends, well, Ellie, anyway …" Tilly pondered a moment, then shook her head. "So what has this Gwyn got to do with his IT consultancy?"

"No idea. Except that it seems like it's her name on the business."

"What a shit. So they've been at it all this time?"

"Tilly, I'm going to forget you said that, because I know you mean well."

"I know. Sorry."

"But," she grimaced, "you're probably right."

"Yeah, but I need to engage my brain before words come out of my mouth. My new chap Ricardo says it all the time." She reached for another chocolate biscuit. "I would find a new solicitor and … hang on, why do you need a new solicitor if that, er, Donaldson and whatsit, think you are a party to it all?" Her hand flew to her mouth. "Oh, is Pete trying to split legally, formalise it?"

"I assume so. I guess all the rest will come next." Viv sighed. Somehow Tilly's directness was at least honest and in a strange way she found it comforting and practical.

"Well, bugger me. But frankly, you're well rid. Anyone who can treat you like this," she waved her hand towards Viv's face, "can go hang, in my book." Tilly screwed up her face for a moment. "Right. So let's get practical. Either a new solicitor will find that it's fraudulent and so you still have the apartment. Or … or I'm afraid you can't prove that you didn't sign it and then you lose the flat."

"Thanks, Tilly, that's so comforting!" It was Viv's nightmare. But it was true. She sniffed and wondered if she was still bleeding. Should she call the police? Oh god, this was all just too much. What if they thought she had brought it upon herself? What if she had to go to court? God, she just wanted it all to go away.

But as she felt for her tissue in her pocket, she touched the voice recorder and knew that might be her insurance. She must listen to it as soon as she was alone again. She felt embarrassed, as well as bruised, by the whole incident and she wouldn't share it until she had heard what was on it.

"So have you got any hidden investments or off-shore accounts or … or treasure or something that he didn't know about and couldn't get his hands on?"

Viv laughed bitterly. "No. I always trusted him and we shared it all. Or at least I shared with him. Clearly not vice versa. Hmmm, except …"

"What? What?"

"Well, two rather interesting items came into my possession recently. I can't tell you how. But there's a key and a crucifix. They may be worth something. At least Rory thinks so. But I can't use them; and anyway they'll be treasure trove."

Tilly swung her attention from the biscuits to Viv. "Hang on! *Rory*?"

"The new vicar at St Michael's. Well, when I say 'new' I think he's been here a year or so."

"Oooh, *him*! I hear he's rather hot. So you know him?"

"Yes, I know him. At least I just met him. He's doing a doctorate at the uni, in my faculty."

"Wow. Is he really like Sydney Chambers as they say? Or James Norton I should say? Grantchester. I've been watching that on iplayer. I wouldn't mind sharing a glass of communion wine with *him*. Snuggling up in the confessional box."

Viv wriggled to find a better position and the pause helped her to gather her thoughts. "Oh no, he's nothing like Sydney Chambers," she lied. "He's dark for one thing." How odd, he had mentioned Chambers himself. But she didn't want to go down that track. It seemed too 'groupie'. "Anyway, I'm pretty sure he's married. They always are, aren't they, vicars? He wears a gold ring on his third finger."

"Ah, then you looked!"

"No! Well, yes, actually, it just happened to catch my eye."

"Oh yeah." Tilly smirked. "But it could be – I don't know, his dead mother's? An eternity ring? A trap to deter panting parishioners?"

"Stop it, Tilly. He looks married. And he mentioned his wife." Why was she gabbling like this? Tilly was staring at her with a strange expression on her face. "Anyway. So … going back to the key and crucifix. Actually you might know more about the dating of the artefacts than me, with your work in that area. In general, I mean, not medieval stuff."

"Metal artefacts, yeah, tapestries and fabrics, no. Okay. Well, let's see them. What's your thinking?"

"I don't know. Ellie and I had a bit of a look on the internet, and found some similar items. Maybe late fifth century. Post Roman but maybe pre Saxon?"

"Good god," shrieked Tilly. "I just read about something …oh, hell, if you've really found something like that … well, we're talking real good stuff!"

Viv struggled to push herself up from the sofa, but Tilly waved her back again. "Tell me where they are and I'll get them. Don't want you to hurt yourself again."

"Oh, I'm starting to feel better. Physically at any rate. They're on my night stand …"

"Oh my … they should be in a safe, girl!"

"That's what Rory said."

"Mmmm, sounds like my kinda guy!" She grinned.

"Come on, Tilly. They all are. Anything in trousers."

"Bit more than trousers," Tilly leered. "Or less. I'm all for a bit of naked throbbing manly flesh … OK, OK, I know. Going to get your treasure."

Barely two minutes later, Tilly was sinking back onto the chair with the crucifix and key nestled in her palms. She looked at them carefully and then stroked them tenderly. "Wow. Just …wow!"

"So what do you think?"

"They certainly look genuine," she murmured. "Funnily enough we've been researching this sort of stuff, would you believe, for a replica for the Roman re-enactment at Sudbury Hall on the 29th. Not my period, but actually it was really interesting. I might widen my scope." Tilly turned them over gently. "You know, they might be Roman influenced."

"Romano Christian, you think? Maybe post-Roman? Surely they were virtually outlawed and disappeared after the Roman withdrawal? Ellie and I found a website with an illustration of a similar one, dated about 490AD." Viv shivered. "They would have been hidden from the Saxons, somewhere safe and secret. See, this marking on the key shaft? And the eyes on the crucifix? Apparently, these were the markings of the smith."

"Well, either they're a very good forgery – or they're genuine and worth a fortune. You need to take these to the museum for assessment." Tilly passed the crucifix to Viv and peered at the key again. "Do you have any old chests anywhere around here?"

"Chests?" echoed Viv. Rory's words earlier that day reverberated round her head and she felt dizzy. She thought of Rory's revelation that morning:

"Viv," he had said to her in the coffee bar, "I was looking into the Wilmingham excavation in the archives. And I found papers by Dr and Dr DuLac of York University. That's your name, isn't it, Viv?"

"Yes, it is. My father was Dr Michel DuLac and my mother Dr Elaine DuLac. They were both involved with archaeology at York University. After their death, when I was eleven, I came to live here in the midlands with my grandparents and eventually went to university in Nottingham. They were both involved in Saxon and pre Saxon research. That's how I got interested. Although I gravitated later towards Old English and Middle English language and literature. I don't remember anything about a dig in Wilmingham though."

"Well, Viv, there was a very significant find of a chest, from post-Romano pre-Saxon times. So significant that it, and its contents, was believed to be of immense value."

Viv repeated to Tilly what Rory had said.

"That's quite weird," said Tilly, turning down her mouth. "So what happened to the chest?"

"Rory said that the papers claim that it was never found following my parents - the DuLacs' - deaths. They had taken it to New York for further investigation. It was thought that they may have had it on the plane bringing it back to England. But it was never discovered in the wreckage. It crashed ..." Viv paused a moment, feeling her isolation again even though it was so many years ago. "It crashed in the Atlantic, well, just off the Irish coast. The wreckage was strewn over a wide area of sea and mountain, and clearly much of it sunk in the ocean." She bit her lip. "It's funny. It was so long ago and I don't think about it much these days but just sometimes it becomes more ... *real*, you know?"

Tilly reached over and patted Viv's hand. "I know, I know, sweetie-pie," she paused and frowned. "Well, to be honest, I don't really, because I have such a large family, sometimes I used to wish I could be on my own a bit more. That's why I came here to get a flat on my own. Peace and quiet. No longer having to shout and gabble to make yourself heard! But I can't imagine how awful it must be to feel that you don't have anyone. And with a mystery as well … goodness."

Viv felt a rush of nausea and wasn't sure whether it was the pain, the shock or the memories. Her head was reeling. And somewhere there was a hazy foggy vision of a letter.

"I think … there was a letter that my parents wrote to me when they were flying over to the States. I got it just before the news of the plane crash and I think it all became muddled up in my head. There was too much to cope with. I was only a child and I was staying with my grandparents while they were away and, of course, in the event, I never returned home."

"So have you still got the letter? Might it give you any clues?" Tilly leaned forward in excitement.

"We hid it away with their effects. My grandparents didn't want me to be constantly reminded of what happened. I've moved three times since then, so various bits have got lost. But I did rescue a box from my grandparents' attic when they died. To be frank, I've not opened it. I couldn't somehow. I just put it away safely. It's in my filing cabinet."

"Well, what are we waiting for?" Tilly pushed herself up and deposited the biscuit plate and her mug on the coffee table. "This is soooo exciting!"

Viv wondered whether she had the strength but struggled to her feet. In her excitement, Tilly seemed to have forgotten all about Viv's injury, and was almost jiggling on the spot.

She led Tilly into her tiny study, hobbling, and searched for the key to the bottom drawer. She kept it in a bank deposit envelope in her desk, pushed to the back of the drawer. Crouching down to the floor, and with a shaking hand, she unlocked the filing cabinet drawer. Viv took a deep breath – was she ready for this? Surely after so many years she needed to be. She lifted out the cardboard box, pulled away the brown packing tape, and, with trembling fingers, opened it. Inside were dusty folders and a small jewellery box where she knew her grandmother's wedding ring lay. Her mother's was never found, nor her body. There was the airmail envelope that she recognised as the last letter she had received from her parents. It was post marked New York, Kennedy Airport. She unfolded the thin paper inside and read:

"Darling Vivvie, we hope you are well and happy at Mama and Grandad's. It's been such a long time since we were with you. But work is nearly done and we'll be back with you very soon. Some exciting news: Daddy and I have made a rather important find at the dig in Derbyshire! We've taken lots of photographs of it and are off to New York to see a specialist who we hope can provide a true valuation. It's a small wooden chest but it contains some very important items from the fifth century! It's so precious that we have lodged it in the bank vaults at Barclay's in St Oswald's Street, and the key is in a safe place at the dig where we can retrieve it when we get back from New York."

So, was the key in her possession the key to the chest that her parents had found? But *that* key was, or had been, at the site of the dig. Presumably in a safe or something. The site which was now abandoned. What had happened to the safe containing the key, and how had it come to her? Somehow it had, across the centuries, and Lady Vivianne, in *her* time, had lost it.

"So what is the key you showed me?"

"I think it's the one from the site."

"How did you get it then?"

Viv tried to tell Tilly something of her experience but her words were making no sense, even to her own ears. Tilly puckered up her brows and screwed her eyes narrow. She shook her head.

"Are you sure you've not got concussion, sweetie-pie?"

"It's not …I wasn't …," Viv began but her words seemed to escape her.

"A nightmare, eh?"

"Well, not in that sense. I …er …oooh, my head."

Viv felt increasingly dizzy and the room seemed to be shaking, the walls juddering and closing in on her. She dropped her head into her hands and rubbed her temples.

"Viv, sweetie-pie, I think you need to be in bed. Here, let me help you." Gently, Tilly supported Viv to the bedroom and helped her undress and pull on her PJs. She plumped up the pillows and tucked her in like a nurse. Then she fetched her copious bag and rummaged inside, pulling out a tube of arnica cream, a couple of paracetamol capsules and a large white pill.

"Here, take these. I'll get you a glass of water from your bathroom."

The ceiling was whirling and Viv did as she was told without arguing. Bless Tilly, she was so kind.

She heard Tilly leave the bedroom and then the click of the front door. She heard waves rushing towards her, rising to meet her, swamp her body, and cover her head. She was drowning, falling into the oblivion of sleep...

Chapter 11

"Morning, Rory," Viv said into the voicemail, her voice still hoarse and thick. She had awoken early after sleeping soundly all night, refreshed although still sore and her lips still a little swollen. Tilly's arnica and her own witch hazel this morning had calmed her skin and a thick application of cover stick and foundation camouflaged the damage reasonably well.

The recorded message was unusual: it sounded to Viv's ears like the first few bars of a mandolin rendition of *Nella Fantasia*. How strange. That was the music she had been listening to on the night Pete left her. Rory's voice cut in and Viv responded, "I guess you're out and I'm just off to work ... er ... but I found out something. It's regarding the Wilmingham dig and I could do with some help to navigate around the site. If you're free, can you come over later when I'm home from the university, say about six? Many thanks ... um ... that's it."

She replaced the receiver of the landline on its stand and grabbed her hobo bag. It's strange how you could never get through to people when you had something really important to tell them. She'd already tried Ellie and got her voicemail too. It was very frustrating. But she had a busy day's work to do, so she'd left the same message on both.

On waking early she had listened to the voice recorder. It was all a little muffled but it was surely clear enough to present to a solicitor. Pete couldn't be allowed to get away with faking her signature and surely that admission would invalidate any claim he had on the flat. Nausea filled her as she remembered Pete's visit and his violence.

Viv swung carefully out of the door, still stiff from the bruising last night, almost colliding with Tilly, laden with bags, in the hallway.

"Hey there, sweetie pie! Any better today?"

"Yes, thanks, Tilly, a good night's sleep on enough paracetamol to knock out an elephant helped. And thanks for all your help last night. I don't know what I'd have done without you."

"Aaww, that's OK, lovey-duck. You're welcome! And actually the big tablet was a horse pill! Ha, ha! Tootle-pops!" *Where did she get these phrases? Goodness, was it really a horse pill? Good god, what was she thinking?*

"One sec, Tilly!" Viv felt a rush of affection for her mad neighbour who had been so kind to her last night. "Can you come over about six tonight? I need support … Got something exciting, maybe dangerous …"

"Ooh. Absolutely, sweetie! But got to rush, late for a meeting. Woops, shit, nearly dropped my samples! Ha! Samples - not wee, of course! See ya later, alli!" Tilly held the outer door long enough for Viv to catch it, then ran off towards her car, a bright yellow Peugeot 206 cabriolet, swiping the remote to let the canvas roof down as she threw in her bags and jumped in after them. Viv smiled as she followed more sedately to the parking area behind the coach house; her neighbour was always pretty nifty for a large girl.

The working day was crowded with a lecture, three tutorials and a team meeting, and Viv discovered many new ways of hiding her hurts. She hardly had time to wonder about the interview results or think about Pete and the apartment débacle, or about Lady Vivianne's Vortigern chest. Only her soreness and stiffness kept a continual back-of-her-mind reminder of the night before.

There was no email about the job interview, so she could forget that for another day. At lunchtime, she sat at her computer eating a bowl of tuna salad that she had thrown together that morning in a drugged yet panicky haze. She managed to drizzle the vinaigrette dressing from the little bowl set into the lid over the salad without dripping it onto the keyboard and ate, despite her still swollen mouth – yes, she was actually a little hungry, a good sign - with a fork in her left hand while tapping the keys with her right and scanning the screen, screwing up her lips so that she could slip the food in between them.

"Look at you!" exclaimed Jo, her colleague at the desk in the corner. "No wonder computer keyboards are more unhealthy and bacteria-laden than loos."

"Well, needs must. Got a lot of work to get through today."

Jo peered at her, screwing up her eyes. "Hey, have you taken a tumble or something? You look a bit swollen around the mouth."

"Yes, well, something like that! But it's OK now."

"You sure?" Jo frowned. Viv nodded firmly and turned back to her computer screen. She didn't want any fuss, or to have to explain anything.

She snatched a minute to phone a solicitor to make an appointment for the first available hour she had that coordinated with their diary window, which was not until the following week. Other than that, her mind was completely occupied with work issues, apart from the niggle of darkness that was now always nibbling away at the back of her brain.

At the end of the day, she closed down her computer, tidied the tutorial reports away into her filing cabinet, and grabbed her bag. A quick "bye" to her colleague who had just returned to the office after her lecture, and she was off to the car park. As she drove home through the rush hour traffic across town and out to the village towards the abbey and the apartment, Viv settled her mind to what she was now going to ask Rory, Ellie and Tilly to do. She had heard the pings of her mobile informing her of incoming mail whilst she was mid-lecture that morning, and had glanced at the screen to check that Rory and Ellie had confirmed. They would each make it for six, six-thirty.

*

Viv was brewing coffee and piling her homemade ginger flapjacks, baked last week and forgotten, from the tin onto a plate when the doorbell rang. A feeling of excitement had replaced (well, almost) her aches and pains of last night. Excitement, and more than a little dread.

She opened the door and Rory and Ellie were standing there together chatting like old friends. Ellie looked at her oddly as they stepped into the hall but Viv ushered them in and Ellie said, widening her eyes, "What is all this about? Is it something exciting?" She peered at Viv and whispered, "Are you OK? I can see ..."

Viv shook her head and mouthed back, "I'm OK, tell you later."

"Wait, wait! Here I come!" shrieked Tilly as she ran down the stairs to join them. Viv held the door for her and she swept inside, unsuccessfully trying to yank down her hemline which seemed to be gathering around her crotch.. "Hi, everyone!" She stared hungrily at Rory. "Ooh, the hot vicar, I assume. Hey, you!"

Rory tugged at his collar and winced. "Tilly, I assume?"

"Sure am." Tilly winked.

"Er, so, you've found something out about the Wilmingham dig then, Viv?" said Rory, raking his fingers through his dark curly hair and grinning at her. "I don't get it. Why do you need help navigating the website?"

"No, no," Viv waved them into the sitting room and poured out coffee from the jug. "Have a flapjack and read this." She handed Rory the old airmail letter from her parents. "It's not about the website; it's about the site of the old dig."

Tilly had squeezed beside Rory on the sofa, as close as she could without actually sitting on his knee, and she caught the opportunity to lean over him to scan the letter, despite the fact that she had already seen it last night. "Wow. This is like a mystery story! So we need to search the dig site for the place where your parents hid the key."

Viv passed the letter over to Ellie. She scanned it quickly and shook her head.

Rory looked across at Viv. "Well, not exactly, Tilly. I think we already have the key." Viv nodded. He could even read her mind.

"Yes," nodded Tilly. "The one I saw last night."

Goodness, I must have been more lucid than I thought, Viv frowned.

"You know what we're talking about, Tilly?" said Rory.

"Oh yes, of course!" Tilly smiled at him. Viv shook her head. She had little recollection of last night, just one or two flashes. Perhaps she told Tilly ... but she wasn't sure *what* she had told Tilly.

Viv was aware that Ellie was frowning and shaking her head. She struggled to think back to her conversation with her old friend.

"So," Rory cut into her thoughts, "we need to locate the place where Lady Vivianne might have lost it. Then we have a connection, a link to the past. In other words, a portal."

"Lady Vivianne? Oh, that's the woman in the vision. But what the hell is a portal?" Tilly wriggled closer to Rory, her thigh squashed against his. Viv smiled as she saw him try to move away.

"I think it's the tear, a rip that Lady Vivianne is reaching through." Viv sipped her coffee. She summarised the story quickly, unsure what exactly Tilly had latched on to last night in her ramblings. Tilly was nodding, Ellie shaking her head, biting her lip.

"Oooh, it's a great story!" Tilly shrugged her shoulders, pouted and grinned conspiratorially at Rory.

"Maybe a bit more than a story, Tilly," said Viv. Tilly turned her head to Rory's serious face.

"Aaagh. This is spooky." Tilly shuddered, inching even closer to Rory, if that were possible. Viv was aware that Ellie was leaning forward, hands gripping her mug.

"The tear in …?" Ellie frowned into her coffee.

"The fabric of the universe," said Rory and Viv together. They looked at each other, startled, then Viv gestured to Rory to carry on. "A portal to another time. It's the multi universe theory."

"What?" Ellie put her mug down on the table and stared at Rory.

"There is a theory – well, a number of theories, actually – that there are more worlds/existences/lives than one." Rory leaned forward. "Basically, it's from Quantum Mechanics. The Einstein-Rosen Bridge. The idea that there are, theoretically, multiple universes, not just one."

"It's a scientific theory?" Ellie jerked her head in disbelief.

"Yes, although of course, not universally acknowledged," Rory conceded. "The idea is that there could be a space-time continuum, whereby there can be instantaneous movement through a space-time-portal, from one time or world to another."

"Dear god. But you don't *really* believe in all this stuff, do you?" Tilly grimaced. "I mean – really, *seriously*? All sci-fi and stuff, like in the movies?"

"I'm struggling to grasp this." Ellie rubbed her forehead. "What on earth are you talking about? This 'portal' thing is …something physical? You mean it's something *in the real physical world*?" Ellie asked slowly. "You see, since Viv told me about her vision thing, I've been thinking …" Her voice trailed off.

Rory spread his hands. "Well, yes. This space-time portal in Quantum Mechanics is, basically, integral to a theory about the nature of what we call 'reality'. Sometimes the portal's sometimes called a worm-hole, or, more accurately when we're talking about movement between worlds, a traversable worm-hole."

"A worm-hole – but obviously not for worms?" Tilly laughed too loudly.

"No." Rory smiled gently at her, and Viv saw her squirm her pelvis. "It's really just a term to identify something in time and/or space that allows different points to connect across universes."

"So … what? That's …. You're saying an actual time-slip from the present day to a previous time?" Ellie insisted. "Physically?"

"That could be one dimension of it, yes." Rory smiled across at Viv.

"Good god!" said Tilly. "Yikes. That really *is* crazy. I thought you were kinda joking before. Or fantasising. I do that. Except not about other-worldy things. Obviously."

"There's a lot of argument about it, as you might expect," added Viv, "And many scientists think it's all baloney and simply a theoretical mathematical possibility, not a physical reality. But what I experienced kind of fits. And many scientists do think there could be something in it."

Viv recapped what had happened in her last journey into the medieval world of Lady Vivianne. And explained to Rory and Ellie about what had happened with Pete, the apartment issue, and his hitting her.

"Oh my god. When I came in I thought I could see bruises under the make-up," whispered Ellie and she pushed herself up from the armchair and wrapped her arms round Viv. The scent of warm lavender filled her nostrils. It was the smell of comfort. "Why didn't you ring me?"

"It was all so startling, and the episode with Lady Vivianne and Sir Pelleas … and when I came round, well, Tilly was there. By the time I was even part way revived it was so late, I didn't want to disturb you and Stuart and the kids, Ellie. And I was OK. Tilly helped me into bed."

"The police …" began Rory, shaking his head. "It's assault."

"No, I just … I can't …it's all too much. Please don't suggest that."

Rory nodded slowly.

Viv noticed that Rory had gone strangely quiet and was frowning. His mouth was set in a voiceless 'hmm' expression. "What is it, Rory?"

"I also had a rather weird experience last night. It was midnight. I'd been making notes late for the seminar today. The rectory was quiet. Mrs N had gone to bed long since and I drifted off and when I woke – just like you the other night – it was still midnight."

Ellie gasped and her hand flew to her mouth; Tilly looked puzzled and started to speak, but Viv already knew what Rory was about to say. It was a familiar story that echoed hers.

"So where was Sir Roland taken?"

"It was a dark vault behind the mead hall. That's all I could make out. But Lady Vivianne's little under-maid, Tilda, whispered through the door to me that she had followed us, nipping in and out of the shadows, fearing a betrayal, and saw where they took me. She managed to open the door, somehow, and I was slipping out as I came round."

Viv smiled, glancing at Tilly. "She's a cunning little soul, that one." She realised that Ellie was looking from one to the other of them, shaking her head in bewilderment, and Tilly sat with her mouth open. "Yes, Tilda reminds me of you, Tilly, just as Lady Eleanor reminds me of Ellie."

"I know it's all very strange," said Rory, moving to reach for a flapjack, then pausing and leaning back in his seat. "Why both Viv and I are involved in this I don't know. I guess that god works in mysterious ways. But I do believe that we have been somehow 'chosen' for a purpose. To, well, lay the ghost, if you like – to put it into a cliché. There's something that we have to do. Something that's calling out to us across time, across the centuries."

The sudden silence in the room was heavy and Viv heard the hall clock strike the last quarter, six forty-five. A feeling of weightlessness and drifting filled her mind. She was like a dandelion clock blown in different directions, floating without will or intent, at the mercy of some 'otherness'.

"Yikes," murmured Tilly.

"I think," Viv began, "it's something to do with my parents' find at the Wilmingham dig. The chest. The key and the crucifix. I just don't understand what yet."

"But it seems just so much of a coincidence, that you two ..." Ellie bit her lip. "I mean, there's some kind of reflection of Tilly and myself there, but I certainly don't time-slip."

"Ha ha! Neither do I," Tilly guffawed. "Although I wouldn't mind getting cosy with those gorgeous hunky knights! And didn't they all sleep around with each other in those days?"

"Not really," mused Viv. "In fact they had very strict codes about sex and marriage, especially the nobles. I guess it was about breeding with the right line."

"So then why haven't Tilly and I travelled back to the dark ages?" insisted Ellie, touching her wrinkled brow.

"Yeah, why do you two get to be so lucky?" Tilly rubbed Rory's arm teasingly. Rory slid further along the sofa, although he was already half way across the edge.

"Some people have a certain sensitivity, I believe," explained Rory. "Especially if they have been going through traumatic experiences in their lives. They become more open to possibilities. Some might say, more suggestable." He paused as if he had said too much. Viv wondered what trauma Rory had suffered, if his logic was right. But she kept quiet and he shook his head. Then he closed his eyes and added in a lighter, but, to Viv's ears, strained, tone. "Viv, these flapjacks are delicious. You cook?"

"Oh yes, my mother and then my grandmother taught me, when I came down here to live with them." Viv smiled at the easier drift. "Granny believed that I should be prepared for the world."

Rory grinned at her, echoing her relief. He had a gorgeous smile that spread across his face and shone from his eyes. It was so intimate and so reminiscent of Sir Roland's looking upon Lady Vivianne, that Viv felt a little wobbly. But, let's face it, he was the vicar, trained to be nice to all his parishioners, especially when they made him coffee and baked goods. And a vicar was essentially a remote person, a step or two removed from his mortal flock. And there was a *Mrs* Netherbridge; of course, to help tend to the needs of her husband's parishioners. He had probably told her all about Viv. On the other hand, his wife might like the gift of flapjacks too.

"I'll bake you a batch if you like … if you think Mrs N would like me to …?"

"But … but … but … Baking be damned! Hang on a minute!" stuttered Ellie, shaking her head so that her tiny gold earrings wobbled. "Good grief! Multiple universe theory, tear in the universe, going back in time … I'm sorry but I can't get a hold on all this. I do, in a way, believe that there are imprints of history in the present world … but that two people who know each other can, at the same time, somehow slip into another world, the same world … I can't get my head round it."

"No," said Viv, biting her lip. "I know. But when it happens to you, like everything else in life, yes, suddenly it seems real. I never thought it would be possible that Pete would betray me – us – or go off with Gwyn, but he has, and then, yes, it *is* possible. Suddenly the world tips over. It's like reality becomes a dream. And a dream, reality."

Viv was aware that Rory was looking at her with … what? Compassion? Contemplation? His dark eyes were soft and he looked as if he wanted to say something, do something. Then the moment passed.

"So," said Rory, placing his hands on his knees, and rising decisively. "Shall we potter over to Wilmingham now?"

"Well, I'm game!" Tilly pushed herself up from the sofa, hanging on to Rory's arm. Rory caught Viv's eye and raised his brows as he smiled at her.

*

They all drove in Rory's car, an ancient, dark blue Jaguar rather like Inspector Morse's but that had seen better days, with its rusting front grill. Wilmingham was just on the far side of Cooney's Mere, beyond the marina.

"I found the area where the dig site was," Rory said as he drove a couple of miles further on from the village, down a lane then a rutted track, to a bleak spot that rose in the distance to a wooded mound.

Rory led them from the layby where he parked the car, along a path that was overhung with tree branches that canopied over their heads. Viv shivered. Somehow the path seemed familiar to her, yet she knew that she had not walked this way before. The leaves rustled, yet as she looked up she saw no movement; all was eerily quiet. Was that the low noise of people moving stealthily through the trees? A soft murmuring, but as she turned towards it she knew that there was nothing. A feeling of horses' movement, a whinnying, a shake of a head, a mane, a prick of ears. A rustle of cloth, a chink of metal.

To her left she heard the flow of water on rocks, yet there was no stream or river. She stopped in her tracks and looked back, heart thrumming; the sound of water echoed in the silence of the trees as it flowed back towards Cooney's Mere. Tilly walked ahead, but Rory and Ellie stopped too, and moved towards her, standing either side. She felt their questioning stares. Viv took a deep breath, trying to still her heart. Tilly turned back to join them.

"Strange. I can hear water. A river. Just over there," Viv murmured, frowning. She felt Ellie's hand on her arm.

"Hmmm. That ditch to our left, in the shade of the trees," nodded Rory slowly, "looks like it could be the location of an ancient river. Now dried up and filled in, of course."

"Possibly," said Viv slowly, "if the Wilmingham dig was revealing the site of a pre-Saxon village, it would have been a transportation river between the mere, the settlement and other small towns."

"Could be," Rory nodded .He looked around as if to locate the landmarks. Then he screwed up his eyes. "Aah."

Suddenly, he swung down the embankment and squatted on the ground, brushing his hand over the weeds and undergrowth. He carefully pulled a leaf from a plant and, climbing back up the embankment, held it out to show Viv, its shiny oval shape pointed at the tip. "It's an ancient variety called atropa belladonna livia, an old plant that grew near the rivers, particularly in limestone, which is what we have here."

Viv stared at the leaf on Rory's palm. He seemed to know so much. She liked that – his learning, his knowledge, his enthusiasm. Then her mind seemed to clear and she drew in her shaking breath, "And belladonna was what they used in Roman times as a herbal medicine. Belladonna and mandrake." She touched the leaf and her heart thrummed as she brushed Rory's skin. She daren't look up to his eyes, and whispered, "And in Roman and medieval times they used it as a medicine. For treating fever and as a pain-killer, an anti-inflammatory."

"Oh, yes, that sounds familiar," said Ellie, gripping more tightly on to Viv's arm. "And wasn't it also used by ladies as a cosmetic? I'm sure I've read somewhere that they put drops in their eyes to dilate the pupils. Make their eyes look dark and sexy."

"Ooh, I'll have to try that," Tilly giggled.

"So it would not have been unusual to have it in your home," said Viv.

"I guess so," said Rory.

"But, remember, it's also a poison. The ancient Britons used it to poison their arrows."

"But what's in that strange name, atropa belladonna … what was it … labia? … livia?" Tilly leaned in to Rory and peered at the leaf in his palm. Her breasts just happened to touch Rory's arm, Viv noticed with a shiver.

"Because Livia, the wife of the Roman Emperor Augustus, was said to have used it to kill him. Hence the name," Viv explained . "So, we call the modern version 'deadly nightshade'."

"Oh, yes, of course," nodded Ellie.

"Ugh, shudder," said Tilly, moving away from Rory as though the leaf might poison her just by looking.

"So, what I'm trying to say, is that belladonna was, first and foremost, a cure-all, a kind of ancient drug, grown near the villages. So…this one growing here," added Viv slowly, "would indicate a river running along to our left, and possibly a stretch of water, a lake, a settlement nearby?"

"I guess so, sounds logical," Rory nodded. But his voice was soft and echoing as if from far away. She seemed to hear it through a mist.

Viv felt the trees moving beside her and the swish of a breeze sweeping the undergrowth. Dizzy for a moment, she screwed up her eyes and looked around her. Murmurings, movements, the thud of footfall passing her, the sweep of a long russet robe beside her, yet as she swung round she knew that there was nobody there.

A few yards ahead the path began to widen into a clearing in the woods, and Viv could see that the grass was oddly coloured in places, as if marking something beneath which had prevented growth. Noises swirled through her head now, growing louder. She felt as if her brain had moved in her skull and reverberated against the side of her cranium. She could hear Rory saying something about the site of the dig … markers … a long, long way away …

It seemed that the leaf fluttered from Rory's hand and drifted across her face, damp and flicking drops of river water into her eyes … a river that seemed to flood over her and into her consciousness …

Viv felt herself move as though something or someone was guiding her gently across the clearing. She saw the sweep of a russet robe between the trees, a flash of terrified eyes. Someone pointing downwards to the earth. A whispered "Here!"

A rush of fear swept through Viv's body. She looked down and saw a dark area of bare earth before her. She knelt and brushed the soil with her fingers, crumpling on the ground, crying, searching …

Chapter 12

"Yes, indeed, I curse you, Sir Pelleas!" Her own words echoed in her ears as Lady Vivianne pushed herself up from the floor of her chamber. Her hands that had scrabbled at the ground now went to her cheeks but her tears were dried. She had not slept, but she had lost consciousness for a long time.

Surely, hours had gone by and she could sense that it was the middle of the night, the darkest hour, and she was trapped, a prisoner. What would Pelleas do to her? Her imagination swept between many dreadful possibilities. And yet she hoped that he would be unnerved by her curse, and too fearful of the knowledge of her mother's magic to harm her. He would not know that she had no acquaintance with it herself.

She could hear the murmurings of the guards outside her door. Where was Sir Roland? What had they done to him? Despair filled her heart.

Then something else: the sound of a girl's cry and the noises of movement beyond the chamber. The scrape of the wooden door. Vivianne caught her breath and sat as still as she could, watching as the door moved slowly open.

"My lady?" A whisper. Little Mathilda's voice.

Vivianne let out her breath. "Tilda?"

"Yes, my lady. But quickly! I have distracted the guards at your door but they will be back within a shout. Come!"

"Oh my dear girl. I cannot thank you enough. What guile and inventiveness you show." Vivianne allowed herself to be pulled by the hand outside into the thick darkness. Stooping low, they scuttled along the path. She stubbed her toes against the stones and suppressed her sharp intake of breath as much as she could. Another hand caught her. She recognised the sweet aroma of lavender and as she looked up through the dark she knew it was the figure of Eleanor beside her. They huddled at the edge of the clearing to catch their breath.

"How … how did you know where I was and what had happened?" whispered Vivianne to Tilda.

"I followed you and Sir Roland, my lady. I kept in the shadows but I saw it all. I am used to the darkness. My father ..." she hesitated, "he used to take me to trap and catch the night beasts for food. Oh, I know that was against the mead council's laws and we should have shared our hunt spoils but Sir Pelleas does not ..."

Vivianne could not help but smile in the cover of darkness. "No, my child, Sir Pelleas does not keep the court's values as my parents used to." She remembered their devotion to courtly chivalry and honour above all, sharing amongst the poorer folk of the settlement, keeping the values of their faith. And she was proud of that, and tried herself to maintain it, but this was one time when she was glad for a little guile. "But for this moment, thank goodness for your father's training."

"So then I found Lady Eleanor," whispered Tilda. "And now we are all together, the three of us, to seek out Sir Roland." Vivianne could sense her hopping up and down.

"You saw where he was taken, Tilda?"

"Indeed, my lady. It was a vault behind the mead hall, beneath the ground. I can find it again even in the darkness. But ..." Mathilda mumbled lower and Vivianne could tell even in the dark that she was hanging her head so that her voice was muffled . "I saw what they did to him as they took him and threw him into the vault ... I ... I heard his screams." Vivianne caught her breath as Tilda looked up to her again. "Then I turned and followed you and your captors, my lady."

"Come," insisted Eleanor quickly, holding tight to Vivianne's arm. "We must do what we can for Sir Roland ... if we are not too late."

Vivianne bit her lip and suppressed her gasp. "Please god we are not too late." She felt for her crucifix to clutch it but remembered that it was not there. Her heart trembled.

Vivianne and Eleanor stumbled after Tilda, only with difficulty able to follow her shadow that sprang quick and lithe like a hill-goat before them along the shadowy paths between the buildings and out behind the mead hall. Vivianne could feel the sharp stones of the path piercing through the thin leather of her delicate slippers. She knew that there were exposed tree roots hampering the way but could see so little that she just had to hope and pray that none of them would trip on the hazards. If only there was a little more light. All she could make out in the dark was the bulky grim shape of the burial barrow beyond the altar-hall at the boundary of the village.

As she looked towards the barrow, she thought that she could hear a whispering, like the wind, softly in her ear. "Come, come, sweet child Vivianne." Vivianne glanced fearfully around her, but there was only darkness. "Do not fear, my child, *my little Lady Vivianne*, come ..." And she knew without doubt that it was her mother. Her mother holding her by the hand and leading her to a ... what, a cave? ... No, a doorway. Nearby. Near the sacred altar-hall. She widened her eyes to scour the darkness but knew she would not be able to see it until the moon slipped out from behind the clouds again.

"Here!" whispered the little maid. Vivianne could see nothing in the darkness but the rear wall of the mead hall, rising up beside them. Then as Tilda dropped to her knees Vivianne narrowed her eyes and peered closely. Gradually she could distinguish the outline of a trap door in the earth below their feet. She gasped. Sir Roland had been thrown down there! Into a closed pit! What – to die without anyone knowing?

Vivianne watched, cold hands clutching her bosom, as Tilda crawled on the ground and whispered through the door. "Sir Roland! I have found you!" There was a muffled noise from the earth. Vivianne knelt down.

A sound, more recognisable as Sir Roland's voice now, competed with the thumping of Vivianne's heart against her ribs. "Well done, Tilda!" His voice was soft but Vivianne heard the effort and the rasping.

Struggling to speak, Vivianne helped Eleanor and Tilda to prise open the wooden trap door. "Do not strain yourself too much, Eleanor! Remember your condition. Let Tilda and myself take as much of the weight as we can."

"I am strong," replied Eleanor. "Do not fear. Who was it who rode the horse from the coast?"

As Roland's head and shoulders appeared they wound their arms under his and pulled him with all the strength they could muster to drag him up and out of his dreadful earthy prison. He was a big man and the first few moments were tense but as soon as his feet and hands found purchase, his strong muscles were able to pull his body, groaning, to the surface. But even in the darkness Vivianne could see that his face was contorted with pain and that he had blood on it and on his body, seeping through the tunic.

He blinked and looked around him. "Vivianne!" he smiled weakly. "You have come to save me. And Eleanor too."

"Yes, but we must get you to a safe place and tend to those wounds," said Vivianne. She was looking down at his hands that he was holding out oddly and saw that they were raw and bloody. He was unsteady and she took his arm again. A memory flickered through her mind and she set her mouth firmly. "Come quickly! There is a place my mother used to go, a way behind the altar-hall where she kept secret infusions. It is like a cave set into the side of the old barrow, and so was not burnt down in the fire, but nobody ever goes there."

Tilda gasped roughly. "They say that place is haunted by the spirits of those who died in the fire!" she whispered, pulling at Vivianne's sleeve. "We would be best to seek shelter at my father's hut, back there."

"No. I am not afraid of spirits. But if you are – Tilda, Eleanor – please go back."

"I am coming with you," murmured Eleanor, although her voice shook.

"Then, my lady, so will I." Tilda hung her head.

Somehow Roland, supported in his barely-conscious state by Eleanor and Tilda on either side and Vivianne in front guiding them half-blindly, stumbled over the rubble that was still, even after all these years, left from the fire. She felt that she could smell the smoke again, and hear the timbers cracking, splitting, falling, feel the hot raging flames that filled her heart. She stumbled, peering into the darkness, desperately trying to feel the confidence that she must show to the others, desperately trying to remember the way.

"This way, my child." A whispering in her ears, her mother's voice, a hand firmly on her arm, guiding her. Her mother's spirit, with her still.

Vivianne trembled as she heard the sounds of night creatures. They were amongst the trees and undergrowth, up in the branches above their heads and following behind them. Flutterings, scamperings and moans. She kept glancing back to check that Tilda, Eleanor and Roland were all still on her heals, reaching out her hand to them. And yet she knew that something, someone was helping her to avoid the potholes, the hummocks, the great reaching roots, and was leading them towards the barrow and the cave's entrance. She was shaking badly by the time she felt for the heavy wooden door and pushed it open.

The cave within was cold and Vivianne shivered as she ushered the others inside. She helped Tilda and Eleanor to lower Roland onto the stone bench and scrabbled to find the flints to light the sconces. She felt Tilda beside her and soon they had enough flickering light to reveal the earthenware pots and amphorae grouped around the walls. She stepped back to the door and closed it behind them. She did not want anyone to detect the light.

"Do you remember this place?" asked Eleanor quietly.

"In a way I do. Although not what it was or what my mother did here. And I have never been here again since she died. I have a faint memory of being brought here when I was bitten by wolves when I was little. My mother used a poultice of evil smelling liquid which she ladled out from one of these jars ..." Her voice trailed off as she searched around for the amphora she could barely remember.

Roland groaned and Vivianne whipped round to see his body fall forwards. She caught him as he dropped, and lowered him more gently to the ground. She tore off her cloak and wrapped it around him. His eyes were blank but her fingers found his chest and, taking a deep breath, she slipped them beneath his clothes. She felt his chest and she knew that he still breathed. For a moment heat suffused her body and she kept her fingers on his naked chest, hoping that her heat would transfer itself to him too. Did she feel a slight stirring – or was that her imagination? Vivianne rose awkwardly to her feet as Eleanor pulled off her own cloak and folded it to cushion his head from the cold earth.

Vivianne looked wildly round. She knew that there was not much time. Tilda moved and in the waft of her robe, the guttering light of the torches flickered sideways and Vivianne saw the markings on the earthen pots. Tiny stylised images of people in various postures. She peered more closely and could make out that parts of their anatomy were enlarged to draw the eye: the stomach, the chest, the throat, even their private, secret places. One was carved with a name but it was indistinct. She felt with her fingers and traced the outline of the word 'Maloran'. Beneath the name was a drawing scratched in the pot. A figure with wounds and gashes on his torso. A leg outstretched awkwardly, clearly broken. And below the figure were runes. Like the one lying at the heart of the cross which marked the burial place of the Vortigern chest.

"Maloran," she whispered. It was the name her mother had spoken in connection with her magic. Was this some kind of a magic potion? Was it one her mother had used? Somehow she felt sure that it was.

Her fingers found another word beneath. Belladonna.

A soft sound beside her made her look round. A glimpse of gold fabric, a stirring of the air. A hand pointing to the jar. A whispered "yes" fluttered in her ear, the warmth of a kiss on her cheek.

Vivianne struggled with the stopper on the neck of the amphora and as she managed to release it, she was regaled with a pungent smell from within. Roland groaned again and she saw, even in the flames, that his face was deathly pale. She would have to risk it. Even as she found the cloths wound round the handles she heard her mother's voice urging her on.

"Vivianne," the air seemed to whisper around her as the flares guttered again. "Do as I would have done. Bathe the wounds with this infusion. Do it."

"Be careful," murmured Eleanor, a hand on her arm.

Vivianne dipped the cloth into the jar and wrung it out in the liquid. Then she quickly applied it to the worst of Roland's wounds. As she did, she felt Eleanor hesitate, then mirror her actions beside her. As they worked, Tilda wringing out fresh cloths and Vivianne and Eleanor bathing the damaged flesh, the pungent smell became light and sweet. Vivianne thought she could smell salt and then lavender … maybe camomile, eucalyptus … Her head felt light and dizzy and she felt something drop from the folds of her robe … She scrabbled around for it on the ground beside her, but she did not know what she was seeking … A bright light at the right side of her forehead heralded a sharp pain that made her wince and blacked out her vision with jagged lines and flashes across her eyes …

Chapter 13

"You OK?" Viv felt Ellie kneel down beside her, wrapping her arm around her back and giving her a hug. Viv realised that her fingers were scrabbling in the dirt, as if she were trying to dig something up. Tilly dropped to the ground too and touched Viv's hand gently, stilling her.

Viv looked up at her friends. "Yes, I … I'm fine … I think." Her right hand fluttered to her temple. The echo of an excruciating pain lingered there.

"You just moved forwards and then fell on your knees. We didn't know if you had collapsed or something?" Rory was standing over her. "Did you faint?"

Viv shook her head, partly to clear away the visions. "No. I must have time-slipped again."

"Oh god! And was I there too?" whispered Tilly, clutching Viv's hand more firmly. Viv nodded.

"Really? But you only just fell down this minute," said Ellie.

"It seems to happen like that for you, Viv. For me it's like a dream, in bed, at night." Rory bent down and took Viv's arm to help her upright again. "Time stands still. In this world, anyway. But it seems that in the other world time can move on. That's not inconsistent with quantum mechanics theory."

"I don't understand. The trigger the first couple of times was falling in to the water, the lake then the canal. But a couple of times … and now …?" Viv shook her head.

"It's as though the portal is becoming more accessible, elsewhere." Rory narrowed his eyes, but Viv felt him hold on firmly to her arm. "Is there anything that's still the same in terms of the portal?"

"Water. There's something about water. Even just drops on my face. But not always even that. Like now."

"Right. I'm just wondering how that can work. Maybe now that Lady Vivianne has … well, let's say, entered you …she's able to draw you through the portal herself."

"It does feel as if I have a part of Lady Vivianne inside me. Oh, god, that sounds like being possessed but it's not like she's evil or anything …"

"It doesn't have to be about evil. It could just as well be that you're a vessel for achieving something good."

"OK, I could take achieving something good!" Viv said shakily. "And, by the way, this time Sir Roland wasn't there." Viv looked up at Rory's frowning eyes, remembering Roland's blank ones. "Well, not really. He was pretty much unconscious."

"Hmmm. I see." Rory looked worried.

Viv took a deep breath. "It's getting rather frightening, if I can just drift off into another world, instantaneously. The sooner we resolve all this, do whatever it is Lady Vivianne and Sir Roland want, the better. 'Cos I have a feeling that it won't end until we do."

"I have a feeling you're right," said Rory grimly.

"Oooh," groaned Viv as a sharp pain stabbed her brow. She rubbed the side of her forehead.

"You're not OK, are you?" asked Tilly, peering into Viv's eyes with a frown.

"I just had a sudden frightful billowing headache, and visual disturbances, zig zags, flashes …it's gone now but it still echoes a bit …"

"Oh, Viv, I've had that," said Ellie, "when I was pregnant. Hormonal, the doctor said."

"Migraine," murmured Rory. But his voice sounded strangled and Viv peered at him. He shook his head as if clearing something from his mind.

"Yes, it *was* a migraine," nodded Ellie, "but he said it can come on suddenly, even if you've never had one before, if you're under stress."

"Well, I guess I'm certainly that! I *have* had migraines before."

"I still get a migraine from time to time. If the light's flickering. Or if there's a strong smell."

Viv remembered the pungent smell of the infusions in the cave, the guttering of the bright flames in the darkness.

Reality and dreamlike fantasy were swirling in her mind. She must try to remember what she was doing immediately before she came back to the present. She remembered the cave, the amphora. Bathing Sir Roland's wounds.

She felt Rory's arm around her shoulders and trembled under his gentle touch. "I hate to say this," he began, "but you look dreadful. I think we need to get you home and to bed."

"Wait. Let me just try again."

"Oh, Viv, I don't think you should," whispered Ellie, putting her hand on Viv's arm. "Be careful."

The words were the same, the voice was the same.

Viv dropped down to the ground on her knees. In the gathering dusk, she felt around in front of her. And as she scrabbled around in the dirt and the dust she thought she heard her mother's voice. "*Darling Vivvie, the key is here, in a safe place at the dig …*" But it wasn't. It was in Viv's cross-body bag. She'd brought it back to the present when Sir Roland had given it to Lady Vivianne.

She felt a hand on hers. She felt the touch physically but she knew that neither Ellie, Tilly nor Rory had reached out to her. They were all standing over her and there was no hand on hers. Yet something, someone, guided her fingers to her bag. Someone whose touch she knew. Her mother? Lady Vivianne? Or were they the same? She pulled the key out and held it in her hand, reaching it out over the bare earth like an offering as the guiding touch commanded. Viv was shaking as she took a deep breath.

"Here it is … Mother …Lady Vivianne …," she whispered, "Take it … help me, I don't know what to do …tell me what I have to do!"

She turned to look up at Rory. "What am I supposed to do?" she pleaded.

Rory dropped down beside her and without a word began to run his hands over the patch of dried barren earth, echoing her own movements. Viv could feel Tilly and Ellie's presence crouching at their side, and could tell they were holding their breath. Tilly's fingers began scrabbling further to the left.

Viv touched a hollow and traced it up and to both sides. It felt like the shape of a cross, a crucifix. She breathed in sharply and her wrecked fingernails dug deeper. They found something hard. She still had the key in her right hand and she clutched it to her breast.

"Here. Let me," Rory whispered. He tore at the ground, then with a sigh he picked something up and held out his palm to her. A piece of pottery.

Viv's hand was trembling as her fingers reached out and took the jagged piece by its broken corner from Rory's palm. She peered at it in the gathering dusk while Tilly and Ellie leaned over to get a better look.

"There are markings. They're a bit odd," Tilly said, furrowing her brow.

"I have a feeling I've seen something like that before," whispered Ellie. "A kind of déjà vu."

"Runes," said Viv and turned her face to Rory's. She held out the shard of pottery for him to take, and he knelt very still beside her. Viv looked up and saw in the darkening light the distant shape of the barrow. Just as Ellie had said, a shimmering feeling of déjà vu slipped around her. She shuddered. The light summer breeze seemed to be gathering strength again. Just as it did before she slipped into Lady Vivianne's life the last time. She heard the rustle of the leaves in the trees around them. Her head pounded and flashes of lights seared her eyes. She felt Rory's hands on her shoulders. He said something but his voice seemed to be far away, echoing in the distance, swirling around her mind.

Viv sensed the movement of the trees and undergrowth around her and behind her, as if some ghostly force was breathing down her neck. It felt like a gathering of power. She thought she could hear murmuring in the dusk, the swish of long robes through the grass. Was that a russet coloured cloak that caught the corner of her vision again?

A cross scraped in the earth. A piece of pottery with runes carved into it. Viv shuddered with the feeling of another world she had seen before trembled through her body. Lady Vivianne, a pottery jar, her fingertips tracing the runes, ghostly whisperings, the cave. The magic. Maloran.

"The cross," began Viv, swallowing hard. "The cross and the pottery marked the spot where the chest was buried in Lady Vivianne's time."

"So, the chest is here?" Ellie's voice was urgent.

"Oh, wow," breathed Tilly.

"No. The chest is in a bank vault, hidden safely by my parents when they flew to New York."

"OK. Maybe the cross marks the original hiding place," nodded Rory, "And where Lady Vivianne and Sir Roland found it, and were interrupted by Sir Pelleas."

"So, is this where your parents found it?" asked Ellie.

Viv frowned. "It doesn't make sense. Sir Pelleas surely must have removed the chest from here when he caught Vivianne and Roland. So where did my parents find it – but more importantly why was I led here, to this cross?"

"There's a link to the cave and magic, maybe?" pondered Rory.

"Because this is where Lady Vivianne's parents hid it in the first place?" asked Ellie.

"Yes, yes," gasped Tilly.

Viv felt a sweep of chill and through the trees the sounds of footfalls and whisperings. "Oh, my goodness. It's the portal, I mean *The Portal*, not just a trigger, like the water, the reflection of the portal, but the tear in time itself."

"The tear in the fabric of the universe where the worlds can touch. So, it's the main portal, the worm-hole." Rory drew in his breath.

"We've found it. The way in."

"Oh. My. God." Tilly whispered, covering her mouth with her hand. And Viv could see that she was trembling.

Viv turned to Rory and saw him bend his head. His eyes were closed as he whispered, "Our Father, who art in heaven ...," his voice becoming quieter and quieter until it was little more than a mouthing. He reached out to Viv at his side and placed his hand over hers. It felt like a priest's blessing at the altar rail. She felt Ellie's arm reaching around her, squeezing her shoulder, and she could hear Tilly's voice faintly echoing Rory's prayer.

The world around her was retreating, fading into a dream. Her vision was again filled with jagged lightning flashes and the pain at the side of her brow stabbed into her brain. Viv was only aware of the key pressing into her flesh through her clothes. Her hand trembled and lost purchase on the metal. She heard it fall onto the hard earth in front of her. And then she was falling, falling into the hollow of the cross and into the hollows in the earth ...

*

Lady Vivianne saw the glint of metal in the flickering light of the sconce flames. She reached out for it and rose to standing.

"What is that in your hand?" asked Tilda, peering round her.

"It appears to be the key which I thought I had lost. How strange." Vivianne thrust it safely into her pouch, as Sir Roland groaned. The smell of the infusions filled her, eucalyptus and lavender and something else that was pungent and seared her senses. She returned her attention to Roland, stretched out on the hard earth floor of the cave.

As she knelt beside him she could see that he had opened his eyes and that they were no longer seared with pain. He was muttering under his breath. She bent over him so close that she could feel his breath on her cheek. "Father … heaven … hallowed … kingdom .."

Vivianne looked up at Eleanor and Tilda. "We have not lost him. He speaks."

She touched his hand. It was warming. Emboldened, she touched his face. Heat was returning, and life was infusing his body again. She hardly realised that she let out a long sigh of relief and closed her eyes. In her mind she recited the prayer with him.

It was when Roland laid his hand upon hers that she opened her eyes and looked into his. "I thought I had … we thought we had lost you, Sir Roland."

He patted her hand and spoke in a halting and rasping whisper. "I am not so easy to be rid of, my lady. You will have to do better than that." His mouth twisted into a painful smile.

"I will find you some wine, sir." Tilda turned briskly and began to inspect the amphorae.

Vivianne rose to her feet, reluctantly moving her hand from Roland's. "This one here, I believe." She lifted the heavy stopper from the top of a large amphora in the corner, and smelt the perfume of rich red wine. It was still there, the one she had seen her mother use so long ago. How could she have remembered that? And yet in her mind she saw clearly her mother ladling out the wine into a gilded chalice. Her glance moved upwards and there was the holder and in it the chalice, shining in the flickering light of the sconces. She felt around the inside rim of the amphora and found the ladle, its handle curved around the stone. She ladled wine into the chalice and took a cautious sip. It tasted perfect even after all these years.

She handed the chalice to Eleanor. "Take care. I have filled it with wine to the brim. He has need of plenty to soothe his pain and revive him further." She turned her back and studied the writing on the jar to give herself time to calm her breathing down to normal and to blink the tears from her eyes. She was so relieved that he was not going to die. He was like a brother to her and had been so since her parents had died. Yes, that was what it was...

Hearing Roland's voice, Vivianne turned back to him. He was struggling to sit up as Eleanor cushioned his head and held the chalice to his lips.

"Ladies, I cannot thank you enough for what you have done for me today," he said and his voice was stronger. "I embarrass myself, a warrior lain prostrate upon the floor for you to tend."

"We tend your wounds, Sir Roland," said Eleanor. "As we would for any warrior hurt on our behalf. Or indeed in battle against a common enemy." She looked up at Vivianne, who nodded slowly. She knew who she meant and the image of the enraged Sir Pelleas and a self-satisfied Guin filled her mind. She saw, as vividly as if it were happening again, now, Pelleas hissing in the darkness, "Never underestimate me!"

"We cannot tend your courage or your heart," Vivianne added, looking down at Roland sitting up proudly, if a little awkwardly, one knee raised as he sipped the wine. "For they are as strong as the oxen that strain at our ploughs in the fields. But we can, and always will, tend your flesh wounds as long as you need that nursing. It is all we can do, and we do it gladly, for one of us."

Sir Roland took the chalice from Eleanor's hand and he did not tremble as he raised it to the ladies. "Your tending has saved my life, I think."

Vivianne smiled and then began to bustle around, tidying up. "We must get you to safety. And we must also find where Pelleas and his men have taken the Vortigern chest."

Tilda giggled as she replaced the stoppers on the amphorae. "I know exactly where the chest is, my lady!"

"Tilda?" Vivianne and Eleanor both turned a puzzled frown towards the little maid.

"What do you know?" asked Roland.

"My lord, my ladies. I watched as Sir Pelleas's men took you both away. They did not see me in the dark. I made sure of that. I hid." Mathilda straightened her back and folded her hands in front of her in the pose of a story-teller. "Then, when I had followed to see where they took you both, I returned with all speed to my father's hut and woke him. Urgently, I told him what had happened and he was only too willing to help me to move the chest before Sir Pelleas's men came back for it."

She bent her head and peered up at them through her lashes. "My father does not think well of Sir Pelleas, not since that time he took all our sheep for his tithe."

"So what did you do with the chest?" Vivianne's heart was thrumming against her ribs. Please god that it was safe.

"We carried it back to our hut and ..." she giggled again, "we wrapped it around with cloth and hid it under the midden. Nobody will look there!"

Vivianne could not prevent the laugh that escaped from her mouth. The midden! No, certainly nobody would look anywhere near the stinking enclosure where the villagers relieved themselves each morning and night.

"Oh, Tilda, you are very inventive!"

Tilda looked puzzled. "Is that a good thing to be, my lady?"

"Yes, my dear Tilda. It certainly is."

Eleanor moved to the door of the cave and opened it to let a sliver of dull light through. "It is near dawn. We must move to where it is safe."

Vivianne paused for only a second before she said firmly. "Tilda, could Sir Roland lodge with your father whilst we think of what to do next?"

Tilda nodded quickly. "He would be honoured, my lady."

"And I have more work to do for the settlement. I will return to my sleeping chamber and try to slip inside again, before the time for breaking fast, so that the guards will not know that I was able to escape. Eleanor, you must return to your own hall and your husband."

"He is aware of my activities tonight," Eleanor smiled. "We thought it best for him to stay in our hall in case anyone came. But I doubt that anyone would have been looking for me in the night."

Roland pushed himself up to his feet and stretched his legs, grimacing. "My lady Vivianne, I do not know what balms you used on me but I think you have your mother's gift of charms." He gathered up the cloaks where they had fallen to the ground, and handed them back to Vivianne and Eleanor with a nod of gratitude.

He moved a little stiffly at first but then Roland's limbs seemed to loosen up and he made for the door. "Come, Tilda, take me to your father's house and after a short while, Vivianne, you make it back to your sleeping hall." He glanced at her, frowning. "Eleanor, it would be best if you could follow her to ensure that she has slipped back into her chamber safely, before you return to your husband. We need to buy some time to retrieve the chest."

Vivianne caught his eye and shook her head at him as she wrapped her cloak around her body. Roland inclined his head. "Yes, my lady, I know that sounded as if I was taking command. But let us argue about that later. Let us all be safe for now." He grinned.

"How well you know me. You are indeed my brother!"

Roland looked at Vivianne strangely for a moment, and then turned to Tilda. "Let us go before the village awakes to the light."

"Do you need to lean on me, Sir Roland?"

"No, but thank you, little Tilda. If I could honour you, I would!"

They squeezed round the door so that they did not need to open it too wide. Vivianne and Eleanor snuffed out the flames in the sconces and checked that there was no trace that they had been in the cave, just in case anyone might find it and guess what had happened that night. Unlikely as that might be, Vivianne still clutched her suspicions of Sir Pelleas in her heart.

As they slipped through the village towards her hall, Vivianne started at every sound. The breeze rustled the leaves high in the treetops, the small dark night-creatures moved through the undergrowth, and the wings of bats and night birds sounded stealthily around their heads.

The muffled noise of a cow-milker across the village trudging off early to the fields made Vivianne stop and thrust out her arm to Eleanor. They held their breath until his footsteps ceased in the distance, before they resumed their cautious steps.

As they neared her sleeping chamber, Vivianne could see the guards at their positions before her door. She signalled to Eleanor to wait in the shadows of the hall as she slipped nearer to the door. Eleanor bent and picked up a handful of stones from the rough path. Aiming round the corner from the guards' position at the door, she threw them with as much force as she could muster. The guards shouted an alarm and rushed round the corner of the hall while Vivianne slipped inside. She ran to the back of the chamber and listened, ear pressed to the rear wall to hear Eleanor's robe rustle as she ran quietly back to her own hall and the safety of her husband.

Hurriedly Vivianne pulled off her cloak, robe and under-dress. She tugged at her hair to appear dishevelled with sleep and lifted her night shift over her head. In her bed snuggling under the covers, she felt her heart thumping in her chest and struggled to calm her breath.

She heard the guards return to their station outside her door, grumbling at each other for their disturbance, blaming one another for the alarm. Their words were slurred and Vivianne knew that they had been drinking their daily allowance of mead for their special duties. She was safe and as she, exhausted, drifted off to sleep she hoped that the others were safe too.

It seemed only a short while later however, that rough shouts and the noise of the door being shoved open abruptly woke her. Sir Pelleas stormed in to her chamber. She pushed herself up in her bed and pulled the covers over her and up to her chin.

"What in heaven's name are you …?"

"Lady! Where is it?"

"Where is what?" She tried to make her voice sound even and puzzled. She knew exactly what he meant.

"You know what," he shouted, roughly pulling the covers from her body. She clutched at her thin night shift. "The chest! My men failed to return for it after imprisoning you and that treacherous *Sir Roland*." He spat out the name and a glob of his saliva landed upon her cheek. She felt it slither downwards towards her mouth. "And when they finally went for it, it was gone. So, where is it?"

Vivianne tossed her head as she wiped the spittle from her face. She raised her chin. "And why do you possibly imagine that I know where it is now? If your men appear to be unable to manage a simple task you give them, perhaps you should seek their help. Maybe in truth they have stolen it between them. Do you really trust those ruffians?"

She was aware of the slight hesitation before he snorted his derision at her. "And I, as you see," she said sweetly, touching her ruffled hair, "have been here in my bed all the time." Under the covers, she crossed her fingers against the lie.

"And Sir Roland has also disappeared."

"Disappeared?"

"From where we …" Pelleas hesitated. "Make no mind. Has he taken the chest with him? Is he in hiding somewhere?" He glanced around the chamber. "Have you hidden him?"

"How could I have done that, my lord? Here I am in my bed with your trusty guards at my door?"

Sir Pelleas glared at her. "I only have to marry you to claim my rightful place as your father's successor. Damn it that I cannot do it until the moon is right. But once that is done, you will be completely under my rule and your father's followers will be unable to counter me." He touched the pouch which she had dropped carelessly on the end of the bed when she undressed, and she held her breath. "And I have a much better - and more willing - bed mate for my pleasure than you, Lady. I will tear this village apart to find the chest. And to find Sir Roland. " He pointed a finger at her. "Mark me, I will."

As he slammed the door closed behind him, she let out her breath. She heard him shout at his guards, "I want every nook, every cranny, every hut, every field, dug up. They have buried the chest somewhere in the village I don't doubt. And I want Sir Roland found and brought in ropes to the mead hall for judgement." He stamped away, shouting, "Come! There is no point in guarding her. I need all the muscle I can muster."

Lady Vivianne climbed out of her bed and lifted the wooden shutter from her window. It was light with a pink and orange dawn creeping over the sky. She shivered. It was still cold as the sun slowly began to rise over the village.

A whisper. "My lady!"

Tilda was crouching under the window opening. "May I come in to light your fire and help you dress and break your fast?" She held up a jar of wine and a willow basket. "I was not certain if …?"

"Yes, of course, come. You are my maid of the chamber now."

Despite her anxiety, Vivianne smiled as she heard Tilda skip round to the door.

"Get back into the bed, my lady, while I light the fire." Tilda glanced around and found the heavy fur-trimmed cloak which she wrapped around Vivianne's shoulders. She fussed over her like a mother hen, tucking the covers over her for warmth. Vivianne half-laughed, for Tilda was but a child, and so determined to be a good maid of the chamber.

Tilda laid the fire with the tinder and logs from the basket in the hearth and worked the stone and flint to raise a spark. It was not long before the fire was blazing well. "I do this for my father all the time," she said although her back was turned to Vivianne and her lady had not asked her. Vivianne wondered if her maid could read her mind.

"Come by the fire, my lady, and eat before I dress you. There is fresh baked bread from the bakery, honey and some cold chicken from the kitchens. I am sorry that it is only chicken and not anything more … more rich, but …"

Vivianne smiled. "Chicken is lovely. Most of the village do not break their fast on venison, goose or swan. I am no different."

"But you are the Lady, daughter of our late chieftain and betrothed to the next." She frowned. "Whatever he is like. So I know I should provide the best for you, my lady."

"You have, Tilda."

"Oh," Tilda scrabbled in her basket, "and I forgot, a handful or two of blackberries."

Vivianne sat on the stool by the fire and Tilda poured wine into a wooden goblet, handing it carefully to her.

"I will find the right things for you for tomorrow, my lady," Tilda insisted. "We had an odd night and early morning."

Vivianne sipped her wine. "How is Sir Roland?" She felt compelled to whisper, in case any guards still lurked outside.

"He is well, my lady. But he talked with my father late and even in the early light I heard them whispering together. It sounded as though they were plotting something."

Tilda shook out Vivianne's kirtle, over-mantle and cloak and laid them on the bed. "But, my lady, there is talk of Sir Pelleas digging up the whole village for the missing chest." She inclined her head to Vivianne and made a knowing expression.

"Yes, I know." Vivianne nodded. "If he carries out his threat we are all in trouble. Are you sure that the chest and Sir Roland are well hidden?"

"The chest is where I told you, and Sir Roland will be hidden if they come looking. We have places to hide things, my lady. My father …"

"Ah, I see. Your father's poachings?"

Tilda nodded hesitantly, and Vivianne smiled. "Good."

But just as Vivianne finished her meal and Tilda had dressed her, there was a loud urgent knocking on the door as if guards were trying to break it down.

"Go to the door, Tilda, before they have it in pieces."

Three guards pushed their way past Tilda into the chamber. They were tall, burly men dressed as if for battle in metal chest armour and they carried long spears and axes like the ones Vivianne knew the Saxons used. Their threatening presence dominated the chamber.

"We are to search your quarters, Lady Vivianne."

"Why? What on earth do you imagine I have here? She fingered her secret pouch that hung at her waist belt.

"Orders from Sir Pelleas. We are to search the whole village and turn it into wasteland unless we find the Vortigern chest and Sir Roland."

Vivianne laughed. "Well, that would be somewhat pointless. If you destroyed the village, I mean."

The biggest guard glared at her and signalled to the others to begin turning the chamber upside down. Tilda cowered against the wall until Vivianne gestured to her to stand beside her proudly at the fire. They watched as the bedcovers were thrown to the floor amidst the rushes, and the ground stamped to detect any sign of a hiding hole. They looked up at the rafters and the thatch and murmured to each other. Finally they made impatient noises and left, slamming the door behind them.

"I am so sorry, my lady," said Tilda as she quickly tidied up. "You should not have had to suffer that rudeness and coarse behaviour."

"My dear Tilda, I am quite sure that all the villagers will have the same treatment. Why should I be any different, especially as ...?" Especially as it was all her fault.

Biting her lip, Vivianne opened the door and stepped outside into the early morning freshness. The air was light and sweet but her heart was heavy. She watched as the guards made their way in the direction of the hut where Tilda's father lived.

Then she heard the urgent cries of the guards. "Here! Quickly! We've found something!"

And her heart stopped.

Chapter 14

Viv felt as though her heart stopped. She took a deep breath and looked round for Rory. He was sitting a little apart from them, head in hands, fingering the gold cross around his neck. He roused himself and moved across to Viv, helping her to her feet.

She all but fell against him. "My god."

"What happened?" Tilly tugged at Viv's arm like an impatient child.

"Tell us!" breathed Ellie.

Rory patted Viv's back absently, speaking over her head to Ellie. "Sir Roland is recovered and Eleanor and Lady Vivianne are safe, but Pelleas has sent his guards to search the whole village to find Roland and the chest."

"So you were in this one too?" Tilly stared at Rory.

"Yes," began Rory, and Viv could hear the slight shakiness in his voice, "but I am ... Roland was ... hiding at Tilda's father's house."

"I don't understand. Why aren't I there too? Or Ellie? If we seem to be reflected in Eleanor and Mathilda in this time-slip thingy? It doesn't make sense!" squeaked Tilly.

"Because," began Rory, frowning as if in pain, "as I indicated before, you and Ellie aren't in the 'zone' if you like, you aren't for some reason susceptible to the time portal. The right ... I don't know ... the right ingredients aren't there." Rory raked his hand through his hair. He took a deep breath. "But the chest is hidden there, in Tilda's father's house, too. In the midden."

"What's a midden?" Ellie frowned.

"It's basically the loo," explained Viv, twisting away from Rory's chest. "It's the enclosure where a household would ... well, store their ... er, human waste, and kitchen waste too usually, before it was taken to their vegetable patch for manure, fertiliser for their crops."

Ellie wrinkled up her nose. "So how could they have hidden the chest in the loo .. er, midden?"

"Maybe they dug a pit behind the actual ..." Viv waved her hand, "manure, but within the midden enclosure. I doubt anyone would go digging around there. The middens used to stink."

"Methane gas," said Rory. "CH_4. I would think it'd be a last resort to search there. But anyway we do know that the chest was found by your parents somewhere at the site, Viv."

"Yes, but I just wonder whether Lady Vivianne ever got it back or whether it fell into Pelleas's hands." She held out her own hands and opened them. "And where is the key? Did I drop it?" She dropped to her knees again and scrabbled in the earth. "No, wait. I remember. I pressed it into the ground in the middle of the cross." She peered at the dints in the earth and although the sky was darkening now, she could make out the shape of the key. The outline but no key. "It's gone. I think ...the portal has received it. I guess it's in Lady Vivianne's pouch at her waist."

"It's passed from one time dimension to another," muttered Rory.

Viv felt shaky. Rory placed his arm lightly around her back and guided her around away from the site. He glanced at Ellie and Tilly over Viv's shoulder. "I think we need to go home and have a drink." Viv could hear a slight tremble in his voice.

In silence they trudged back to the car. Viv glanced at her friends and thought that she had never seen either of them look so shaken. Even Tilly walked slowly, almost slumped.

"Sit in the front," said Ellie and thrust Viv into the car. "I need to get home to my hubby and kids, gather my wits and touch reality again. What with all this ... universe portal stuff. Can you drop me off, please, Rory?"

They said little as they drove back through the darkening village, each immersed in their own thoughts. After he dropped Ellie off at her house, Rory turned to Viv and said kindly, "Would you like to come back to the rectory for a cup of tea, or a brandy, or something? I don't think you should be on your own for a while."

"I can stay with her," offered Tilly quietly, but Rory stilled her with a look. "Mmm. But on the other hand ... just drop me off, Rory."

Rory glanced at Viv, eyebrows raised. Viv felt the need to be with him, just the two of them, for a while. She didn't want to let go of the experience yet. Although she had no idea whether Mrs N would be at the rectory.

"Yes, thank you, Rory. That's kind of you. But just a quick drink. I still have some prep to do for tomorrow's tutorials."

*

Viv sat on the battered sofa in the rectory sitting room. Rory told her with a smile that the bishop rather grandly called it the 'drawing room'. He sounded back to his normal confident self. Viv felt more herself, again part of the real world, in this calm soothing place.

"It's a lovely room, with the big fireplace and the panelled walls. I like the portrait paintings of the previous rectors too."

"All a bit too grand for us, really. It's early Georgian apparently, so an interesting history. Some might think it's spooky, but I like it."

"I like it too. I don't think it's spooky. There's a peaceful, gracious feeling about it. As if it's blessed. Which I guess it is, as it's a rectory." Viv looked around the room, with its old leather sofas, dinted by so many rears, its large French windows framed by long velvet curtains and opening out onto a stone terrace and a dark sweep of lawn. She saw the framed photographs on the bureau and wondered if she could have a closer look, or whether that would be rude. "Actually, I think it's gorgeous."

"Thank you. And your place is great too. The coach house. I bet there are stories to tell there. But let me go and get us drinks. Tea or brandy or wine – or what?"

"Oh, d'you know, I think I'll have a cup of tea, strong and sweet, if you don't mind. Can I help?"

"Coming up. No, you sit there and ground yourself again after all that at the site."

The rectory was quiet apart from Rory, who she could hear moving around in the kitchen down the hall, clattering cups and filling the kettle. Other than that, all she could hear was the ticking of the grandfather clock by the front door and the sound of the occasional traffic outside.

Viv pushed herself up from the sofa and sneaked to the bureau to look more closely at the photographs. She felt quite weird. They all showed Rory with a beautiful woman. She looked lovely even in jeans and her hair was short, blonde and gamine. In most of the pictures, they were holding hands or his arm was draped around her. Clearly this was Mrs N, his wife. Viv breathed in sharply. So much love. You could see it in their eyes as they looked at each other. Lucky lady, sighed Viv. Then she picked up one that was slightly behind the others. It showed Mrs N in a loose smock dress, clearly pregnant. Viv bit her lip. Pregnant? So where was the child? Rory had mentioned his wife but not his child …

The door opened and she swung round. Rory carefully placed the tea tray on a side table and with a frown took the photo from Viv's hand and replaced it on the bureau.

"Sorry."

"It's fine," he said, after a moment. "Don't worry about it. People are always curious about their rectors or vicars. I guess we're an odd breed. So. Now let's have some tea. I've found some biscuits. Not as good as your flapjacks, I'm afraid."

Viv sat down again, feeling awkward, despite Rory's words. "So, where is Mrs N tonight?"

Rory looked up from pouring the tea into the mugs. "Mrs N?"

"Yes."

"Oh, er … sorry. Yes, she's at one of her meetings. Always one committee or another."

Viv wondered about the child, but suppressed her curiosity; she didn't want to be intrusive. And of course, for all she knew the baby might not have made it. Or might have died of some awful childhood disease. She had no desire to open up old wounds.

"You know," Rory said abruptly, "I think we should track down the chest in your parents' bank vault – well, if it's still there. How long ago was it, if you don't mind my asking?"

"About twenty years now. I think I need to go through my parent's things properly too. It's time."

Rory reached over and touched her hand, saying gently, "Do you want me with you when you do? Sometimes it's easier when someone else is there too."

Viv looked at his deep dark smoky eyes and thought she could lose herself there. They were so full of concern and love … well, maybe not love in a relationship sense; after all, he had a wife, but maybe in a really caring brotherly way. Rectors were supposed to love their flock, weren't they? Goodness, her hands were shaking and her heart quivering. He was sitting so close to her. She could feel his heat. He smelled of … what? That same woody bergamot fragrance that reminded her of Sir Roland. It was so heady and almost made her feel dizzy.

He smiled. Such a gorgeous smile. Full lips. Heavens, what was happening to her here? Yes, she would answer yes and then he would need to come over to her flat to search through her parent's box, and he would come with her to the bank where the chest was supposed to be …What was she thinking? He was married. A wife and child. Well, possibly a child. She must not be attracted to him. He did not mean it in that way. She must take his friendship and care for what it was. The care of a vicar for a parishioner.

"Yes, I'd like that. Thank you." She nearly forced herself to add "Reverend" but couldn't quite get the word out of her mouth. It somehow didn't gel any more.

"Good. Then let me know when you feel strong enough to do that and I'll try to fit it in."

"Tomorrow." The word was out there before she could help herself. "What about tomorrow afternoon? I don't have a full diary after two o' clock. Does that suit you at all?"

Rory's expression was one of surprise. "Well, that's fine with me too."

"I think maybe I'd better get off home. I've some work to do for the morning. Thank you for the tea and biscuits."

"OK. Let me drive you back."

As he pulled his Jaguar into the parking area at the back of Viv's coach house building, and reached over to open the door for her, his face was close to hers and she flushed. She said a flustered "thanks" to cover it up, and before she turned away to get out of the car, she noticed that he raked his hand through his dark curly hair, and her heart fluttered.

She waved as she walked towards the corner of the building. She watched as he swung the car round and drove fast out to the lane. The security light flicked on as she crossed the cobbled courtyard to the front door.

"Wow!" Tilly's head popped out of the front doorway. "He is sooo gorgeous."

"Are you stalking me?" smiled Viv, pulling herself out of her dream world. Tilly stood aside to let Viv through into the hallway. Viv scrabbled in her bag for the keys to her own front door. "And how could you see? It's dark round the back."

"I'm not stalking you. Just waiting up for you to come home safely after all that stuff this evening. I was worried. And, anyway, I saw the security light in the car park come on through my bedroom window at the back, where I happened to be … er … tidying my bed, and I looked out. Of course. That's all, Viv." She grinned. "I saw your guy Rory open the car door for you – the interior light came on. All evening I've been thinking – wooh, he's sooo H.O.T!"

"And married," said Viv, pushing her key into the door.

"Married? Well, he didn't look too married as he leaned over you. Gosh, I thought I was going to see some action there!"

Viv turned and hid her face as she opened the door and stepped into her own hallway. "Oh, Tilly, you have such a wild imagination." She twisted back. "He's married with a child. I saw the photos in his sitting room."

Tilly's face fell. "Really? Oh no. I'm so sorry, Viv. What a pity. I thought we'd got you fixed up after all that stuff with Pete, and the portal mystery."

"I know you mean well, Tilly, but really, it's too soon. I'm off men for the present. I really can't risk it again. Reverend Rory is just a friend who's helping me out at the moment. More like a brother." Viv caught Tilly's smirk. "I'm sorry, Tilly, but I must get myself some supper. I'm starving and it's late, and I've got work to do."

*

Viv balanced the salad bowl on her knee as she jotted notes for her tutorials the next day. She wriggled to a more comfortable position on the sofa, cosy in her PJs. The music from her iPod gently wafted through her mind but the aria from La Boheme was abruptly interrupted by the shrill sound of her doorbell. God, what time was it? Too late for any caller. Unless there was some kind of emergency.

She pushed herself up from the sofa, trying to calm her breathing. Her hand slipped on the door handle and she wiped it down her pyjama bottoms. As she opened it cautiously she realised who it was standing there in the dim light. Her first impulse was to slam the door shut again in his face, but she thought that he would only keep ringing. Her hand flew up to her cheek, touching the memory of his blow.

"Hi, Viv," said Pete in a low voice. "Can I come in?"

"Pete, it's late and I have no intention of letting you in after last time." She took a deep breath. "I don't know how you have the nerve to come here again."

"Oh, Viv, I'm sorry … so sorry for what I did." Viv began to close the door, but he thrust out his foot and hand to stop its motion. "Please, Viv. I must have been mad – some kind of temporary insanity. I have no idea why I did it."

Viv shook her head. "*What*?" She held the door firm.

"I can't believe I hurt you. I can't believe I went with Gwyn. It was all a mistake. A big mistake. It's you I want."

She screwed up her eyes. "No. You have a baby on the way."

"Oh, you heard about that?" Pete's head dropped and he shuffled but did not move his foot or hand from the door. "Look, we can – I can support her and her child, but we, you and I, can go back to normal. I only went because she told me she was pregnant. I … I didn't know what to do, Viv … Please, please let me come in, let me be with you, take me back. I love you. We've always loved each other. We can't wipe out all those years, can we?"

For a moment, Viv hesitated. People make mistakes. We all do. If he truly was sorry … if it was a madness … if he really loved her, wanted her … couldn't they go back to being together again, together against the world, safe and secure in the apartment …the home they'd made …? Viv sighed. She looked at his face, so familiar again after that awful aberration. Pleading, abject, sorrowful. It was what she wanted. Wasn't it? To be safe again, to be in a close relationship, a family.

She shivered. A whisper in her ear, echoing across the centuries: "You should not have had to suffer that rudeness and coarse behaviour." No, nothing could erase that, and she would never trust him again because of it, and because of all that he had said and done. He'd still had an affair, after all. He'd still got someone else pregnant. He'd still hit her. He'd still walked away. He'd still lied and been so devious. "My little Vivvie …" Her family was still there, in her heart. She drew in a long strong breath. "My Lady of the Lake".

"No, Pete," she said softly. "I'm sorry, but that is over. You must do whatever you need to as far as Gwyn is concerned. And your child. And I hope you do; I hope you make a go of it with her. But I'm afraid you shattered "us". I can't ever be with you again."

*

The hall clock struck midnight. Pete had slunk away and Viv's heart twisted within her. She crawled back to the sofa to struggle with the preparation for her lecture and tutorials the next day. But as she did, she bit her lip and tears threatened her eyes. Had she done the right thing? She could have been comfortable in Pete's arms again now. Yet, even that image was tinged with doubt and shadows. At least she had been true to herself. And it wasn't anything to do with Reverend Rory. Was it?

There were so many problems on Viv's mind that she found it difficult to focus. Her mind kept drifting to Rev Rory and as it did she felt the fluttering and flushing that began in her heart and suffused her whole body. Just as quickly she tried to squash her emotions down. She couldn't … she mustn't think of him as anything but a friend, a brother. Yes, the brother she never had. Her turmoil reminded her of Lady Vivianne, and she felt for her dilemma so keenly.

How was she to help Vivianne get rid of Sir Pelleas and make a life with Roland? Yet still keep her parents' inheritance for her – the ladyship of the settlement? Sir Pelleas seemed to have so much support in his usurpation. How could Lady Vivianne break that and set herself free without being forced to leave her home? Viv couldn't see a way out. Both she and Rory now believed that they had some kind of mission to touch the world of Vivianne and Roland, one and a half thousand years ago, through the portal, to do whatever was needed so that the world of the dark ages could right itself. And maybe so that their own could right itself, too. Neither Pelleas nor Pete could be allowed to win and damage others. But what did she have to do and why?

Finally, Viv pushed her work aside, closed her eyes and leaned back on the sofa. She snuggled up in her comfortable pyjamas, no longer needing to wear sexy nightwear for Pete. She felt the relief amidst the sadness of a relationship gone wrong. She let the music of Il Divo continue on the iPod and swirl around her mind. Her head was spinning, and as she fluttered her eyes open for a moment she saw the room juddering and drifting in and out of focus. She thought she could see wood smoke drifting across her eye line. She could hear sharp calls across the air, the thumping of many footfalls nearby. The air around her felt light and sweet, not dark and weary. She saw guards making their way in the direction of a hut where she knew, somehow, that Tilda's father lived.

Then she heard the urgent cries of the guards. "Here! Quickly! We've found something!"

Lady Vivianne clutched her cloak and furs around her and kept her trembling hands pressed to her chest. She felt a hand on her arm and jumped, swinging around.

"Oh, my!" she breathed. "Tilda, you startled me."

"My lady …"

"Tilda, just stop pulling on my sleeve, please."

Tilda lowered her hand but not her head. "My lady, I must go with all haste to my father's hut and see that all is well. No, do not come with me. That would look very suspicious. You must stay here and appear unconcerned."

"Yes, you are right. But I hate to abandon you and Sir Roland."

"My lady, you are certainly not abandoning anyone. You have done more, much more, than your duty already, I know that."

"Thank you, Tilda. You are wise beyond your years. Now, go – run and see what is happening, and please to return soon to tell me. I shall be waiting impatiently for news."

Vivianne watched Tilda run off towards her father's hut. She bit her lip and beneath her cloak she wrung her hands together. She paced her chamber, then, knowing she had to find something to do, to look as though she were busy and unconcerned, she walked out and down the narrow street to the baker's house. Through the door that stood open onto the street, she could see that the fires of the ovens were already blazing even in the early morning as the baker prepared the bread for breaking fast. The smell was delicious and for a moment overcame Vivianne's senses and her agitation with its soothing warmth. She breathed it in deeply.

The baker turned from his bread paddle and noticed her. "Oh, my lady, I did not see you there. It is unusual that you grace the bakery so early in the day. What did you require?" He wiped his hot floury hands on his apron and looked agitated.

"Hmm. I … er … I woke and suddenly felt consumed with a passion for a loaf of your wonderful fresh baked bread …" she stopped, realising that he would find that strange, since Tilda herself had come for bread earlier, but it was all she could think of on the spur of the moment, and with her mind full of imaginings about what was happening at Tilda's father's hut.

But the baker smiled, and bowed his head, as he used to when she was a child, and for a moment it seemed that his mind had slipped back into better times. "I am flattered, my lady, that you love my bread so much. I have a secret recipe, you know, passed down from my father and his father. It cannot be shared, of course, but I can only say that it contains certain rough meal and seeds …" He continued to speak lyrically of his recipe but his words floated over Vivianne's head as she heard shouts and the thudding of boots outside.

"Please excuse me," she said, turning towards the noise. "I must see what is happening. I do hope it is not danger."

"Indeed, my lady." His face recovered its tension." I must continue my baking or the loaves will not be ready for the rest of the villagers, and then my taxes …"

Lady Vivianne slipped outside, trying not to draw attention to herself. Guards ran past and dust flew up from their boots. It looked like a whole army running past. She had to know.

"What is happening? Is there danger?" she called to one she recognised.

"Yes, indeed," shouted the guard breathlessly as he ran with the crowd, glancing back as he passed. "Betrayal … enemies …able-bodied men … Sir Pelleas!" was all she could make out.

"Oh my Lord," whispered Vivianne under her breath. She stretched up on tiptoe to see if Sir Roland was in their midst but she could not see through the mêlée. "He has been discovered. And maybe the chest, too."

She pushed her way through the crowd and towards the back of the huts. Her breath was raw and seared her throat as she gasped.

There were no guards, none of Sir Pelleas's warriors in sight. They must have all thundered back to their lord's hall or the mead hall. Vivianne looked around cautiously. Where was everyone? It was eerily quiet back here, in contrast to the noise of the main thoroughfare with the thudding boots of the guards and cries of startled villagers beginning their day, roused with sleepy eyes to see what all the commotion heralded. She heard the cockerels crowing and the hens clucking for their meal. Away in the fields she could hear the shouts of the men working the land for vegetables and herding in the cattle for milk.

But here, the absence of any loud noises, save for her own heart.

Had they all been captured and taken already: Sir Roland, Tilly and her elderly father?

Chapter 15

Lady Vivianne squeezed through the stockades around the patches of worked earth at the back of the huts. She could see the cabbage and kale sprouting fresh green from the dark soil. She smelled the stench of the midden at the back of Tilda's home before she saw it and noted that the stockades were intact and the ground smooth and flat. Nobody had dug anything up here.

A whisper over the air. "Lady Vivianne!"

She swung around to see Tilda peeping out of the crack of the open door at the rear of the hut. "Tilly. What has happened? Are you all safe? What about Sir Roland? And your father? And the chest?" Vivianne clutched her cloak around her, knuckles white.

"We are all safe," whispered Tilda, beckoning her to come inside. Vivianne could not help hearing the amusement in her maid's voice. "Come. Quickly."

Lady Vivianne ducked under the low lintel and peered into the darkness of the house. She could smell the smoky fire in the hearth at the end of the room and see the glow of the flames. A figure in a dark cloak moved aside to reveal the lamp's light and the place was dimly illuminated. She could now make out Tilda's father sitting huddled by the fire and a couple of straw beds to one side. A noise made her swing around, but all she saw were the hens clucking in and out of the doorway and a sheep shuffling in a pile of straw on the furthest side of the hut. The air smelled stale and earthy, an animal smell of damp wool and fowl, but Vivianne smiled to see Sir Roland moving towards her, his heavy cloak wrapped around his muscular body.

"My lady, are you well?"

"Certainly I am well. But you ... your wounds?" She could hear her own voice catch and break.

"Lady Vivianne, you are most truly the daughter of your mother. The herbal infusions worked their magic on my flesh and on my spirit. I am well. I am whole again."

Vivianne smiled, and even though the light was dim in the hut, she knew that Roland smiled too. He came closer until she felt his breath on her cheek. He smelled of sheep and dung, but her heart beat thrummed loud in her ears. "Sir Roland," she whispered.

"My lady, you are indeed a sorceress. The Lady of the Lake." His lips brushed her cheek. "But in a magnificent way."

Her heart filled with a remarkable sensation that she had only sensed vaguely before. But, she realised, always in Roland's presence. She lifted her hand and touched his shoulder.

Tilda coughed. "My lady … Sir …could I pour you some honey mead?"

Vivianne felt her face flush and stepped quickly away from Roland and made to smooth her dress, although it had not been creased. "That would be very welcome." She moved nearer the fire where she knew her blushes could not be detected. "And I want you to tell me all that has happened since you ran off. Did the guards find the chest? I saw them running towards the hall. Where are they going?"

"Sit down beside my father, here," gestured Tilda, filling wooden cups from a large jug.

Vivianne turned to the elderly man who had stood up for her. "My apologies, Hrothgar. It was rude of me to fail to greet you properly. I was so overcome that Ro … that you were all safe."

The elderly man gestured her to sit on the stool nearest the fire. "You grace our humble abode, my lady."

"I do not know how I can thank you enough for your kindness." She felt tears prick her eyes as she sat and Hrothgar sat on the stool beside her.

"Mathilda, child, you must tell Lady Vivianne about what has befallen."

Tilda handed the cups of warm mead to each of them and then sat on the floor at Vivianne's feet, and Sir Roland stood at her side. "My lady," she began, plucking chicken feathers from her skirts as she sat cross-legged. "I found my father here in the darkness with the lamp unlit and the fire cold, busily whittling the willow sticks and weaving them into baskets as always. He often works without light. He says it helps his eyes to simply feel his way with the willows. But I did think it odd that the oats were not yet ready in the pot on the fire for breaking fast, and that father seemed a little breathless as he worked." She sighed.

Her father reached out and patted her knee. "You are a good girl for noticing such things. But tell my lady what happened."

Tilda smiled, sipping her mead. She folded her hands over the cup in her lap and resumed her story-telling pose. "I might have known that he was hiding something. He quickly told me that he had ensured the chest was well hidden and at that moment I saw a movement in the straw by the sheep." She pointed to the far corner of the room. "I can see well in the dark. My mother used to say I was a night-wolf. But ... it was then that we heard the shouts and heavy footsteps. I began to tremble, my hands shook so much, I had to clutch on to my skirts to hide their shaking. Then four guards pushed their way in through the doorway and stood there trying to see into the dark of the hut. 'Light a lamp, old man!' they shouted. 'How can we see what you are hiding in this gloom?' Slowly my father rose from his stool, bending and rubbing his back, as I had never seen him do before. The guards were becoming impatient. Father was just slowly fumbling with the lamp and rubbing the sticks for a flame, and I was biting my lip, dreading a raised fist to hit him. Then there came the sound of the horn outside and a yelling on the road. 'Guards! Thegns! Quickly to the mead hall. By Sir Pelleas's command!' Oh, my lady, I held my breath ..."

"Why?" Vivianne shook her head, trying to follow the tale. "I mean, why was there shouting?"

"My lady, they shouted, 'The Picties have come ...!'"

"The ... what?"

"The Picties!"

"Picts, Tilda," murmured Roland. "Scots marauders from north of the borderlands."

Tilda nodded. "They are two days' journey away from *our* borders. Only two days! So the shouts told me."

"So did the guards leave?"

"Yes, indeed they did, my lady. They ran out and we heard their heavy footsteps join the others running to the mead hall at Sir Pelleas's command. My father looked out onto the road and many guards were kicking up the dust as they rushed past. My father came back inside and stretched to straighten his back as normal."

"At least I bought a little time," snorted Hrothgar. He sat upright and erect, his cloak almost falling from his shoulders.

"That was well done," smiled Vivianne, handing her cup back to Tilda with a nod of thanks, as did Roland and Hrothgar. "And I take it that Sir Roland was hidden in the sheep straw where you saw the movement?"

"Yes, he was indeed. He was so covered in straw and sheep dung that I had to clean up his cloak."

Roland, grinning, brushed imaginary straw from his tunic and boots. "And a wonderful job she did, although I still smell of animal." He took a deep breath. "But two days journey and a battle mean that we have a little time. They know that I am missing from their prison and they think that I am hiding out somewhere, so my absence in battle would not be remarked … and yet I should be fighting for our land, for your father, Lady Vivianne, for your heritage."

"But not for Sir Pelleas?"

"I have done so before, but with a heavy heart. Yet clearly the protection of your homeland is paramount, lady. But also the protection of you yourself …" He rubbed his forehead for a few moments, while Vivianne's thoughts swirled around her head; she knew what he was thinking. She watched him pace to the far end of the room and back and knew he was struggling.

"My lord Sir Roland, you must go." She stood and squared her shoulders. "God knows I do not wish it, but I know that you will feel less of a man, less of a warrior, if you do not. You have your pride as a Romano-Briton to uphold. And we will be fine." Her eyes met his. "I will be fine. Have I not shown that already?"

He strode towards her and grasped her shoulders. Vivianne could feel his heat through her robe and cloak. "You know me well. And I know you to be a strong lady … with magical gifts to surround you."

"Sir Roland," interrupted Tilda, jumping up and rummaging in the willow chest at the end of the beds. "Here, smear this woad on your face and wear my brother's helmet. He died bravely in battle with Sir Pelleas at the start of his chiefdom, but this helmet he wore previously in the Great Battle alongside Sir Tristram." She swiftly crossed herself. "He was blessed in this by the holy High King Arturius. Sir Roland, you need not be recognised. Use my father's cloak and clasp."

"And use *my* father's horse," Vivianne added quickly. "The stallion was hand-signed by my mother before he rode him out to the Great Battle. He has magic upon him. He will bring you safely home."

"I will ride well to the back until the forest, then take the short-cut and face the enemy full on at the front." Roland smeared his face until it was dark and pulled on the helmet with its crest and nose-guard. "I can collect my shield and spear as I go for your father's stallion – I assume he is in the royal stables."

"Yes, he is exercised but rarely ridden to battle, for fear of disturbing Sir Tristram's spirit." Vivianne held her breath to stop the watering of her eyes, and distracted herself by fumbling in her pouch. "Here, take this." She held out to him the cross her mother had given her.

Roland caught the hand she held out as he took the cross, and bent his head to kiss it. He looked up at her and as their eyes met, her heart stood still.

"Return safely to us," she whispered, before he smiled, then turned swiftly and disappeared out of the door.

"I will see you gone," called Hrothgar after him and hurried out.

Vivianne turned away from Tilda towards the fire, and murmured a prayer. As the words formed at her lips she realised that they were not hers. She smelled the scent of her mother at her side, felt her touch on her arm, heard her words that entered her heart and left her lips. She stood still for a few moments, hands clasped at her breast, eyes closed. She breathed in, long and slow, then exhaled, controlling her breath outwards as she collected herself and regained her composure. Then she turned back to Tilda.

"Thank you." She bowed her head. "But can you tell me why your brother was not wearing the helmet alongside Sir Pelleas, if it was blessed by Arturius in the Great Battle?"

"He … he was ordered to leave it behind, and not go into battle wearing something blessed as Christian and something that only nobles wear."

"I see. And he died in battle without it?"

"Yes, I am afraid that he did. He was bare-headed as befits a humble fighter, and as befits the son of a willow worker."

"But my father did not think so. He gave him the helmet and had him blessed. He was clearly noble in battle with my father."

Tilda bobbed a curtsy. "Thank you, my lady. You also honour my family."

"Your mother?"

"She died of the fever two winters ago. But I look after my father. He works hard for us."

"And so do you, my dear." Vivianne knew that she must stop her chattering but she found it a comfort in the moments after Roland had departed, and prevented her tears. Now she realised that she was clutching her skirts in tight fists and as she loosened them she was aware of the crumples in the cloth. She seemed incapable of dismissing from her mind the image of Roland looking into her eyes, his deep dark eyes pouring tenderness into hers. Her heart felt as though somebody was squeezing it hard, and her head felt light, her legs shaky. Tilda's face was moving, swaying, rising up to the roof, in and out of focus. A voice drifted in and out of her mind and she knew it to be her mother's. *My Lady of the Lake* ... and she heard strange music, and a soft chiming of a bell ...

*

Viv's body jerked awake. The hall clock was chiming. She glanced at her watch. Twelve midnight. She must have drifted off. Yet she distinctly remembered hearing the clock strike midnight as she fell asleep. Didn't she? Her ipod softly emitted the gentle music of Il Divo. A phrase echoed in her brain. *The Lady of the Lake.* DuLac. Of the lake. Lady Vivianne's mother was the Lady of the Lake and she had inherited at least some of her magic. Her own mother was involved somehow. But surely DuLac was her father's name, and so hers? Yet the magical stuff came down through the female line. It didn't make sense.

She clicked off her iPod, and, thankful that she had already changed into her PJs and was ready for bed, struggled to her bedroom and fell upon her soft quilt. How could she sleep? So many thoughts, so many puzzles battered her mind.

Yet she was unutterably tired.

*

When Viv awoke the sun was streaming through the bedroom window between the curtains and a beam illuminated dancing motes in the bright light. Pete used to hate these Laura Ashley curtains that hung with wooden rings on the dark oak pole. He said they never shut properly and

154

used to pull them together so hard that they always ended up overlapping untidily. She had no objection to a sliver of light in the mornings. She never wanted the black-out curtains that Pete claimed he needed.

She felt the sun's warmth and the promise of a lovely day again. She missed Pete, she missed having someone else around the flat, but the quiet and the ease, the feeling of relief at not being pressured to pander to his needs and to please him, was a new recognition in her heart. Did that mean she hadn't loved him as much as she thought she had? Viv lay for a moment, relishing the peace although her dreams had been disturbed and she felt like a rag doll with the stitches unravelling. Rolling over and pushing herself upright and out of bed, she stretched her neck and lower back.

After her shower, she did a few yoga asanas in her underwear and bare feet. The salute to the sun made her feel more energised for the day ahead. She had a meeting first thing, a couple of tutorials and a draft assignment to check for an anxious student. Then she was meeting Rory in the atrium to make their investigations at her parents' bank. She knew that the chest had been stored there in the vaults for twenty years now. As far as she knew, nobody but herself knew that it was lodged there. She slipped her identity documents and her parents' letter from her memory box and hid them in her bag, hoping that they would be enough to convince the bank manager that she was entitled to retrieve the chest and that it was now her inherited property – and in fact had been for many years.

Viv made a bowl of porridge in the microwave, scattered a handful of blueberries on the top, knowing that this was about the only food she could swallow easily these days, especially in the mornings. As she made herself a quick mug of instant coffee, her mobile pinged a text onto her screen. Peering at it, she realised that she had missed one text already. The first was from Rory confirming that he would meet her in the atrium at two o' clock. As an afterthought he had added that it might make more sense if he picked her up from her flat this morning so that they would only need one car. He was so thoughtful. She hadn't even got as far as working out the logistics. He'd written it at 7.45 and a glance at the kitchen clock told her it was now 7.55. She tapped a quick "that would be great" reply and added "any time after 8?"

The second text was from Ellie: "Are you OK? I was worried yesterday; it was like you were someone else! Take care xxx". Viv smiled. She and Ellie were the only people she knew who put semi-colons in text messages and rarely used abbreviations. Viv sent a hasty reply to Ellie, assuring her that all was well, knowing that her friend knew her so well that she wouldn't believe her and would probably ring her or come round tonight.

The outer doorbell rang, which meant that Tilly had probably not gone off to work yet. As she opened her own front door she heard her neighbour's heavy footsteps thudding down the stairs. She opened the door and all she saw was Rory's gorgeous smile that made his dark eyes twinkle. Viv's legs felt shaky.

"Hi! Oh, Rory Rev, you look even more sexy this morning! In the daylight. Wow!" called Tilly from the bottom of the staircase, a huge hobo bag over her shoulder. "After all that last night – wooee. I slept like the proverbial log. Oh, what a divine man!" Her eyes raised up to the ceiling and she bent double with loud giggles, hand over her mouth. "Oh god!" which made her giggle even more. "Of course, you're the man of the cloth. Divine. In both senses. Sorry. Slip of the tongue. What am I *like*?" She turned to Viv, heaving her bag further up her shoulder, and waggling her eyebrows. "Wow."

Viv glanced at Rory who moved inside, away from the doorway, looking bemused. "Morning, Tilly, and bye. See you later maybe. Have a good day!"

"You *too* … mmm." Tilly squeezed through the doorway banging her bag on the lintel as she went. They could hear her singing "How great thou art" as she rushed round the corner to the car park.

"So-o-o," murmured Rory, with a grin, holding the outer door for her as she picked up her briefcase and locked her own door. He took her case from her hand, carrying it round to his car. He clicked the old Jaguar's remote to open the boot and as he bent to place the briefcase alongside his own rucksack, she couldn't help but notice his well-fitting slim jeans skimming a nicely rounded bottom and muscular thighs. "OK, off we go. Work calls."

Viv jerked her eyes quickly away from his backside and felt her cheeks flush with heat. Stop this, she urged herself, he's married and he's a vicar, both no-go areas. She slipped onto the front seat as he held the passenger door open for her, and sank into its soft leather curves. Rory opened the driver's door and eased his tall frame inside. He stretched his long legs and started the engine.

"Last night …" they both started together.

"Sorry," smiled Rory, turning towards her as he reversed the car and drove out of the parking area and onto the lane. "You first."

"After you dropped me off here last night," she began, "I was prepping for today but … it happened again. I time-slipped. They seem to be becoming more frequent. There's almost an urgency about it."

"What happened to you?"

"I … er, Lady Vivianne went to Tilda's father's hut. The soldiers were all along the road through the village, shouting. Apparently they had turned up at the hut but had to hurry off to join the others. There was news of the Picts approaching the settlement. I remember they said they were about two days' journey away. Sir Pelleas had ordered all the warriors, all the able-bodied men, to make the army to stop them reaching the village."

"Hmmm," murmured Rory, nodding.

"The Picts were dangerous enemies," Viv added, wondering if Rory already knew this. "They came on many raids from the borderlands of Scotland way down south to the midlands, destroying settlements, pillaging them, raping the womenfolk, then taking their spoils back north to Scotland. Particularly after the Romans left, they were less effectively pushed back at the wall."

"So what else did you find out?"

"Sir Roland who was hiding at the hut, followed them, to do his duty I suppose. He's very loyal to Lady Vivianne's father. Did *you* … time slip at all?"

"I can't say I time slipped. But I had a very vivid dream. When I woke up this morning I could remember everything. About …"

Viv glanced sideways at him. "Which bit? Taking the cloak and helmet and rushing out after the army?"

"No, not so much that. More about looking at Vivianne, into her eyes … and the feelings I … Sir Roland had …" He turned a little towards her and smiled. "She's … *was* … beautiful. Actually, she reminds me of you. There was a definite connection there … it reminded me of … well, I won't go there."

Viv's heat suffused her whole body, rising from her thighs to her face. She surreptitiously raised her left hand to her cheek. She was burning. She felt shaky and as though she had to gasp for breath. Her heart thrummed, beating an uneven rhythm in her chest. "I ..." she stopped. Rory was looking at her with a strange expression.

"To be honest, I looked into her eyes and I was ... lost."

Viv slowly drew in her breath. She remembered Roland's eyes too, dark, smoky, full of love; the touch of his hands on her ... no, Vivianne's ... shoulders. She imagined Rory looking at her like that, holding her shoulders in that way, drawing her to him ... stop it! She warned herself. But she couldn't help taking another look at his strong profile, the way his thick dark hair curled round his ears and at his neck.

Rory drew into the university car park and pulled up in a space near the entrance. He turned towards her and took a deep breath, "Viv, we need to ..."

"Hi!" came a voice at the side of the car. "Rev!" Both turned and Rory opened his door. "I didn't know the priesthood was so well paid!" The chap was stroking his hand along the Jaguar.

"One of my fellow doctoral candidates," Rory murmured to Viv. "Sorry." He stepped out of the car. "No, it's not well paid at all. This was my mother's until she decided she wanted something smaller and lighter. And I got it for a very reasonable price!" He smiled at Viv who had got out of the car and walked round to Rory's side. "Actually she wanted to give it to me. But I don't think that's right."

"Mad. I'd have taken it for free," said the chap. "Anyway, must dash."

Viv and Rory, carrying her bag, made their way to the revolving doors of the main building and into the atrium. Viv knew that she had misinterpreted all that Rory had said in the car. She had wanted to misinterpret it. But she must be sensible and realistic. She was vulnerable, coming out of a relationship, having such a shock – doubly so with the shock of the news about the flat. Of course she imagined it all. He wasn't meaning her at all. It was his wife he was thinking about. Losing himself in his wife's eyes. Reminding him of ... what? ...maybe when he met her. The first time he kissed her. Fell in love with her. Of course it was nothing to do with her. Oh god. What if he had seen the warmth ... attraction ... in her eyes? He was going to say, Viv we need to talk about your misguided feelings … wasn't he? What a fool she was. Oh god, how embarrassing.

She took her brief case from him and said, too brightly, "Thanks, Rory. See you at two here in the atrium for the trip to the bank. I'll ring the manager to let him know we're coming. You're very kind to support me. Appreciate it."

Ignoring his quizzical look, with a wave she ran up the steps to the lift for her office on the fifth floor. She didn't look back.

Chapter 16

Viv opened her email inbox and saw one message from the Dean of her faculty. Her heart jumped. For a moment she couldn't bring herself to open it. Then, taking a deep breath, she clicked on it. She scanned it, mouth dropping open, then she read it through again more slowly, taking on board every word. He apologised for keeping her waiting for the decision on the promotion, but there were a number of candidates they had to interview, and unfortunately one of the panel was taken ill and they had to reschedule. The field was extremely talented … blah, blah, blah … but he was pleased to offer her the post. She was the most qualified in the field. It was a majority decision of the panel and they were sure that in the longer term she would be a valuable member of the senior team. However, it would, in the first instance, not entail a salary rise, in view of her lack of senior management experience. She would be on a trial for a period of one academic year on her current salary level. If this was acceptable to her and she was still interested in the role, a formal letter of appointment would follow.

It wasn't that she had forgotten about the post and the interview, but there had been so much else on her mind, so much to occupy and invade her thoughts, that she had pushed it to the back of her thoughts. For one thing, she had not wanted to hope because she didn't want to be let down. She didn't want to suffer a repetition of the plunging feeling of falling and drowning that she had when Pete left and when she received the letter from the solicitor. She had applied for the senior post before all that, and probably wouldn't have done so if she had already felt the humiliation and anger of the betrayal. She wouldn't have felt strong enough. As it was, the interview had taken most of her courage and single-minded strength to, at the very least, give a good account of herself.

She shook her head and read it one more time. The joy of the appointment was diluted by the fact that she would be doing the job without the extra money. That would have been so useful in the current situation. But she had to accept it, hoping that it would work out in the end. She gritted her teeth and took a deep breath before replying that she would be pleased to accept, and that she would do her best to fulfil their faith in her.

The rest of her inbox was less interesting, but kept her busy responding to students and colleagues. A lecture and two tutorials meant that she grabbed an oat bar and a banana to eat at her desk between activities and just made it down to the atrium for two o' clock. As she hurried down the walkway she spotted Rory near the reception desk, talking to the receptionist who gazed up at him adoringly. He was leaning in towards her. For some reason, Viv felt a little annoyed at the girl's batting her long, mascara-ed eyelashes. Then, almost immediately, chided herself for such an unwarranted feeling and let herself smile brightly.

Rory looked up as she approached him, and grinned. "Goodness, you look positively beatific!"

"Well, yes. I've had some great news. I've been offered the job I was interviewed for." She didn't add the disappointment about the salary.

"Wonderful! I'm so proud of you! Brilliant! That certainly calls for a celebration. What about we go for a meal tonight, after we've sorted things out at the bank?" He paused as he stared at Viv's face. She knew she was frowning at him. "Or … er …just a drink?"

"What about Mrs N?"

"Er … well, she has WI tonight. Oh, I see, you haven't met her yet, have you? She did say she'd love to meet you sometime. And, no, I haven't told her about the time-slip thing – at least not in terms of the experiences, only in abstract philosophical terms, if you see what I mean."

"But you can talk to her about *anything*?"

"Yes, of course … well, not exactly *everything*. There are some things I don't share with anyone at all."

"I see."

"Hey, are you OK? You look a little confused." He slipped his arm round her back and patted her shoulder in an avuncular fashion.

"I'm fine, just the excitement of the promotion, I guess." Viv glanced down at her watch, more to hide her face than anything else, as she was perfectly aware that there was a large clock behind the reception desk. "But we'd better get a move on. I arranged a two-thirty appointment with the bank manager."

Rory raised his hand in a goodbye gesture to the receptionist but kept his other hand on her back as he guided her to the revolving door.

*

"Welcome, Dr DuLac," nodded the bank manager as they arrived half an hour later. He reminded Viv of Mr Mainwaring in Dad's Army with his rotund, red-faced appearance, toothbrush moustache, round spectacles, and rather formal, stilted manner. He shook hands with her and then with Rory, looking quizzically at his dog-collar. "*Humph …* Are you family, reverend?"

"No, a friend and supporter," said Rory. "Close friend."

"Reverend Netherbridge has kindly offered to come with me, in case there's anything upsetting in the safe." Viv glanced at him and smiled. Rory grinned comfortingly in return.

"Good. Good … *humph* ... Come this way, please." The bank manager ushered them to his office at the back of the bank, and gestured to the leather chairs in front of his large oak desk. "Please be seated. Now, first of all, I'm afraid that I must ask for identification."

"Yes, of course. Your assistant told me that I'd need to bring various papers." Viv dipped into her bag and pulled out a clear document wallet which contained some of her parents' papers from her memory box, including their last will and testament, and her own passport, driver's licence, and the last letter she had received from her mother. Rory passed over his ID.

The bank manager studied them for a long time, frowning gravely. For a moment, Viv's heart dipped as she wondered if he was, for some reason, about to refuse her access to her parents' safe box in the vaults.

Eventually he looked up. "All seems to be in order, Dr DuLac. Reverend Netherbridge. I will accompany you myself into the vaults … *humph* ... We have a *procedure*." The way he said it made Viv shiver.

The vaults seemed to Viv to be like something out of a heist movie. Heavy metal doors and grids with access ID codes and eye recognition. Viv wondered whether there were priceless treasures like the crown jewels or the Staffordshire Hoard hidden in there. The bank manager led them through and, standing in front of the wall of large safety deposit boxes, turned to Viv and said, clearly with effort, "I knew your parents, Dr DuLac. I was just a young junior assistant. They were …*humph* … very kind. Lovely couple. Very clever, of course. They brought in some precious items to add to their safe. Most precious. And I had to deal with matters when the name was changed." He shook his head. "I offer you my condolences on their ...*humph* ... their departure. So long ago now, but still, such a shame."

"Thank you. It's good to know that they were well thought of. But it *has* been a long time. Twenty years or more. It's time for me to open their safe and sort out their things, finally. As an only child, I inherited everything. But I don't really know quite what "everything" is. And until now I haven't investigated. I've only just been able to sort through the box at home that was passed to me. At least, I didn't really sort through it, just found the items I needed to bring here."

"Of course. You were but a child." He sighed. "Sometimes it takes a long time to be able to do this. I had one lady last month who had taken fifty years to open her family's safe. But I think she had fallen out with her family and so there were *issues*. She was the last of the family. She said she had to do it before she died." He peered over his spectacles at Viv. "I must say, if you'll excuse me, Dr DuLac, *humph*, but you look so much like your mother."

"So," said Rory, stroking her back a little in comfort. "Shall we open it before you lose your nerve, Viv?"

Viv felt herself holding her breath as the bank manager unlocked the safe. Rory must have sensed it, as he moved his hand on her back. She shivered.

"I will leave you in privacy, Dr DuLac, Reverend Netherbridge, to examine the contents in peace. I have to lock the outer door, of course, but when you are ready, please press this button here and I will come to let you out." The bank manager seemed to almost bow and retreat backwards, but as he let himself out of the door of the vault, he added, "I hope neither of you is claustrophobic?"

As she heard the clank of the outer door being locked, Viv took a deep breath. "OK. Let's do it." She peered into the darkness of the safe and saw a box and a number of files. Carefully she drew out the box. It was wooden with gold-coloured furniture. Rory took one end and together they lifted it onto the table in the middle of the room. It was not as Viv had imagined. When she had thought of the chest she had pictured something that looked like a pirate's treasure chest, although she was aware that image was a much more recent stereotype.

This one was a flat-topped box, but it had a gold lock for a key and beautiful carvings picked out in gold leaf over the top. The gold gleamed in the harsh light of the single bulb that hung from the ceiling. Viv brushed her hand lightly over it. Probably the last people to touch this were her parents, as they prepared to fly off to America. They expected to return from New York and do whatever they needed to do with the chest. Viv thought it was smaller than she had envisioned, but then she remembered her mother's last letter where she had described it as a "small wooden chest". Perhaps in her mind its growing importance to her and Lady Vivianne had enlarged it in her imagination.

"It's locked," said Rory, bending over the chest, as Viv lifted out the files from the safe and placed them on the table next to the chest. She turned back to the safe and groped inside again, but it was now empty.

"Oh, lord. I sent the key back to 499, didn't I? But I felt … *compelled* somehow to do that. I guessed that there may be a key in here. But there isn't. Now we can't open it." Viv felt around the lock with her fingers, thinking of her mother opening it, closing her eyes and seeing again her slim figure in work jeans, her long dark chestnut hair twisted up into a top-knot. And as she detailed the image in her mind, it shifted and reshaped into the figure of Lady Vivianne in her long robe and cloak, lifting the lid and taking treasures out of it, slipping treasures in. She heard the thud of the lid closing, a whisper of Lady Vivianne's prayers over the box, and the gasp of her mother as she opened it for the first time, kneeling in the muddy channels of the dig site.

The vault echoed with whispers and murmurings. A soft voice rose and fell rhythmically at her back, but Viv couldn't make out the words. Her fingers fumbled at the lock, its cold metal warming under her touch. Something felt loose.

"It's not locked." Viv began to push the lid up and she felt Rory's hand beside hers helping her.

"But I'm sure … I …"

"Look." Viv nodded at the gold hinges raised from the wood and patterned with images of what appeared to be dragons. "Those are the dragons of Lady Vivianne's line. The dragon from the banner they took into battle."

Rory turned his head to her. "You saw that?"

"I …er …" Viv frowned. War banners? She hadn't any recollection of seeing any such thing in her time-slip. Who might she have read about with a dragon for a symbol? Uther, was all she could think of. King Arthur's kin. "I … I don't know. That's weird."

"There's something," Rory began. "It's vague. I'm trying to pull it back from my memory. Sir Roland. A battle. Or do I know it from iconography? Of course, there's St George and the dragon, but that's much later."

"Oh my god!" a shriek escaped from Viv's throat as she folded back a dark green cloth which had been covering the contents of the chest. "Just look at these!"

She carefully lifted a gold goblet from the box in one hand and a large bejewelled cross in the other.

Rory took out a helmet and examined it, turning it in his hands. "I recognise this. It's like the one Sir Roland was given by Hrothgar. It has the nose guard and the peak. But it's not the same. The engravings are different. There are icons."

"Where?" Viv peered closer, the goblet and cross still in her hands.

"See here, Viv. Christian icons. Early Christian cruciform. Dragons too, weaving through the cross."

"So whose was it, do you think?"

"It must be a king's battle helmet."

"Ah, a high chieftain. They were considered royal in those times."

"And the icons are for protection in battle, amulets."

"That sounds like a mixture of Christian and pagan?"

"Yes, it was at that time. It's what I'm particularly interested in – paganism, magic and early Christianity. Often at that time, all three were melded. It was really a time of transition."

"So, if this is a king's helmet, do you think it could have belonged to Sir Tristram, Lady Vivianne's father? He was, after all, the king or chieftain of the settlement or the region?"

Rory turned the helmet over in his hands and felt its surface with all its relief images and indentations, its jewels and embellishments. "It could well be, Viv. It must be worth … well, a king's ransom!"

Viv took out her iPhone and began to photograph the artefacts.

"There are papers in these files, too." Viv moved the ancient objects carefully and slipped a sheaf of papers onto the table. There was a plastic pocket underneath the pile too. "This is clearly not from the dark ages!" She turned it over in her hands. "My parents obviously slipped this in the safe with the treasures. But locked away – it must have been important and private."

She peered at the papers. They were copies of newspaper cuttings of twenty years ago, relating to the archaeological find at the Wilmingham site, legal documents referring to the authenticity of the objects and witnessed declarations of their finders. In the plastic pocket were more papers, protected with covers, and a large A4 envelope, addressed to Viv.

She looked up to Rory and caught her breath.

"You need to open it," he whispered gently. "Here, or at home?"

"Here, while you're with me."

Viv slid the flap carefully up and drew out the documents inside. The first was a letter from a solicitor addressed to "Dr Petersen". Who on earth was that? Puzzled, Viv flipped through the other sheets, something to "Drs DuLac-Petersen", then finally "Drs DuLac". Viv scanned through them: a legal change of name. A scribbled note at the top of a sheet telling her that the DuLac name must always be retained, even though she might marry one day. The final sheet, a copy of her birth certificate, Vivianne DuLac. She handed them to Rory to read. She felt disorientated; so in a sense, she should have been Viv Petersen, but her parents had decided, for some reason, to use her mother's name, DuLac.

"Oh." Viv remembered something that the bank manager had said, "to deal with matters when the name was changed". So that was it.

"Interesting," Rory said. He shuffled the papers, turning them over. "Oh. There's something on the back of this one. Oh, my Lord." He held it up for Viv to see.

She gasped. "It's a drawing of Lady Vivianne!" She clutched the edge of the table to steady herself. It was a rough sketch, as if drawn in a hurry before the memory faded. In a scribbled hand, her mother had written: "mother to daughter".

"To pass down, mother to daughter," Viv murmured. "Where did I hear that?" She glanced towards Rory and saw that he was peering at the laminated pages. "What are they?"

"Well, they appear to be formal documents, but they're written in an odd script. The letters are difficult to make out, but I think I see some odd words in Latin," he pointed.

" … and some, look there," Viv gasped, "possibly an early form of … no, it can't be Anglo-Saxon … it's not right. Similar, but … could it be some kind of Brython, early Briton, Celtic language?" She leaned across to look more closely. "Goodness, I can hardly make out the letters, never mind the words. It's much earlier that the original scripts I've studied in Anglo-Saxon … *Beowulf* and *Bede*. But then those were … what?... two hundred years later than Lady Vivianne."

"It's like a detective puzzle."

"Yes, medieval documents are like that. In the late fifth century most of the communication was oral, the poems, the tales. But some were written down, mainly by the priests - religious and legal texts, and they were generally written in Latin."

"So the average person couldn't understand them."

"No. But this is a mixture. And even through the covering I can see that the paper is old, thick like vellum, clearly fragile in places." Viv met Rory's dark eyes. "My god. I think we have something very rare and important here. Something that might shed light on the dark ages."

Rory nodded slowly. "Good grief. No wonder your parents protected the pages. At least I'm assuming it was them, after they discovered them at the dig."

"Look here!" gasped Viv, "This word looks like 'Vivianne'. And here, 'Nymue', 'Roland','Pelleas' – that name appears over and over again. This is something about our Sir Pelleas, perhaps?" She began to snap more pictures of the documents.

"Who was 'Nymue'?"

"Lady Vivianne's mother. But the name comes up in a much later text, from the fifteenth century, written in Middle English, but based on traditional tales of many centuries earlier. Do you know Malory's *Le Morte D'Arthur*? The later medieval tales of King Arthur and the Knights of the Round Table. Launcelot and the holy grail … and the Lady of the Lake?"

"Oh, yes. Excalibur and all that."

"But the thing is, there were many names for the so-called lady of the lake. Vivianne, sometimes spelled with one 'n', sometimes spelled Ninianne, Vivien, but also Nymue or Nimue. The letters V and N were at times interchangeable."

"Viv, what was your mother's name, again?"

Her hand seemed to flick up to her mouth of its own accord, and she breathed in sharply. "Oh my god. It was Elaine. Another name used for the Lady of the Lake." She was shaking, her hands, her whole body shuddered. "Passed down from mother to daughter. Oh, Rory, what on earth does this mean?"

"For a start, if these documents were found by your parents at the Wilmingham dig …" Rory looked confused.

"Well," Viv murmured, "then it could indicate that the Malory tales were based on much, much earlier stories, dating from at least as early as 499. And that some at least could have been based on real people, and maybe corruptions of real events."

"Ah, okaa-ay."

"But what I meant was … what does it mean for me? Am I in some kind of ancestral line of ladies of the lake, with magical powers and …?"

And then, somehow, she *knew* the truth. She was a descendant of Lady Vivianne, wasn't she? It had to be that. Mother to daughter. Powers passed on from generation to generation. So there was the connection.

Rory slipped his arm around her and patted her back. "Look. It just means that in the past generations of your family there might have been ladies with senses that were particularly attuned to imprints or shapes on the air, in the fabric of places … We do know that you have time slipped, that there is something that is 'haunting' you. Not in any bad way, not evil, but in order to right wrongs, to re-attune history. Does that make any sense to you?"

"I suppose so."

"And remember that I time slipped, too." He squeezed her shoulder and lifted her chin up towards him. "Are you OK?"

She took a deep breath in and as she did so, she remembered that both Vivianne and Nymue were, in Malory, strong forces for good. "I think so. It's just that it's a lot to take in. I need to think about it all."

Rory began to lean in to her and for a moment she thought he was going to kiss her. Then he seemed to hesitate.

And in that second there was a disembodied voice,

"Dr DuLac!"

Chapter 17

They both jumped. Rory stepped away from Viv and her mind cleared. The voice was, of course, that of the bank manager, issuing from a speaker on the wall. She looked at the papers scattered across the table and glanced at her watch.

"Oh goodness, we've been in here for nearly an hour," she said as she began to pile the sheets together again. "I want to take these documents home to take a better look and I think I need to get an expert to identify them, age them, and maybe translate, if they can. "

"And the artefacts?"

"I want to leave them locked up safely here for the time being. I need to think about what to do with them."

Together they checked that the pieces were securely arranged as they had found them and that the cloth protecting them was back in place. They lifted the chest and slid it back into the safe. Viv pushed the door closed and then pressed the button to indicate that they were ready to leave.

The bank manager opened the doors and stepped inside. "Is everything satisfactory, Dr DuLac? Can I lock the safe again?"

"Yes, thank you. But I want to take these papers home."

He frowned as though that was not quite appropriate. "That is fine. But I have to register that on the inventory."

"You have an inventory for the items in the safe?"

"Yes, of course. Although it doesn't give details of the items as such. That is a private matter for the owners of the safe."

"I see, but I'd like to read it."

Rory murmured his assent. "It might give us an idea of what your parents thought of the items."

When the bank manager had locked the safe and the iron doors, he took them back to his office and unlocked his filing cabinet. With nimble fingers he flicked through the files and pulled one out. "Here it is." He glanced at it and neatly selected a page before handing it across the desk to Viv. "Not much information, I'm afraid."

Viv held it between herself and Rory so that he could also read it. It was a list headed with the name of the dig, its catalogue number, ID code, and an estimated dating of 530-550 AD, artefacts with an earlier dating of around 480 AD. It listed a wooden chest, containing a war helmet, a cross, an altar goblet, and a file containing papers and documents to be investigated.

"Oh. There is also an envelope," said the bank manager, holding it out to Viv.

She eased it open and saw that there was a letter in her mother's handwriting. She read it quickly, and glanced at Rory who frowned. "I need to take this home too. And the list."

"I will need to take a copy for our files then. Of the list, not of the letter. In case of any need to check ..." his voice trailed away. He took the list from Viv and slid it into the small photocopier in the corner of his office before passing the list to Viv and the copy back to the file.

*

By the time they had found Rory's Jag in the multi-storey car park and driven out onto the road back to the village, Viv's stomach was rumbling. She wasn't sure whether Rory could hear it but he said, as he navigated the roundabout, "OK, so let's just take a break. What about that celebratory meal for your promotion? We could go to The White Knight in the village? There are new owners and it's really quite good now. We went the other week and it's been refurbished, new menu. Good, fresh, bistro-type meals. What do you think?"

Viv shuffled in her seat and watched the houses of the new estate at the edge of the village drift past. "Er ... well, won't your parishioners be curious? Won't it be a little ... um ... awkward?"

"My parishioners? Why would they be curious, or make it awkward?"

Viv hesitated, unsure how to express her concerns. She couldn't very well say 'because you're married'. That would seem somewhat presumptuous. As if she considered herself a threat to his wife. That he might fancy her. That having a meal together constituted a date, that they were having an affair, that a divorce might result. "Er ..."

"Oh," Rory laughed. "You mean that they would be gossiping about us. Well, let them. It's no big deal. I'm sure that the gossip about Pete leaving has already whipped round the village."

Viv felt even more confused. "Well ..."

"Two friends eating dinner together rather than making it at home. Convenience. Don't worry. It's fine. They know me."

Viv wasn't sure how to take that. But her thrumming heart wanted so much to accept. If he, as vicar, didn't mind, then she supposed she shouldn't either. Probably he meant it as part of his job, caring for his parishioners. And they'd think he was wonderfully kind, not 'oh god, he's got a family at home.' And, after all, *her* reputation wasn't at stake. Folks would, in reality, probably either imagine that she was still with her partner, 'married' as they saw it, and therefore safe with their rector, or had heard that Pete had left her and would think that Rory was taking care of her – in a priestly sort of way.

Within a few moments she had successfully convinced herself that it was all fine. The thought of an evening with him was delicious. "Yes, that would be lovely!" Rory turned slightly towards her, grinning. "Great!" He turned off towards the centre of the village and the green, with its Saxon cross in front of The White Knight, a charming white building with touches of local dry stone walling. He pulled in to the car park which wound round the back of the pub and drew to a halt under the spreading branches of an old oak tree.

Inside, the décor was much more effective than the last time Viv had been there: no longer drab and dated, the walls were painted white and the medieval beams newly varnished. The tables were either scrubbed pine or draped with snow white linen cloths. All were laid with gleaming cutlery, large church candles and fresh flowers. Each table nestled in its own corner or booth.

"They've certainly done the place up well. It's beautiful," said Viv as her eyes took in the detailed touches of solid antique furniture and artefacts. "I haven't been for ages. It was so run down. It always reminded me of a city old man's pub. I expected to see McCawber – or Fagin – sitting in the corner. But this is just my sort of thing."

Rory grinned. "I'm glad."

When they had been shown to a table, Viv excused herself and made her way to the ladies'. As she took off her work jacket her fingers trembled. A whole evening with Rory. Then she shook her head at herself in the mirror. No. Don't go there.

She pulled her tiny brush from her bag and tidied her hair, fluffing it out. It looked burnished in the warm light of the ladies' room. Nose powdered and lips refreshed with gloss, Viv heard the faint whispering: 'lovely.'

Viv swung round, but there was nobody but her. She turned back and stared into the mirror. A slight rustle at her side. She could have sworn she could feel a faint breath in her hair. She watched in the mirror and saw the movement of her hair as if blown by a gentle breeze, felt the soft caress of fingers at her cheek. She felt a sense of great love. Of smiling tenderness. For a fraction of a moment she saw … *thought* she saw a shadow in the glass, a shape beside her. Then, nothing. Just a shape on the air, which had gone as swiftly as it had appeared.

The ladies' room door opened, and a woman in jeans and a tight pink sweater stared curiously at her. Viv grabbed her make-up pouch and stuffed it back into her bag, as she smiled at the woman.

She smiled back and bent her head to one side. "Sorry, but aren't you Tilly's neighbour?"

"Yes, I am." Viv gathered up her bag, adjusting the drape of her silk scarf. "Are you a friend of hers?"

"Yeah. And colleague." She leaned in towards Viv. "I'm so sorry to hear about that rat of a husband of yours. What a bastard. But chin up. Better off without him, duckie."

So Tilly had spread the news.

"And I'm glad that gorgeous vicar's looking after you." The woman winked. Viv grabbed her jacket and headed for the door, trying to keep the smile on her face as it froze into a rictus grin. Breathing a sigh of relief as she slipped between the tables to where Rory was sitting, Viv cursed Tilly under her breath, and as she slipped into her seat opposite Rory, she told him quietly what had happened with the pink-sweater woman.

"Well. In some ways, I guess it's better than having to keep answering people's queries about where Pete is. They all already know." He reached across the table to touch her hand. Electricity leapt up her arm and left her breathless. "Less hassle for you, in the long run." He smiled and her heart stumbled. "White or red?"

Viv studied the menu to hide her flushed cheeks. "Ooh, let me see. It's a super menu. I think I fancy the beef stroganoff with brown and wild rice … or maybe the salmon in hollandaise sauce …?"

"Good choices. But I'm sticking with the good old steak and kidney pie."

"I always think," said Viv after they had chosen the wine and the waiter had taken their orders, "that it's better to choose something you couldn't or wouldn't make at home. Otherwise it seems so extravagant – if you can make it yourself for a fraction of the price! I don't often make stroganoff, that's why I settled on it."

"So you're a good cook – I mean as well as the flapjacks?" Rory sipped his red wine, raising his dark eyes above the rim of the glass. "Could you bake a great steak and kidney pie?"

"I think you'd have to ask someone else that! But I like cooking, and baking. When I have someone to cook for. I don't bother for myself. My mother taught me from an early age, then my grandmother … oh, that reminds me. The letter that was at the bank." She pulled it out of her bag and read it through again. "So mother was able to read some of the document in the safe files, and was planning to get her colleague to attempt a better translation after they returned from New York. It's odd. It almost seems that they had some kind of premonition that they may not return and wrote down their thoughts and plans before they went. Lodging it all in the bank safe is strange, though. As though they didn't trust anyone else, but me. And then, how could they possibly know that I would come to find it all in time?"

"Yes, that part is odd. A bit of a gamble. And of course you didn't go to the bank for many years. It could all have lain there forever."

"But it didn't," pondered Viv. "It all happened now. An opportune moment."

Their meals arrived and Viv was able to eat hers with a fork in her right hand and read out parts of the letter to Rory at the same time. "It says here that the document is, as we suspected, an odd mixture of Latin and Celtic. She says that it records the misdeeds of one Sir, or Lord, Pelleas, who appears to be a thegn of the chief Sir Tristram, husband of Lady Nymue and father of Lady Vivianne. It provides detailed and valuable evidence that Pelleas was responsible for the deaths of Tristram and his wife in a fire that he had set. Arson! Oh."

"And the document was written by ..?"

Viv scanned the page. "Oh. Sir Roland! And witnessed and confirmed by … Malloran, priest and spell-weaver, Arturius, high chief in Wales, and someone called …Hrothgar!" She looked across to Rory. "I know those names. Malloran was the name in the 'magic' medicine cave, and Hrothgar was the …"

"…the name of Tilda's father."

Viv caught her breath. "And Arturius was the one who they said blessed Hrothgar's son in battle. I always thought that Arturius was the origin of the King Arthur tales, a Celtic chief who stood against the Saxon, Angle and Jute invaders. Maybe so." She felt odd seeing the names written in her mother's handwriting in the late twentieth century, about these characters who peopled her 'dreams', her time-slips from the late fifth century. It made them real, actual people who lived that long ago in real time, not visions or ghosts. "They lived and breathed, these people."

"Didn't we know that?" smiled Rory, eating his pie with obvious relish.

"Yes, in a way. But the time-slips are so strange that I keep feeling a certain weirdness about it. A kind of *haunting*. I'm not sure whether this makes it better or even more weird!"

Rory rested his knife and fork on the edge of his plate and gulped down more of his wine. "So read me the part about the misdeeds of Sir Pelleas."

"She says that the document lists the reasons for the killing of Tristram and Nymue as evil, usurpation, and … er … ambition to become the chief of the settlement. It says he had no grounds for his claim to the chieftaincy, having come to the mead hall as a child, a lower warrior from the Saxon tribe in the south. It describes his vow of loyalty to Tristram as a lie. And it declares that the writer, Sir Roland, suspects that Pelleas desires to marry with Lady Vivianne in order to strengthen his claim to the mead hall."

"As we also suspected. Interesting."

"Yes. And my mother says that the document also claims that Pelleas is already betrothed secretly to another, 'a lady of deceit' who is in the trust of Lady Vivianne, and in this way they plan to deceive the whole village into believing that they are honourable, yet aim to bring the settlement into the control of the Saxons from the south."

"Phew. So maybe the purpose of all this is for us to ensure the document gets to Lady Vivianne and Sir Roland, so that they can reveal the evidence of Pelleas's treachery?"

"How?"

"Let me give it some thought. And in the meantime, Viv, please finish your stroganoff before it gets too cold."

*

"That was a lovely evening, thank you for suggesting it," said Viv as Rory opened the car door for her at her apartment's car park and helped her out, handing over her work briefcase from the boot. "But you should have let me pay half."

"Absolutely not. You'll find that I'm quite old-fashioned in some ways." He looked up at the security light. "And it looks as though that light's gone for a burton, so let me see you safely round to your door."

"I rather like 'old fashioned'," smiled Viv, feeling mellow after all that wine and discovery.

As she reached in her bag for the front door key, Rory touched her shoulder and a shiver ran through her body, a warm delicious shiver. Should she ask him in? Or would that send out the wrong vibes?

"And don't ask me in for coffee," said Rory quietly. "It might give me ideas I probably shouldn't have."

Viv let herself into her flat and gulped, standing still for a moment, her eyes closed. She struggled to suppress the longing for Rory to hold her, kiss her. What was she thinking? Pete had hardly slammed the door and there she was imagining herself with someone else. His wine bottles were hardly empty, his flapjacks barely eaten and there she was dreaming of the rector! It was all happening too quickly. Nothing good could come of this.

"For god's sake," she chided herself, throwing her keys on the table. "No, no. He's only undertaking his pastoral duties with a parishioner, being a good priest. I'm misinterpreting his words."

Yet she replayed his last comment before he opened the door for her and strolled away into the darkness. Ideas he probably shouldn't have? Did he really fancy her? But the wife! The wife!

She made a hot chocolate in her Tassimo and sunk onto the sofa to sip it. She made herself dwell on the conversation, not the man. Gorgeous, kind, caring, and sexy as he was … She forced herself to focus on her difficult decision. What was she to do about the chest of undoubtedly valuable artefacts and documents, if they were indeed genuine?

If she had them valued and they were genuine, she could be set to gain enough financially to buy the apartment from Pete, if she needed to. She had no idea what would happen about the property if his forgery was accepted as such, and therefore the document invalid. Presumably then she wouldn't have to buy him out? But if she had a fall-back plan, then at least she would feel safer. Then there wouldn't be any more hassle and she would be free, completely independent. It certainly would go a long way to delete Pete's horrible behaviour to her. She knew that she now felt no desire for him; his words and deeds had killed her love, and that even if, sometime in the future, she came to think of him with equanimity, she could never recapture that feeling she used to have for him as her partner. He needed now to go his way, and she hers. It even made her feel more in control that it could be possible for her to enable that to happen, of her own free will.

Even as she imagined she had decided to go down that route, she remembered Lady Vivianne, Sir Roland, the injustice of Sir Pelleas, who seemed no longer a 'Sir' in her mind. Viv, Rory, and Pete. As she thought about them all, they merged one into the other.

The room slipped and shifted. Dimly she heard the hall clock strike … was it eleven or twelve? A great sadness poured through her body. She drew in her ragged breath. She could hear the rustle of straw and saw a shadow at the door. Her cheeks were wet with tears and her heart was full with dread. She should have told him before he left. She should have said what she felt deep in her heart. So that he could stride away with that in his soul. All her upbringing which demanded restraint and dignity and level-headedness, all her parents' urgings to consider always the consequences of her actions, all of it swamped her heart and mind. And yet … and yet, she also heard her mother's voice softly whispering to her, "in the end, love is worth more than all else together, *my little Vivianne …little Viv …*"

Viv jerked back to her own reality. The sofa was firm and solid beneath her. She looked around at her apartment, the sitting room she loved to relax in, the furniture she had chosen with Pete, the mementoes of their travels, the reminders of her parents, the significant points in her life.

And she knew what she had to do.

Chapter 18

"You're crazy!"

"But you need the money to buy out Pete if you need to. *And* he doesn't deserve to have his own way!"

Ellie and Tilly's raised voices and wide gestures showed their feelings only too well.

"Are you really going to let him get away with it?"

"He's such a rat, hit back at him!"

Viv signalled them both to sit and passed the glasses of wine over to them from the tray on the coffee table. She switched on her iPod resting on the dock and the soothing sound of Mozart reached out to her. She sank in to an easy chair and lifted her glass to them. She had updated Ellie and Tilly about everything … well, everything except Rory and her feelings for him. That had to be kept a secret in her heart. She had made her decision about the treasures and she knew in her heart that her decision was the right one.

"No, I have come to a decision. I've really thought it through, believe me. And there are a lot of issues involved. I can't just 'keep the stuff', Tilly. It doesn't work like that."

"But to disappear it back to the dark ages – that's mad!"

"It's where it belongs." Viv felt a great calmness descend upon her as she said those words, and knew them to be true. "And Ellie, I'm only in the same position as I was before I found them."

"But it's your inheritance from your parents. They want you to have it. All this time-slip stuff is all about that. The chest, the treasure."

"No. I don't think it is, you see. I think it's about restoration and righting the wrongs of the past. My parents already left me an inheritance. I just used it wrongly. To support Pete's business venture. I didn't know what was going to happen. OK, it turned out to be misguided, in retrospect. But I did it out of love at the time. And that's what matters."

"So surely you have the means now to right the past in terms of Pete's actions." Tilly sighed.

Viv took a deep breath. "I can sort something out. Maybe it won't come to that, if it's proven that my signature was a forgery. After all, I have the tape recordings. But if not, I can sell the apartment and move somewhere else, even if it's a small temporary place until I get back on my feet. But I have the chance to do something I will be proud of. And I think that my parents would be proud of."

Tilly snorted. "I think that gorgeous hot vicar has invaded your brain, sweetie. All priestly 'doing the right thing'." She gulped her wine and flicked imaginary crumbs from her bright pink trackie bottoms.

"No. He has had nothing to do with my decision. Actually he tried to change my mind this morning."

Ellie placed her glass back onto the coffee table with deliberation and looked across to Viv. Her frown had lightened, but she still grimaced. "Well, if that's what you've decided to do, than obviously we'll support you all the way. If you're sure."

Viv smiled at her. "I am."

Tilly sighed loudly. "I still think it's crazy. I mean, the history's done, finished, caput. You can't change it. Whatever happened, happened. Whether this Lady Vivianne and Sir Roland got it together or not, whether they became the leaders or whatever, whether the settlement survived – all that has happened, nothing can change it, for good or bad."

"It's not about changing the whole course of history, though. But I suppose that depends on what you think history, time dimensions, time portals are all about." Viv leaned back in her armchair and bit her lip. What did she think about it, philosophically? Her whole view of the world had changed, inevitably. If time could be changed, why not history; after all … She wanted to talk to Rory about it, discuss the implications. She realised that she'd never been able to talk to Pete at that level.

She became aware that they had all slipped into thought-filled silence. Even Tilly was still.

"Look," Viv sighed. "The chest and the treasure have to be either donated to a museum or sent back to where they came from in 499. They aren't mine to sell and profit from. My mother says in her letter that they found the chest at the site of a settlement dating back to the late fifth century, behind a building that may have been either built partially of woven willow or was a willow weaver's house. My feeling is that I need to return it there and then, maybe, Lady Vivianne would have the evidence from the document that Sir Pelleas had won his place by foul means."

"It's an intriguing story, I'll grant you that," Tilly grunted. "But tell us again about what was in the chest and what the document said."

As Viv picked up her iPhone and began to point out the details of the contents of the chest, the helmet, the goblet, the cross …beautiful, gleaming, set with jewels she could only imagine the worth of … she closed her eyes, the better to recall what she had held in her own hands. To feel that helmet, with its crest and dragon embellishments, and to know that it, or something very much like it, had protected the head of the handsome, kind, loving, Sir Roland all those centuries ago. Had he survived the battle against the Pictish marauders, or had he died in the fighting? Had Sir Pelleas discovered him? Was he injured or did he return to Vivianne's arms?

What she did not tell them was that she had gone back to the bank that morning and withdrawn the chest, slipping it into a black bin bag, and taking it, much to the bank manager's consternation, in the boot of her car, back home. She smiled as she thought that the poor bank manager didn't even know exactly what was inside, or its significance. In her apartment, she tucked it to the back of her wardrobe, and instead of feeling anxious, she felt strong. It wasn't that she didn't trust her friends; it was simply that she felt a desire to keep the physical chest private at the moment.

Viv was aware that her iPod moved on from Mozart to Nella Fantasia. She told Ellie and Tilly about Hrothgar's house, the dark room lit only by the flames from the fire in the hearth at one end. And she remembered it all as it came back to her so vividly: Tilda, smiling in the flickering light, reaching out to her, then her expression concerned, frowning, and she herself feeling strange, dizzy, hot, her heart thrumming loudly in her ears, crumpling …

*

She felt nauseated and weak. A face peered into hers. She was aware that she lay on the floor, hard and damp beneath her. Inhaling slowly, she smelt smoke and the earthy odour of straw, animals, and manure. A pad of cloth beneath her nose, the sweet scent of lavender and camomile. She struggled to sit up and felt the heavy robes that dressed her body. Raising her hand she touched the soft fabric of her bodice, the furs around her neck and chest.

"My lady," came a gentle, young voice, "You fainted clean away. I managed to hold you and lower you to the ground so that you did not fall heavily and hurt yourself. Do you feel well now?"

"Y-yes, I thank you, Tilda. I seem to be making a habit of this. I seem to recall hearing strange noises and … oh, I do not know. Such peculiar things." Lady Vivianne rubbed her brow, feeling dazed. "A dark room that became light…"

"This room?"

"No." She looked around her. "No. I am sure of it. There was no flickering firelight. It was a room which had a light on the roof but it was constant; the flames did not move, a magic light, I think. A room with so much metal, like stacked boxes, and a … helmet? It is hazy, like the smoke of a fire … or a thick mist …" Vivianne shuddered.

"It is well now. You are safe here." Tilda watched as her mistress looked around the room; Lady Vivianne was taking it all into her mind and puzzling over it, frowning. "We are in my father's house, my lady."

"Yes, of course. I know that. But I do not know … it was so vivid …" Vivianne struggled to raise herself and Tilda helped her to her feet. She brushed her robe and cloak, smoothed the furs and took a deep breath. "Any news of the warriors?"

Tilda's brow wrinkled. "No, my lady. They only left a short while ago. They had to claim their horses from the stables behind the mead hall so they will have only set off a few breaths ago. They will still be riding out to the borderlands."

Lady Vivianne crossed herself and bent her head. "Then I pray that he … they return safely."

"Indeed, Lady Vivianne," came Hrothgar's deep crackling voice as he entered through the low doorway and stomped into the room. "He found Sir Tristram's stallion and has ridden out at such a gallop that I am sure he has joined the back of the throng. They head for the forests at the border."

Hrothgar glanced over to Vivianne and said low, "Lady Vivianne, I need to give you something which I pray will help you when Sir Pelleas returns from battle." He rummaged in the willow chest and, grunting, lifted out an object wrapped in a russet cloth. He brought it over to Vivianne and carefully opened the folds of the cloth. He held it up to her.

"An amulet!" she whispered. "But it has Sir Pelleas's name upon it." She looked up quizzically at Hrothgar. The old man turned it over and Vivianne saw the sign of Malveus the pagan devil, its amber skull with black jet at its eye sockets.

"He has sold his soul to the evil pagan cult, my lady, I am sure of it. I found this in his chamber when I delivered baskets just before he was voted as chief. I slipped it into my pouch as a protection against any retribution to your parents' loyal followers after their death. I have not needed to reveal it. But I know it is here for Mathilda and myself. If Pelleas and his men turn against us, I can defend us with it. And, of course, yourself and the faithful Sir Roland."

Vivianne bit her lip and lowered her head in thought. "I heard tell a long time ago, tales of the malicious Malveus whom no man has ever seen, and of the mysterious pagan ceremonies when Saxon men took the goblet of wine and cut each other's wrists with their axes, dripping their blood into a charmed dish to mix their life blood with the others of evil intent."

"They say that many a Saxon has given his life to Malveus. And that they sold their souls to him for power. Many claimed Celtic and Brython settlements, and even Roman, as their own and seemed untouchable."

"Then he means great harm to me, to my family, to my helpers." Vivianne looked towards Tilda.

"My lady, I will never leave you. I will fight for you even though I die."

"I hope to goodness that never has be your choice, little Tilda." Vivianne smiled at the furious expression on her maid's features. "And Hrothgar, do you think, then, that Pelleas had a hand in my parents' death?"

Hrothgar grimaced and nodded slowly. "I do indeed. I saw Pelleas and his men that day, with brands, approaching the sacred hall when Sir Tristram was at his prayers within. I shouted but I thought that nobody heard me. Then one of his traitors grabbed me and I thought I was to be killed. One of his look-outs at the edge of the village ran up to tell them that Lady Nymue was returning early from the mere and my captor threatened that if I spoke what I saw, he would ravish and kill my wife and my daughter. And God forgive me, I kept my silence. Who would believe me, a poor willow-weaver, against them, anyway?"

"And my mother saw the fire and ran into the sacred hall to my father. They would have died together at the altar." Vivianne fought to check her tears. "And Sir Roland?"

"He was not much older than you, my lady, but enough to have already just been initiated in the Witan and made a man. He had recently come in to his inheritance and title, but he had been out hunting and had not seen what happened at the sacred hall. It was a time of great fear, whispering and uncertainty. He listened to me and we decided to write down our knowledge and beliefs. It was all we could do - so that others after us would know. We signed our names and also your mother's guide, Malloran, committed his to the document, for the magic. He said that he had seen it all in a vision. Then we sealed it and it was hidden. We were able to slide it under the lid of the locked chest, your father's Vortigern chest which Sir Roland kept secretly. We vowed we would use it when the right time came."

"And the right time never came?"

"Oh, it came, many times, but of course we could not open the chest to retrieve it. It needed the true magic of Lady Nymue's kin to open it. She had cast a spell upon it to protect Sir Tristram's treasure."

"But I ...?"

"We needed to be mindful of utmost caution, my lady. You were a child, and especially vulnerable. We had to bide our time and weigh up the dangers, for you especially." He grimaced. "Perhaps we were wrong and waited too long."

"And since then you have kept your faith together and your secret?"

"All to ensure your safety, Lady Vivianne. We suspected what Pelleas was planning – to marry you when you came of age, and gain final justification for the Witan council's vote in his favour as chief. We saw that just before the voting, a large group of Saxons appeared in the village. Pelleas welcomed them as his friends and worthy inhabitants and protectors of our settlement. It is said, in whispers, that they entered the council hall as the thegns gathered and they made so much noise with beating their axes against their shields that they drowned out any opposition. I do not know. I was not there."

Vivianne saw that Hrothgar surreptitiously wiped a tear from his cheek, and she reached to his arm and touched it gently.

"But I do fear," he continued, his voice breaking, "that he plans to make the settlement into a cult village, for Malveus. Your parents' heritage and influence would be destroyed and the place recreated with entirely different values. It breaks my heart."

"I see that already happening, though it takes a long time to change a community like that. But the memories of my parents are fading for many but the most loyal."

"I think that there are more of us than you imagine, my lady," said Tilda eagerly. "We await a sign, and then I believe that Pelleas will be overcome and good will prevail."

"I do so hope that you are right, little Tilda."

*

Vivianne returned to her chamber with Tilda. The village seemed quiet, ominously so. The sun was sinking and there was a chill in the air. She watched the deep shades of orange and burnished red streaked across the darkening sky. They looked like splashes of blood, and Vivianne prayed that it was not an omen.

She knew that if Sir Pelleas returned victorious and won again the acclaim of the people, if Sir Roland was in any way hurt or weakened, then it would be the beginning of the end for her parents' heritage. And the settlement would become more firmly Pelleas's and would be a place that she did not want to live in and could not support. Whatever happened, she also knew now that there was no way on this earth that she could be married to Sir Pelleas. She would have to flee and perhaps try to make a home somewhere else. She wondered if Roland might feel the same way. But, of course, if Pelleas had any notion of her thoughts, she and Roland would never even make the border alive. Unconsciously, she tugged at her robe in distress as she walked through the quiet pathways towards her hall.

Her chamber was dark and cold. Tilda set about laying a fire and lighting the torches on the walls. She settled Vivianne, deep in her thoughts, on the seat by the fire and poured wine into a goblet to warm her. Vivianne gestured to Tilda to pour some for herself, but the maid, clearly mindful of convention and place, shook her head. But Vivianne insisted and finally Tilda did as she was commanded. While the wine

184

settled, she drew back the covers on the bed and took her lady's bed wear from the chest under the window. Tenderly, she refolded the shift and placed it at the end of the bed along with furs to ward off the chill.

Vivianne pointed to the seat at the other side of the fire and when Tilda hesitated, she rose, picked up the goblet of wine from the top of the chest and guided her maid firmly to the fireside.

"Tilda, I feel that times are changing. I hope and pray that it is for the better, but I have determined to spend the coming days at prayer. I shall make a small altar from my wooden chest and a kneeling step from my maid-stool, and here I shall devote myself to prayer and to bringing those loyal to us back safely from the battle. There is no danger in doing so openly, because Sir Pelleas and all his men are at the fighting place. But I would be glad if you would bring me sustenance and tend to me."

"Of course, my lady. You know that I will be happy to do that for you. And …" Mathilda hesitated, "…I shall be pleased to join you at prayer, if I may?"

Vivianne smiled. "With the greatest of pleasure. I shall be glad of the company, even in my silence."

*

Lady Vivianne had no idea how much time had passed. She only knew that every day and all day long she knelt at the little altar, covering her eyes, opening them only to gaze again at the little cross her mother had given her and which she had propped up against the wall. She ate the food that Tilda brought her, in quiet reflection, just as she received the words every day that told her there was no news from the battlefield. She knew from her maid that the men who provided the sustenance for the village, the bakers, the cooks, and the farmers remained at their duties, as did those who were needed for maintenance work, the leather and metal workers, the potters and weavers. But otherwise the settlement was quiet and often the only activity on the streets was the chatter of the women at their gatherings to report any news or gossip.

Whenever she could between her tasks, Tilda kneeled beside Lady Vivianne, and together they felt stronger.

Then, as Lady Vivianne prayed her morning devotions, she heard a noise. A lone rider, by the sound of it. She and Tilda looked at each other with fear. Quickly, Vivianne rose, crossed herself, smoothed her robe and slipped quietly outside with Tilda close behind, breathing heavily.

Dust rose in billows as the horse and rider approached along the holloway, easing speed as he came to the village street. Then Vivianne saw that he held aloft the banner of Sir Pelleas, and heard his shouts.

"Sir Pelleas and his thegns return. Victory is won. The Picts are forced back to the higherlands. Our lands are safe again!"

Cheers and clapping broke out as villagers came out to the street to hear the news, but Vivianne turned to Tilda with a heavy heart.

"Oh Tilda, I am glad but fearful, so very fearful, now." She shook her head and bit her lip until she tasted blood. "And I wait to see Sir Roland back safely again."

"My lady, there is nothing we can do. Let me make you some mulled wine on the fire. It will help to soothe you."

"I must hide the altar now that Sir Pelleas and his thegns will return. Quick. Help me. The herald is not usually far in front of the warriors."

*

They heard horses' hooves as the host returned to the settlement, their noise seeming to echo across the village, and they glanced fearfully at each other. They were sitting by the fire sipping mulled wine as there came a loud knock on the door. Without waiting for a response, Sir Pelleas's side thegn lumbered inside, his cheeks red and forehead dripping with sweat. He bore fresh wounds to his face, still bleeding, and held his left arm awkwardly. Vivianne hardly had time to rise from her stool before he bowed peremptorily to her and said, "Lady, you are summoned to the mead hall. You will have heard of the victory and securing of our boundaries from the Picts, but my lord Sir Pelleas has other announcements to make." He bowed again and was gone.

Vivianne caught her breath. What of Sir Roland? Where was he? Had Sir Pelleas discovered him, hurt him, imprisoned him again – or worse?

"My lady, we should do as we are commanded. Otherwise worse may follow." Tilda wrapped a dull brown hessian cloak around Vivianne's shoulders, hoping, she suspected, for them to be hidden in the crowd at the mead hall.

But that was not to be. As soon as she entered the hall, Sir Pelleas approached her, arms wide open as if to embrace her. She stopped. Pelleas hesitated only for a moment, before quickly side-stepping her and, flinging an arm firmly around her back, swept his left arm expansively to the gathered thegns, shouting out, "See, my beautiful lady comes to welcome me home, to celebrate with me my victory and to rejoice in our union!" He gripped her shoulder so hard that she winced. He noticed and pulled her head round to meet his kiss. His lips were soft and wet against hers and he pushed his tongue into her mouth so far that she almost gagged. As he withdrew slightly he breathed into her face, "Do not dare to move away. Do not dare to show anything but devotion to me. I am watching you."

His threat made Vivianne shiver.

"See!" Pelleas turned aside and shouted to his assembled thegns. "She shivers with desire for me. She tells me that she cannot wait for my bed!"

The thegns, high with their victory and the thrust of battle, roared with lusty delight and banged their spears on the floor so that Vivianne felt the ground beneath her shaking.

"You will move with me to the dais," Pelleas growled into her ear, gripping her tighter and pushing her towards the raised section at the end of the hall.

"Your fingernails are bruising me, sir," Vivianne spat between clenched teeth. "You hurt me." She tried to wriggle away but the more she moved, the more he dug his nails into her.

"Ha! But you know nothing. Wait until you are in my bed."

He pushed her onto the seat on the dais and glared his warning at her before turning to the room. "I have brought you victory over the enemy! And I have vanquished the enemies within!"

Vivianne's heart stopped. Did he mean Sir Roland? Was he found?

"And now we will have a queen, a Lady for the Chieftain. My lady Vivianne and I marry tomorrow!"

Vivianne swooned.

Chapter 19

"Sit up!" hissed Pelleas into Vivianne's face, so close that she felt his spittle on her cheeks as she was shaken to consciousness by his rough hands. He paused a moment to signal to his herald scōp to proclaim the victory and, numb with horror, she heard the clear timbre of the poet begin to tell of the lord Pelleas's bravery and cunning in the face of the brutal barbaric Pictish hordes, his great leadership when warriors hesitated and he thrust forth into the spears of the enemy.

"Sir Pelleas with spear-hand aloft gave the cry for the arrow-warriors to draw back their arrow-arms and let fly the sharp-tipped feather-sped weapons into the devilish hordes," he sang. "Over the stockades they flew faster than the galloping horse or the swooping eagle, and into the swarm of barbaric infidels. Cowardly cries of the dying barely whimpered above the beating of the drums and the roar of spears on shields. The shield-wall moved forwards and, spears aloft, Pelleas's men, following his own valour, broke through the crumbling defence, and charged."

Sir Pelleas turned from Vivianne to acknowledge the cheers and shield banging of his warriors. She realised that she had been holding her breath and drew air into her lungs, though it tasted of sweat and dirt and deception. He stood in front of her to hide her from view in case her expression revealed her distaste. But as she peered around him she could see that the hall was not full of warriors, that those in front of Pelleas stood in thin lines spread across the hall, sturdy fighting men with loud voices. Behind them stood a crowd of villagers, quietly listening to the scōp, like the still, carved figures in the sacred hall. Vivianne had not seen the warriors' return, but surely they had not all come into the hall for their lord. Where were the rest?

Her mind was on the fate and whereabouts of Sir Roland as the scōp finished his song. Then a roar went up to the rafters of the great hall and as Sir Pelleas stepped to the side, she could see that two warriors handed Pelleas a huge banner. It bore the symbol of the red dragon.

"I, your lord Pelleas, have captured this banner from the Pictish enemy on the battlefield as a sign of my ... of our victory. The very banner they had stolen two Beltains ago from the Welsh drawn up to the north to battle. This shall be hung in this mead hall as a sign of our greatness. And above it shall be hung my helm to remind you all of my leadership in battle."

"No!" came a strong voice from the back of the hall, and as Pelleas moved to see the intruder, Vivianne saw that it was Sir Roland, and she gasped. His eye was badly cut and dried blood streaked his face and neck; dirt caked his hair and his robes were filthy and torn. But he was alive. He strode through the crowd and they parted for him in bewilderment. "He stole it by stealth as he skulked around the rear guard of the Pictish horde."

"This is nonsense!" shouted Pelleas, red-faced and sweating heavily. Vivianne could see the dark wet patches beneath the armpits of his robe. "Do not believe this *ceorl*," he spat. But Vivianne could hear the bluster in his voice, the trembling.

"Certainly he fought some of the enemy. But it was from behind as they advanced and he stole the banner from the young bugle boy whom he thought kept it and whom he killed with one slash of his spear, beheading him from the back."

There was an audible gasp across the mead hall.

"This is not honour," a voice was heard to call.

"It is untrue. Lies. Evil lies," shouted Pelleas.

"But, you see, Pelleas, warriors, thegns and all, as I rode to join the battle, I had seen the ambush that Pelleas had allowed his men to face, and I also saw Pelleas lurking at the rear, reluctant to follow his men into the trap. I guessed what was to befall and galloped around through the woodland to the enemy rear guard. They were pushing forward and so I was able to drop the Welsh banner behind to see if Pelleas would be such a coward as to pretend he had won it. God knows, it is mine!"

"You ridicule me! How dare you, Roland. Your words are lies!"

The crowd turned to Sir Roland who had made his way to the front and stood before Pelleas, his feet planted firmly apart and his head held high.

"It is mine," Roland insisted, "because it was my father's. I swear before God. But if you doubt me, look at the bottom right hand corner and you will find my family's crest, and beside it the Welsh shield of

Arturius from my mother's side. My father and Arturius fought together."

Then Pelleas made his mistake. He hesitated and in that moment, the headman of the Witan council stepped past the warriors and held the right side of the banner up. He dropped the banner and turned to the crowd.

"It is true. These crests are exactly where Sir Roland proclaims."

"But he … he was not at the battle!" Pelleas's voice shook.

"Yes, he was!" came voices in the doorway. Everyone turned to look. Several warriors stood at the back of the hall and Vivianne could see many more behind, outside the building. Pelleas's warriors raised their spears and axes, but the council headman lifted his hands.

"There will be no drawn spears or axes in the mead hall. Those who do so will be damned as we all know."

Slowly they let their weapons drop. From the back of the hall, the warrior spokesman said in a loud voice which echoed round the great room. "It is as Sir Roland says. Those of us near to him saw all this. But we saw a man clad in unknown cloak and helmet. We did not know then that it was indeed Sir Roland. He rode back round to our troops and gave us the command for the rear flanks to retreat to a point where they were able to wing to the left and right, whilst the enemy advanced into the ambush valley. Sir Roland led the charge through to attack them there and the wings converged again and followed on. We routed them. They fled. And Sir Pelleas having escaped the other way round, massacred the rearguard of the enemy from behind as they fled and was able to steal the dragon banner as if it had been won nobly in battle."

"That is madness!" shouted Pelleas, stamping his heavy feet so that the dais shook. Vivianne trembled knowing that Pelleas would never allow his traitors to win. Deep voices echoed him across the hall and Vivianne realised that she was chewing the inside of her mouth in confusion and fear.

But all except a few of Pelleas's closest thegns hesitated, and a low confused murmuring broke out in the hall. Then the first warrior's voice rose above them. "You saved your own skin at the expense of your men. You left Sir Roland to face death in the fight. It was he who won the honourable victory!"

Vivianne gasped and at once Pelleas swung round towards her. He grabbed her round the neck and pulled her up from the seat and round in front of him, his left arm immobilising her body against him, his right raising his spear. She bent her arms and scrabbled to reach his arm, clawing at him, but he only laughed. It was only then, that, facing the crowd, and her eyes sweeping the faces, she saw a fearful Guin at the side of the hall, biting her lip. Their eyes met, and Vivianne saw the hesitation, the doubt, and did she also see a glimpse of shame? But Vivianne realised in that moment that Pelleas was fully intending to marry her for the security of his position and to keep Guin as his bed partner, using herself only as perhaps a breeding mare.

"There is nothing on this earth that will induce me to marry you, Pelleas. You can kill me first," she whispered, her voice straining against his arm which pressed against her throat. "Your world is falling apart, Pelleas!"

And with that, she pushed her rear against him, hoping to break his hold but realising with a sharp intake of breath that he was actually aroused. "Hmm, I do desire a fiery one," he spat into her ear.

She raised her knee and kicked her foot back and upwards with as much force as she could muster, and even through her robes she could feel the point of contact. She heard the winded out-breath as he doubled up behind her and his arm released her neck. Gathering up her skirts, she jumped from the dais and ran.

"I have more proof! I shall bring it to the mead hall," she called back. "Evidence to damn him to eternity!"

The crowd fell back and as she rushed past Roland she knew that he turned to follow her. As she ran through the great door of the mead hall, she heard the voices raised again as the crowd turned back to Pelleas, moving in to surround him and his warriors.

A wind was gathering and she saw the dust of the roadway rising up and swirling. In her mind voices were melding together. Her mother. Someone else, a strange voice, muffled and indistinct, drifting in and out, louder and softer. She stumbled, but she felt strong hands catch her and Roland seemed to bear her along as she fled towards Hrothgar's house and to the back, and to the midden. She did not need to say anything to him, as she dropped to the ground and scrabbled at the earth to uncover the chest. He held her back and found a digging implement at the side of the midden, thrusting it again and again into the soil.

He dug and dug. But there was nothing.

"It was here. I know it was," said Roland, pushing the metal again into the earth. "This where Hrothgar and I buried it."

"Where is it? Has someone stolen it? How could that be? The earth is not disturbed."

"Oh, Vivianne. My love."

Vivianne stood up straight and fell into his open arms, and he held her close, stroking her back in comfort as her tears coursed down her cheeks.

Chapter 20

She tasted the saltiness of her tears and the gentle stroking at her shoulders.

"Viv! Viv, are you OK?"

The fogginess of her mind began to clear and Viv struggled to open her eyes, blinking away the fear that had seemed to consume her. She took a deep breath and then released it sharply. The voices of first Ellie, and then Tilly, registered as if from far away.

"She's coming round."

"God, that was weird. She sort of went into a trance for a moment."

"She fainted."

"Viv!"

She shuddered. "Phew. That was … goodness …"

"Did you do this time slip thing again?" Ellie and Tilly's faces retreated from hers as they sat down again on the sofa. Viv glanced around her. All was normal. As it should be. It was almost as if she expected the fears to follow her, but they hadn't. The clock was ticking. The music from her iPod dock continuing its steady beat in the background. Nella Fantasia.

"Yes, it's taken my breath away." Her voice in her own ears sounded gravelly even to herself.

"Here." Ellie held a glass of wine under her nose and she shifted up in her armchair and grasped the stem, taking a welcome gulp. Her throat felt sore and somehow flattened as if a strong pressure had been applied to it. She raised her hand to rub it; it felt quite tender under her fingers.

"Oh, golly goodness," breathed Tilly, peering at her, head to one side. "Your neck looks really red and … kinda like someone's strangled you."

"I need to speak with Rory," Viv said, draining her glass. Tilly immediately filled it again, although Viv signalled 'no'. Jerkily, she tried to tell them about what had just happened to her.

"So time moved on – what? – several days at least, in 499 while Lady Vivianne awaited, praying, the end of the battle?" puzzled Ellie. "I thought this time slip was instantaneous. Or the same time movement as … as here?"

"It's not the same time movement as here," mused Viv. "I knew that already, although, yes, a passage of many days *is* odd. I mean I hadn't experienced that before. But it was as though time was irrelevant, Lady Vivianne was hardly aware of time passing, I felt. Maybe that matters."

"What happens now? Ouch, got an itch." Tilly pulled her top away from her bosoms and peered down. She delved in and retrieved a pea, which she placed on the coffee table, still frowning down into her top. "Pesky things, peas. That's my egg fried rice dinner for you. Wow, d'you know I can't even see my tum down here. Beyond my boobs. Great obstructions. Too dark. But I know it's there."

"Yes!" Viv jumped up. "That's it! Wonderful, Tilly." She grabbed her neighbour and bent to plant a kiss on her head. "I'm going to ring Rory and see if he can come over right now. We have something vital to do." She reached for her mobile from the coffee table.

"Viv, do you know what time it is? Eleven. You can't ring and summon him over this late."

But Viv was already listening to the ring tone, the mandolin *Nella Fantasia*. It suddenly cut out and a croaky female voice answered. Viv startled then plunged ahead.

"Is … is that Mrs Netherbridge?" Viv heard both her friends' sharp intake of breath. "Er … I'm so sorry to disturb you so late but I think it's rather important. Is your … is the reverend available? It's Viv DuLac here."

"Oh yes, he's spoken about you." Mrs Netherbridge was suffering from a heavy cold. Her voice was nasal and deep, almost like a man. "He's still up, working on his computer. I'll just call him. One moment."

"Hello? Viv? Are you OK?"

"Yes, Rory. But there's something we have to do. Quickly."

"I know. I'll be over there in five." The line went dead.

*

Rory was true to his word and only just over five minutes later he was ringing the doorbell. Even as she opened her mouth to explain, he raised his forefinger to her lips and said, "No need. I know."

Viv nodded and showed him where the bulging black bag was hidden. He lifted it out and carried it round to his car.

"I can't come with you," said Ellie, "I must get back home, Stuart's baby-minding, it's very late and anyway, it feels really creepy, even more creepy than before, and I think I've had enough of creepiness."

"No, me too," shivered Tilly. "It's all so weird. No, actually over the edge of weirdness. Sorry, sweetie-pie. Count me out this time."

As Rory drove her towards the Wilmingham site, Viv felt her heart pounding. She touched her pocket and sighed. Rory turned to her and said, "Are you OK with this? Is it really what you want to do?"

"Yes, absolutely. I've thought about it so much. It's the right thing to do."

She caught Rory's smile and turned back to look at the dark road ahead. She did not know where her own personal road led, whether there was darkness ahead, but maybe that's what it was all about. You can't see it, but you know it's there.

Viv felt Rory reach out to her and place his warm hand on her knee, as if he knew. How could someone she had barely got to know, make her feel as though she had known him forever? How could someone, when she had lost her trust in men, make her feel that she trusted him implicitly? He would be her friend, her close friend, for always, she knew it. They connected, on a different level, a higher level, than she had ever reached before with anyone. That was enough. Her heart filled with a simple peace. The gesture said to her that he was with her, supported her. He did not need to say those words. His warmth and strength flowed into her being. It no longer mattered exactly where they were headed. She would be OK.

The Jag jolted over a rough bump in the road as they diverted onto the narrow lane and Viv laughed, "I think you'd better keep both hands on the wheel!"

Rory pulled up at the edge of the wood. He handed her a torch and carried the chest, wrapped in its dark covering, as they slowly took cautious footsteps along the holloway, the trees reaching gnarled witches' fingers over their heads. It seemed to Viv that they were protecting them, the carriers of history, of salvation. Viv swung the torch from side to side a little so that they did not trip on the exposed roots or stray from the pathway. With her other hand she felt the objects in her pocket, holding them safe. Above their footsteps, she heard the wind rustling in the tree tops, gently as if encouraging them on their way. She heard soft whispers, voices calling low, measured and somehow comforting.

Footfalls at her back. Viv swung around, her torch searching behind. But there was nothing, only darkness as the path to the ancient village swallowed them in its air. Rory hesitated too, until she swung the torch back to light up their way ahead. The footfalls passed them and ran off into the dark night. Yet Viv's torch illuminated nothing but the empty path in front of them.

"OK?" whispered Rory at her side.

"Yes, fine." She sensed his smile.

The briefest glimpse of a russet robe whisking into the trees.

A voice like a wave smoothly creeping into her and pulling out again, filled her head, guiding them onwards. Her feet seemed to move of their own accord. Tiny lights, like fireflies, danced ahead, calling them on.

The overarching protecting trees shrank back and the clearing opened out before them.

"Shine the torch ahead," whispered Rory. "Yes, there. Look."

Viv could make out the pottery, the cross in the moist peaty earth. The portal. Rory bent down and lowered the chest just in front of the markings of the cross. They knelt down.

"You know," he said, "I was reading that the rich soil of the river valley, the reed beds that we saw back there in the daylight, make ideal conditions for preserving ancient artefacts, even timber structures, textiles, leather. No wonder your parents were so excited about the finds here. I should think it was like touching the lives of the past. It's like York, similar conditions – and even more so up there."

"I'd like to find out more about their discoveries, what happened, what it was like."

"Before …" Rory began. "I need to tell you. I also read up about the Lady of the Lake. Those names Vivien, Vivianne, Nymue, and indeed, Elaine, are names associated not only with the Arthurian Lady of the Lake but also with the Water God."

"That rings a bell! They were the spirits of the mere, linked with magic and certainly capable of doing things that would have been inexplicable in those days. Oh, and Nymue is even named as walking out of the mere without being wet." Viv closed her eyes. An image of Lady Vivianne as a child watching idly as her mother rose from the mere like a spirit. And cuddling against her on the horse, the cloak warm, dry, comforting. Yet Lady Vivianne's clothes were wet from the lake. And her own, too, from the mere. Maybe the "magic" was dissipating.

"Rory? Something I'm puzzling about … it seems that I'm a distant descendent of Lady Vivianne …"

"Ye – es,"

"And that link, as well as maybe having been through a traumatic experience with Pete, may have been a trigger to my time-slip into the body of Lady Vivianne."

"Ye – es."

"But what about you?"

"In terms of …?" He seemed to shrink away from her a little.

"Well, do you think that you're a distant descendent of Sir Roland?"

"Ah!" Rory exhaled sharply. "That link." Then he reached an arm around her shoulders. "I really don't know. Maybe someday I'll find out that I am. Perhaps I should do some investigation. But in a sense, to me, it doesn't matter as much as the other things I'm interested in, no, *absorbed* by - magic, miracles, religious rituals. Are they all, maybe, very close to each other? There are things we can't explain. We look for the answer – how did he do that? How did that trick work? All must be explained, have a logical reason in the real world – whatever the real world is. But does that actually matter? As Shakespeare said, 'there are more things in heaven and earth, Horatio, than are dreamt of in your philosophy.'"

Viv leaned her head onto his shoulder. "Things beyond our comprehension," she murmured, and he squeezed her arm. "I'm getting less and less able to distinguish. I hardly know what we mean by 'real' anymore."

"Understandable. And of course I've always dabbled in the 'unreal' world - religion. That's my calling." His voice seemed to trail off as if he was deep in thought.

They knelt like that for a while until Viv shivered. "You're getting cold," said Rory, "OK, let's do it. The task we came to do."

Viv slipped her hand into her pocket and took out the silver cross. Carefully she slid the bag off the chest and raised the lid, gently sliding it under the green cloth inside, along with the goblet, the large crucifix and the helmet. Now they were all together again, and she snapped the lock closed once more. She took a deep breath and together they slid the chest onto the cross carved in the earth. With their hands still upon the wooden lid, Rory whispered a blessing and a prayer for its safekeeping and return to its true owners. In her head, Viv called to her mother, and Lady Vivianne, and Lady Nymue, to receive it and use it well. She closed her eyes as she felt Rory's hand slide onto hers, warm, comforting.

She saw behind her eyes … tears, a thin faint light slipping through the darkness, growing as it approached her, becoming more intense, enfolding her in warmth and glowing like the sunrise.

She felt the chest move beneath her fingers, yet somehow she could still feel the warmth of the wood, the shape of the clasp and the lock.

But she knew that it had slipped away to where it truly belonged.

Chapter 21

Lady Vivianne became aware that Roland's hand on her back had stopped its stroking. She raised her eyes, still wet, to his dear face and followed his gaze. A flash of gold glinted. He dropped down to his knees and she knelt beside him. He reached out and brushed the earth away. The chest. Roland lifted it up out of the soil and stared at it.

"I could have sworn …!" he began, but did not finish his sentence.

Lady Vivianne was scrabbling the soil away as if the earth tainted it. Her trembling fingers found the key in her pouch and she slipped it into the lock. Slowly she lifted the lid, and slid the green cloth away. She gasped and crossed herself, unable to speak.

She caressed the pieces inside and shook her head in wonder.

Roland reached across her and pulled out a document. "What do we have here?"

He opened it out and frowned as he read. Vivianne leaned in to peer over his shoulder. She knew what it was. Hrothgar was right. "Can you read it?" she croaked. "These words are strange. Or perhaps it is the way of the writing."

"Yes. It is written in the Romans' language with some of the Celtic vernacular words. And I know it. I signed it. See, here." He pointed to the signatures at the foot of the page. "My own hand, and that of Hrothgar and Malloran."

"It is as Hrothgar told me. And it declares …?"

Roland grinned. "It tells us that Sir Pelleas has been completely discredited with no hope. He is no more. His hold is utterly broken." He hugged Vivianne to him. He read it out to her and translated to the local Brythen-Celtic language she was more familiar with. "We have your evidence."

"And Hrothgar also has …" There was a movement behind her and she swivelled round and stood up. "Hrothgar?"

"Here it is. Pelleas's amulet in proof, too." Hrothgar pressed it into her palm. "Have this to prove his intentions for our beloved home. And go!"

"Yes. We must take these to the mead hall immediately. When the Witan hears this …" Roland leapt to his feet, but Vivianne restrained him.

"Wait. Let us hide the chest safely away. We only need to take the document."

Quickly the two men carried the chest into Hrothgar's house and hid it under the straw of the animals' bedding, where Roland himself had hidden. He enticed the sheep to lie over it, with bribes of food.

"Now go, quickly." Hrothgar ushered them off, flapping his old hands. "And return in due course to tell me the outcome."

*

The mead hall was still echoing with angry voices and shuddering with the thrusting of spears in the air, ignoring the head of the council's efforts to stop them. Back on the dais, Pelleas was surrounded by his men, guarding him from the others crowding them in. As Lady Vivianne and Sir Roland entered the hall the mob at the back began to turn and as they did so, they fell silent. Bit by bit, the voices grew still as the pair moved forward and the crowd parted for them. Even Pelleas's men hesitated. They stepped up onto the dais where everyone could see them, and Pelleas and his men seemed to shrink back.

Vivianne unfurled the document and held it up. She was aware of all the eyes upon her, and her voice almost faltered. Her task now was great and she no longer had the passion of fury to strengthen her words. She cleared her throat and thought of her mother and her father, and then her melodic tones rang out across the hall.

"This, as those closest to me can see," she said, as she turned the paper over and necks craned forward, "is the original document, signed and sealed with the stamp of five years ago just after the tragic and untimely death of my parents, Sir Tristram and his queen, Lady Nymue. It tells of Sir Pelleas's treachery. He started the fire in the sacred hall, which killed them."

The hall erupted with gasps and shouts.

"Lies!" screamed Pelleas, and his men echoed him. "Why would I do that?"

"Because you wanted to give our settlement over to the cult of Malveus. You wanted to sell us." Horrified gasps filled the air and she held something above her head, "This is the amulet of Malveus with Pelleas's name engraved upon it, to prove the document."

"That object is not mine!"

Angry yells reverberated from the walls and spears were shaken aloft. Vivianne raised her hand for quiet.

"This document here is true and it is signed by Sir Roland …"

"Pah" shouted Pelleas, "*He's* the traitor. Perhaps *he* started the fire."

"And Hrothgar …" the hall became quieter, "And Malloran, my mother's guide …"

"And me, Arturius," came a strong ringing voice from the doorway at the back of the mead hall.

The crowd gasped and swung round to see a huge giant of a man at the door. Vivianne thought that she could see a shimmering aura around him. It may have been only the light behind him from the open doorway, but she drew in her breath in awe at the sight. He bore no shining arms but a long staff, and he commanded the room as if he had a thousand men behind him. The whispers flooded the hall. "Arturius. The High King Arturius."

He held up his hand and immediately the hall became silent. He seemed to hold everyone in his thrall. How strange was his appearance here at this particular moment of her need? But then she remembered her mother's words: "he is my magic, he and Malloran" she used to say although little Vivianne had no idea what she meant. Now Vivianne felt a power emanating from this man as if he were not a human being like the rest of them, but one of the ancient gods, some supreme being who filled their hearts with, not fear, but awe. Every person in that place was waiting for this man's next words, even a silenced Pelleas. Arturius lowered his hand and swept his searing gaze from one side of the hall to the other, taking in every person, every heart. The tension was palpable.

"I have seen enough evidence here from our strong and brave Lady Vivianne," he began, his voice resounding to the rafters, "to intervene in the affairs of your settlement. I was not High King when I witnessed that document," he nodded towards Lady Vivianne, "but I am now. And I would say to you, Pelleas, and your henchmen, that you need to go from here and never step over these boundaries again. I will personally see to it that you do."

Pelleas lifted his head to the rafters and let out a great roar, like a captured animal surrounded by the hunting dogs. He swore and cursed them all, especially Arturius, and even his own men gasped at the blasphemy of his words. He raised his spear-arm in defiance and charged towards the door of the hall, eyes looking neither left nor right, but screaming "I curse you all!"

"Pelleas," the vigorous voice of Arturius rang out. Pelleas paused and turned to Arturius. "In your pride you have dealt great evil here. You have with deliberation tried to destroy the true order of the people's lives. But unfortunately for you the line remains in Lady Vivianne, and she, along with Sir Roland, whom you tried to ruin, will lead this good community to high endeavour and abundance. I have no use of you. And I brand you for ever more." He flourished his staff and Pelleas's hand flew to his right cheek where a jagged black wound appeared, the sign of evil cut into his flesh. The crowd gasped.

Pelleas swung round and threw a glare of hatred towards Vivianne, then turned and strode from the hall. Her heart was beating so strongly that she thought she might faint. She could breathe the taint of malevolence left in his wake, and she shuddered. His men hesitated, then glancing around them at the angry, vengeful faces in the hall, quickly followed their leader out. One by one, as they left, Arturius marked them with his staff, and Vivianne could see, even from the dais, that they left with a dark scar on their cheeks.

The great hall rang with shouts and battle cries, and some of the warriors ran out after Pelleas and his men with fearful eyes. When Vivianne had gathered her wits again, she looked around the room, but she could see Guin nowhere. If she had any sense about her, she would flee over to Wales, where her ancestors had lived, to her family and people, now that Pelleas had abandoned her. She could hide there. Vivianne's people would not seek her out or harm her. She would be quietly forgotten, Vivianne was sure.

Sir Roland wound his arm around her. "You are my brave soul-mate, and I hope, perhaps … my wife?" And he gently lifted her face towards him and kissed her on the lips in front of all the people remaining in the hall. Lady Vivianne pulled away for a moment, embarrassed, then hearing the encouraging whispers around her, smiled and murmured,

"Forever through time, and even after death," and she pulled Roland's head down to her and kissed him firmly on his mouth.

As they separated reluctantly, Vivianne heard a frantic squealing and clapping. Mathilda was jumping up and down in delight in front of the dais. Vivianne held out her hand to her little maid and pulled her up beside them.

"And you," she said softly, "will be my personal high maid for as long as you desire!"

"Oh, my lady! And maybe also your nursery maid?"

Vivianne smiled. "Mathilda," she chided. "That is a little too soon to think of." But her body told her otherwise.

*

Viv opened her eyes as she felt the warmth of Rory's hand stroking her back.

"It's gone," he whispered.

She felt a lightness around her. She no longer heard noises in the branches or saw fleeting wisps of people between the trees. The air felt calm and she knew a great peace in her heart.

"I think I did the right thing."

"I know you did." Rory turned towards her and drew her up to her feet. He looked deep into her eyes and his were dark with desire. His strong hands cupped her face and he leaned in towards her. Her heart stopped and her body suffused with wanting. He was going to kiss her. At last. Oh yes, Rory. She could feel the heat radiating from his body … She moved automatically in response, then stopped. Her head fought with her heart. Her pulse sounded a loud thrumming through her whole body. Oh god, what was she doing. She gasped and drew back.

"No! I … we … can't."

"I'm sorry, Viv. I'm so sorry. Clearly I misread the signs." He stepped back from her and grimaced. He raked his hand through his hair and her heart stopped. "Oh dear. I do hope I haven't spoiled everything?"

"Spoil what?" demanded Viv. She couldn't understand why he was being so dense. "I don't go with married men."

Rory frowned. "Well, I should hope not."

"You're married."

"Am I? Who to?"

"Mrs N. Oh, *please*, Rory. I don't play games."

203

Rory stared at her. Then burst out laughing.

"For goodness sake, Viv! Mrs N is my mother!"

"Your ... your mother? But I spoke to her on your phone. Tonight."

"Yes. Of course. She lives in the rectory with me. Well, one wing of it. It's too big for me alone, and since dad died ... well, it just made perfect sense. We do share the cooking and so on, but what with the bistro, I think she's getting rather fed up of having to do that at home too, especially with my odd hours. Sorry, I'm burbling. But ... goodness, you thought ... I can't believe it."

"Why not? I've never met her. When I spoke to her, briefly, on the phone, she clearly had a cold and cough so I couldn't possibly tell her age."

Rory reached out and stroked her hair. "My mother – Mrs N – is the kindest, loveliest, most supportive mother a chap could want. And why would I call my wife 'Mrs N'?"

"But I saw the photos in your sitting room."

"Oh Viv." He took a deep breath. "Let me take you back to your apartment and tell you everything. I can't talk here."

*

"I loved her very much," said Rory, as Viv handed him a soothing hot chocolate. "She was my wife, my everything. I was starting out after my ordination, settling in to a new parish. We were welcomed with enthusiasm into the community. It was a very busy urban area. I had high hopes of raising the profile of the church there, getting a youth group going, a mother and baby group, family oriented services. And when Sarah became pregnant, we were delighted. So many plans."

He paused and Viv gently laid her right hand on his thigh. He seemed not to notice but looked straight ahead at the painting of Wilmingham Woods on her wall, gripping his mug of chocolate.

"She was nearly due. But she insisted on going out shopping for some baby things she'd forgotten. I wasn't there. I was at a diocesan meeting. She collapsed at the shopping centre and was rushed to hospital. She'd had bad headaches but we thought they were just her normal migraines, which she did have from time to time." He reached out and placed the mug onto the coffee table. Of course, thought Viv, that's why he reacted when she and Ellie were talking about migraines and pregnancy. "But this time, she had raised blood pressure – well, it was through the roof.

The doctors said it was toxaemia, pre-eclampsia." He paused and raked his fingers through his hair. "It was all too late. She lost the baby ... and her life."

"Oh, my god, how awful." Viv's left hand flew to her mouth. What on earth could she say?

"Of course I blamed myself. Because I wasn't there for her. And the church because that's where I was. I lost my wife, my child, and my faith. At least, I questioned my faith. I battled with myself for so long. If there was a god, how come he did this to us? We didn't deserve it. She had so much more to give. We had so much to give as a family. I had so many discussions with my curates and the archbishop, I can't tell you. I lost my way. But I knew that there was something there. There was an answer – I just couldn't find it. When I was a bit more compos mentis, and felt I should go back to work, they insisted I go away to a new, quieter parish and after a while to take a sabbatical."

"So you're here."

"So I'm here and taking time out to research for my doctorate. The archbishop was establishing a synod group investigating religious iconography and allowed me a sabbatical to do research for him. Mother moved in – that was the idea – it was a much bigger rectory and she could still have her own life. She could set up the bistro she'd always wanted."

He lapsed into silence and Viv didn't want to break through his thoughts and memories, clearly so painful for him, with words that may have seemed trivial and unfeeling. She could hardly move her hand away at this moment; it might seem like a rejection. Yet she wasn't sure that it was appropriate to be touching his thigh. She stroked his leg, struggling to seem comforting, and yet she felt deeply for him. Her breath caught as she flushed hot, her heart thumping. She was so aware of his presence, his physicality, his strength, his body beside her, his warmth. His thigh was muscular, hard. She moved her head slightly to drink in his profile, his thick dark hair, his strong roman nose, his chiselled chin, his large soft lips. Her legs were trembling, her whole body filled with a delicious ache. She hardly dare breathe again.

Rory raked his hand through his hair again and she longed to do the same, to run her fingers through his curls and to stroke the nape of his neck, to stroke his gorgeous face and soothe away his pain.

He started to reach for his mug of chocolate on the coffee table but then hesitated, leaned back and felt for her hand, linking his fingers into hers. She felt the electricity between them. As he turned towards her, she saw that he was smiling, as though he had, in the end, found something that was precious to him. "I'm so glad I could say all that to you, Viv. Get it off my chest. Because I don't want to live in the past. I don't usually tell people, well, never, actually, apart from certain church people who had to know, the archbishop and so on. But you, I feel I can tell you anything now. I want to look to the future. With you."

"Yet you still wear your wedding ring," said Viv. "Do you really want to move on?"

Rory smiled. "Viv, it's a signet ring, not Sarah's. A while after she died and I'd taken off her wedding ring, I put it on that finger, because it felt so naked."

"Er, and not at all to deter unwelcome advances from young attractive parishioners?"

"Hmmm, you've seen through me!"

He squeezed her hand and her world seemed to stand still. He reached for her face, and gently caressed her cheek, her ear, her neck. She sensed her whole body melting and turning to liquid as he whispered, "So may I kiss you now?" He smiled and his eyes crinkled at the edges as he drank her in. Was he really seeing in to her soul? She leaned in to him, and as he stroked her shoulders, and downwards, cupping her breasts and moaning softly into her hair, she let her hands explore his strong chest, his waist, his hardness below.

This time she did not pull away, and as his lips met hers and his feelings merged into hers, she felt as though a lake of warm welcoming waves flowed over her and she knew herself to be drowning in him.

Chapter 22

Lady Vivianne nestled into the strong arm of Sir Roland that enfolded her shoulders, and smiled up at him. She felt Mathilda's hand tugging at her sleeve and turned to chide her again for such a childish habit, but realised that her maid was anxiously trying to catch her attention.

"My lady, my lady," she was whispering urgently.

Vivianne wrenched her eyes from Roland and saw a large commanding figure standing before them.

"Arturius," she said quietly. "I thank you for your intervention and your support this day ..."

But Arturius raised his hand to stop her. "I should have come earlier. But there were troubles on the western borderlands." He shook his flowing dark locks and looked with that stern frown into her eyes, as though he looked into her soul. "And you, my lady, have done it all. You have saved your settlement. And you, Sir Roland. I am immensely grateful and proud of both of you that you have the strength of mind and independence of spirit to stand up against the evil that threatened it. You shall both be most royally honoured. Firstly, though, my men are, at this moment, clearing all that remains of Pelleas's evil power over the people, and with your permission they will cleanse the mead hall."

Vivianne inclined her head in thanks. "I would appreciate that. And I will then fetch my mother's infusions and libations from her cave to bring sweetness and peace again to the hall."

"I hope that you will, as the true heir to your parents' title, court, and all the settlement lands, restore the values and practices of noble courtesy that they upheld. It is your inheritance and your burden. Use it wisely." He looked round and signalled to the warrior who held the banner which Pelleas had so lately proclaimed his own. "Kneel." Vivianne and Roland glanced at each other and did as they were bidden, kneeling in front of the great Arturius. He took the banner and wrapped it around both their shoulders as if binding them together.

"This banner is indeed that of Uther Pendragon to whom both of you, through different family lines, are linked. As you are to me." Vivianne

207

raised her eyes to him. "I would wish for you to be betrothed, as I believe that you do too, and from this moment you are one." Vivianne turned to Roland who smiled at her and she saw the love in his eyes. "But ..." Arturius added and her heart skipped. "You have to invite me to the hand-fasting. I suggest this Beltain." He winked, and then turned to stride out of the mead hall to the cheering of those who had remained there.

Lady Vivianne hardly had the time to take another breath, for as she and Roland stood, she heard a rumpus at the door and a messenger ran in, followed closely by a crowd of warriors.

Red-faced and panting, he shouted to the company in the hall, "My lady, Sir Pelleas is gone!" He bent to regain his composure and drew himself up to his full height, pulled back his shoulders and said, more strongly: "We followed him to the mere and we stood on the bank and watched as he strode into the water. He kept on walking as the water crept higher, until the floods were lapping at his throat. Then he sank down and the mere covered his head and he drowned."

Vivianne closed her eyes tightly and felt Roland's hand grip her own. "Thank god," she murmured. "Thank god he and his evil are gone from here. I am sure that his own pagan god will take him to his breast, but we are rid of him here."

Her thoughts were dimmed by the people in the hall cheering and yelling.

Voices clammered together. "Where are his henchmen? His own warriors?"

The messenger raised his arms aloft. "They are all fled. We chased them from here and many men are now dispatching them over our borders and away."

"The mere where he drowned." Someone shouted, and the noise abated. "Nobody will want to go there now. I say we name it 'Cūning's Mere' to remind us and to scorn his ambitions."

Cūning's Mere. King's Mere. Pelleas was no king, although he wished to be. The name would show the people it was haunted by the evil he brought. And although her mother and those before had her had used it for good, now it seemed tainted. For now those waters would not be the holy ones of the Lady of the Lake but a reminder of the black heart of the would-be king, Pelleas. Lady Vivianne scanned the crowd with her eyes. "Yes, we will do that. It is right."

Yet she hoped and prayed that at some time, in the distant future, the lake would be, once more, the province of the Lady of the Lake and her kin.

And now, to her surprise, she watched as the crowd bowed to her and the warriors raised their spears in salute. This was a new start to their settlement, a new era.

Sir Roland let go of her hand and took a step to the side, addressing the people. "We must have a full Witan council and name the thegns to build a new constitution. But before that, I suggest," he glanced at Vivianne and as though she read his mind she nodded, "we hold a feasting."

A great roar of approval resounded through the hall. Lady Vivianne smiled and raised her face to the rafters. She knew in her heart that there was something, someone, who had helped them through, a spirit, a shape on the air. And she silently thanked them and sent her prayers and her peace flying through the wind and the light, across the centuries.

*

As Viv awoke the next morning, she felt lighter than she had for a long time. Images of Rory's body filled her mind and she relived the wonderful feeling as he kissed her so deeply that he touched her very soul, and as their bodies merged into one. She could still smell the scent of his bergamot skin on hers and the sense of peace and rightness that enveloped her. She knew for certain that she had not felt that way for years, not even when she first linked up with Pete; she realised now that somehow there was always a slight tremor of uncertainty, long, long before he left.

She touched her body as though she must have changed in the night. She could hardly believe how different she felt in herself: strong, happy, excited about the future. She had gained the promotion she had wanted for a long time, and she was proud of herself that she had done it in the midst of one of the most difficult times of her life. And most of all, whatever happened, she no longer felt alone. There was just one uncertainty left eating away at her heart. The apartment …

In the mirror a fresh, peachy, glowing face smiled back at her. Even though Rory had eventually torn himself away from their intimacy and kissed her goodnight, to let her sleep, she knew that sometime soon he would stay. And then …

The telephone's ringtone interrupted her daydreams.

"Hello," she frowned, not recognising the number on the screen.

"Hello. Am I speaking to Dr Viv DuLac?" came a rich female voice.

Viv affirmed. "Who is this?"

"It's Jane Rosen here, of Rosen and Brookes. You made an appointment to see me next Wednesday but it so happens that I have a cancelled appointment later this afternoon, so if you would like it, it's yours."

Viv readily agreed; it would be a relief to find out her position, whatever it may be.

No sooner had she clicked her mobile off, than it rang again. This time the caller name clearly told her it was the Reverend Rory Netherbridge.

"Hi, Viv." Her heart quivered as she heard his deep voice again, and she pressed the phone closer to her cheek as if it was his face she held. "I just wanted to say 'good morning' to you before you go out. Shall we have lunch?"

Viv told Rory about the solicitor's appointment and he insisted that he would go with her for support. She smiled into the empty room.

*

Jane Rosen was an elegant slim woman in her thirties. She welcomed Viv and Rory into her office and looked questioningly at Rory in his clerical collar, as she indicated the leather chairs in front of her desk.

"I'm here to support Viv," he smiled, glancing sideways at her. "But we are ... together."

"Ah," Jane Rosen said, nodding her blonde head. "That's a plus."

Viv passed the voice recorder over to the solicitor and gave her a full summary of the context of the incident, including Pete's leaving with Gwyn. As the solicitor clicked the recording on and Pete's loud rough voice filled the room, Rory squeezed Viv's hand tightly. When it finished, a silence fell upon the room.

"Well." Jane Rosen sat back in her swivel chair and clasped her hands together. "Frankly, this is dynamite. You did well to have such foresight. Your ex-partner's claim will undoubtedly be quashed and I will need to discuss with his solicitor about the way we proceed. Personally, I think you have grounds for a charge of abuse, as well as an overturn of the fraudulent claim. I would also say actual bodily harm, but you would need to have photographs of the damage, bruising and so on, or x-rays."

"No, I didn't go to the hospital so there's no evidence. And really I just want to ensure that my property is left intact. I don't know that I want to go through the awfulness of a law suit for abuse against my former partner."

"The problem there is that he could possibly claim a share of the flat anyway as a cohabitee and maybe he contributed financially to its upkeep or contents? However, we can negotiate with his lawyers on the basis of your generosity in not bringing a case against him."

"Goodness, that sounds like bribery or blackmail," said Rory, leaning forward, and running his finger around his collar.

Jane Rosen laughed. "I guess it sometimes does. But it's simply negotiation for the best settlement and frankly I'm sure that neither party would want to drag this through the courts."

Viv sighed. "No. I have no heart for that. Just as long as I can have my apartment – or as much of its value as possible. But preferably the apartment itself. I don't want to move out of the village if I can help it."

Jane Rosen smiled. "You seem to have no desire for vengeance. That's good. You'd be amazed at how unusual that is in these kinds of fall-outs, and especially when it involves an old friend of yours."

"I wish her no evil, nor him. It just makes me sad. But vengeance won't make anything right."

"I admire your sang-froid, I have to say. Right. Well, I'll send off a letter to your ex's solicitor and we'll see what they say. I think the chances are that he'll cave in about the apartment and that can be settled quite quickly. But I'm also going to look into the issue of the forgery itself. It is a crime, after all."

*

It was on a sunny Saturday morning in late autumn that a thick letter arrived for Viv, and she sat on the sagging leather chesterfield in the rectory sitting room, reading it. She loved the old rectory and had come to know almost every inch of it since the summer; she spent so much time there with Rory and Mrs N. It was home now, even more so than her apartment at the abbey down the lane, although she wasn't sure that she could ever sell the flat she had loved so much, whatever happened. It was now a bolt-hole (not that she exactly needed that) but these days it felt cold and lonely if she was there without Rory.

The golden light reflected from the copper beeches around the lawn outside the French windows shone on the thick pages that trembled in Viv's hand. It had taken months for the matter to be legally pursued and a judgement made. During the protracted course of law, Viv knew that Gwyn had fled back to Wales and was now with a childhood sweetheart who had never left the village where they grew up together and, amazingly, had promised to raise Pete's baby as his own. Gwyn had written to her to tell her and to pour out how sorry she was at what she had done. It appeared also that she had discovered that Pete was not entirely the man she had hoped for.

Rory slipped his arm around her shoulders and pulled her to him. She could feel the warmth of his body against hers.

"So what does it say?" asked Mrs Netherbridge, leaning her elegant body forwards from her sofa opposite them. "Do we crack open a bottle of bubbly?"

Viv bit her lip. "Basically, Pete has been charged with forgery and fraud. The solicitor had to take that route. The apartment is mine … all of it … legally." It felt unreal, after all that they had gone through.

"At last!" breathed Mrs N, clapping her hands in such an old-fashioned gesture that Viv laughed. "Now you two can start making plans." She pulled her steepled hands to her eau-de-nil silk-draped chest, and smiled delightedly.

Rory hugged Viv even closer. "Yes." He looked into her eyes and his smile was full of the love she had come to see and feel over the past months. "If you'll have me?"

"Rory, for goodness sake, ask her properly! It's high time you made an honest woman of her! And stop those parishioners' tongues wagging."

With a wink to his mother, Rory slipped from the sofa onto one knee. *Goodness*, thought Viv, *do people still do that? But how romantic it was*! He took her hand in his and smiled. Her heart flipped and her body shivered.

"Dr Vivianne DuLac, will you do me the honour of marrying me and becoming a poor rector's wife?"

In response, Viv lifted her mouth to meet his.

Acknowledgements

With grateful thanks to all those who made this book possible and bore with me to its completion:

To my husband, Clive, who brings me constant supplies of coffee and makes dinner when I become lost in my writing and forget the time.

To my beautiful daughters, Tam and Mel, and my lovely grandchildren.

To my publishers, Endeavour Press, for their support and encouragement, especially Amy, Jack and Jasmin.

To my wonderful critique partners who give me so much support and a huge amount of their time, especially Susan Fisher and my good writer friend and "twin" Dorinda Cass, and my editors, Mandy James and Debz Hobbs-Wyatt, who give me so much help and many suggestions for improvement, not forgetting my review buddy and fellow Endeavour author Emily Murdoch, and my good friend Pauline Barclay.

To the encouraging and supportive members of the RNA: including Ros Rendle, Sue Bergen, Kath McGurl, Jane Linfoot, Christina Hollis, Alison Morton, and especially those of the Leicester and Birmingham chapters, Lizzie Lamb, Alex Gutteridge, and a very special thanks to Amanda Grange who persuaded me to write this novel in the first place, having enjoyed my children's medieval fantasy timeslip, S.C.A.R.S.

Author's notes

The idea for *A Shape on the Air* has been brewing in my mind for a long time. I had been reading about, and mulling over, the notion of time slip and especially the concept of 'worm-holes' and the Einstein-Bridge theory of portals into other dimensions of time and space. I felt that this was a more 'logical' (in some ways!) and scientific explanation of those everyday glimmers of 'déjà vue' and perceptions of the past that many of us experience, those intimations that maybe the spirits of history are embedded in the fabric of old houses and ancient geology. So, what if we could take it further and, somehow, slip into the world of the past, another world but one to which we might have a personal connection, through our own family links which still reverberate through us; some kind of glimpse of shapes on the air.

My time slip story is set in the present day (Viv) and in the 'dark ages' (Lady Vivianne). One thread in Viv's narrative is the notion that the dark ages tend to be misconstrued as primitive. As a specialist in early medieval language, literature and history, I am excited by this idea. Let's look at the more recent discoveries about the world of late fifth century Britain, for example the site near Lyminge, Kent, where an early feasting hall has been unearthed. I am also intrigued by the exploration of the bronze age settlement at Must Farm in the fens, dating from long before the setting of *my* story, yet revealing a sophistication of crafts, utensils, clothing, domesticity and foreign trade which I am convinced would have become a surviving part of the British psyche. Both of these discoveries are mentioned in my story.

The historic part of *A Shape on the Air* is set in 499 AD still in the period we call the dark ages but on the cusp of the Anglo-Saxon era. The term 'the dark ages' refers to the time between the ending of Roman rule in Britain around 410 AD when Honorius demands the return to Rome of the legions and administrators, and the establishment, developing gradually from around 450AD, of settled Anglo-Saxon-Jute communities, the new 'Kingdoms' and of a new culture towards the end of the century. We have long perceived this time as mysterious, dangerous, even barbaric. The glory of Rome had gone from our island with the withdrawal of the legions; the Roman Empire, under threat from Germanic tribes, was collapsing. We believe that the threats to Celtic-British communities or small 'kingdoms' (I won't call them 'tribes' which seems to me to connote primitivism) led Vortigern, High King of the southern Britons, to call upon Angles, Saxons and Jutes from overseas to help quash the Picts and Scots who threatened his land. In my story, Vortigern sends gestures of support northwards to Lady Vivianne's parents, Sir Tristram (a Romano-Briton or Brythen) and Lady Nymue (a Celtic-Briton), in the shape of gold and weapons. Their settlement, in the midlands of Britain is threatened by Pictish raids, as we see in Sir Pelleas's battle, but is not essentially unstable. The threat is more internal: the conflict between Lady Vivianne and Sir Pelleas (from pagan Saxon invader-stock). An alliance between Lady Vivianne and Sir Roland (a Romano-Briton) would have been a much more comfortable and stable union for their community.

So, Britain was now embarking on a new age, alone without its Roman protection and orderliness. But was it 'dark' because it was primitive, ungoverned, lacking in culture and sensitivities?

What happened to the culture and yes, even spirituality of Roman times, and of pre-Roman Britain? Religion, beliefs, gods and their effect on mankind were strong influences on Roman life, demonstrated in their art and craftwork; icons and imagery of beliefs or superstitions (call them what you will) were rife. Or was Britain 'dark' because we simply don't know to any degree of certainty, because of the paucity of archaeological or documentary evidence, what it was like? What if all that did not crumble and disappear from everyday life after the Romans left Britain? After all, why should it all be forgotten in the disappearing flash of Roman swords from our shores? Wouldn't the British still retain something of their Roman past and indeed of their pre-Roman ways?

Today, we still have our Roman roads, our sites of Roman towns and villas, some have been adapted, some in ruins. Were these splendid constructions simply abandoned in 410AD and left to rot as the occupying forces left, as we have long believed? I argue that during the long Roman occupation, rather than two opposing and alien cultures, there would have been a mingling, intermarriage between the invaders and the 'native' Britons, Celts, and other groups, that these resulting communities would have perhaps settled, compromised and accommodated each other's ways. In my story, the inter-marriage of Lady Vivianne's parents intermingled Christian values and rites with more magical ancient deism. Bringing in to my tale 'king' Arthur (Arturius), probably a Celtic leader of this time with Roman connections, as well as a legendary figure of literature, also signifies the mingling of cultures and beliefs.

After the withdrawal of the Roman legions and administrators, the people, the so-called 'abandoned' Britons and remaining Romans who had established homes and families after inter-marriage, would have used Roman effects in their subsequent buildings and settlements, and likewise would have retained aspects of their cultural heritage that were important to them, their craftwork, their art, their beliefs. Granted, there would have been challenges and tensions between different cultures which by the late fifth century would have comprised a complex mix deriving from native groups (Celts, Britons), remaining Romans, occupying warring migrants (Picts, Scots), and new invaders (Saxons, Angles, Jutes). Many Celtic-speaking Britons would have adopted the Christian religion of their forebears and of many converted Romans, yet with the sweep of the Saxons northwards after the Roman withdrawal, paganism returned before a more widespread Christianisation in 597 with Pope Gregory's emissary St Augustine. Thus the religious conflict between Lady Vivianne and Sir Pelleas.

It seems to me that the resultant culture within settlements would have been more like our own contemporary multi-ethnic communities, with diversity and, yes, maybe dominance by a particular group, but with a desire for some of the peace and security of the Roman occupation and a willingness to integrate where possible. And a will to develop and grow towards a 'brave new world'? I believe so.

But were they lacking in the sensitivities, artistic abilities, craftsmanship and beliefs of the pre-Roman and Roman times? Surely not. I claim that there must still have been the cultural and religious folk memory which survived the turbulence and uncertainty of the times. As an academic, I want to believe in the logic of unbroken continuation and developing richness of the world of the Romans, Celts, Britons, and Anglo-Saxons and that the 'dark ages' are only so-called because of our own ignorance.

A post-script about language: I have used a writer's licence variation of modern-ish English for dialogue in the 499 AD sections and some Anglo-Saxon terms. We cannot be certain of the language and especially the midlands dialect of that time, probably a mixture of Celtic and Latin, so I have tried simply to give a flavour (for example the use of kennings in Sir Pelleas's herald's report) without linguistic accuracy. I have also used terms which would not have been in use in 499 but which added to the accuracy of descriptions of items we now recognise (for example cloisonné garnets in the mead hall). And please suspend disbelief for Hrothgar, the poor willow-worker's ability to read, write, and sign the declaration against Sir Pelleas!

Dr Julia Ibbotson
2017

And now for some references you might like to read:

Fleming, R (2011) *Britain after Rome* [Penguin: London]

Wood, M (2005) *In Search of the Dark Ages* [Ebury, BBC books: London]

Crossley-Holland, K (ed) (2009) *The Anglo-Saxon World: an anthology* [OUP: Oxford]

Zaluckyj, S (2013) *Mercia: the Anglo-Saxon Kingdom of Central England* [Logaston Press: Logaston, England]

Campbell, J., John, E., and Wormald, P (1991) *The Anglo-Saxons* [Penguin: London]

Printed in Poland
by Amazon Fulfillment
Poland Sp. z o.o., Wrocław